SEEN

SARAH'S JOURNEY

OLLIE LLEWELLYN

MOKUZAI DESIGN UK

SEEN By Ollie Llewellyn

ISBN (Paperback) 978 1 9195411 0 5

ISBN (Hardback) 978 1 9195411 1 2

ISBN (Ebook) 978 1 9195411 2 9

Published by Mokuzai Design UK

mokuzaidesignuk@gmail.com

Ollie Llewellyn is the pen name of N.J.Twinney

All correspondence accepted by email: mokuzaidesignuk@gmail.com

For Bronnie

CHAPTER 1 - THE BEACH

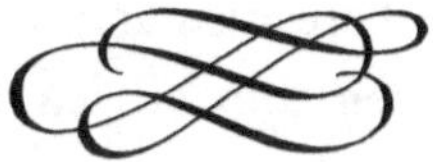

Cold sand pressed against Sarah's fingers. She hadn't expected that. June in Normandy was supposed to be warm. The morning air from the Channel stung her skin; it woke her up with a sharpness that caught her off guard, but she was more alive than she had been in months. Everything around her seemed foreign, unsettling, and new.

The air tasted of salt, seaweed, and something she couldn't quite name. It was unmistakably French. Maybe it was the smell of bread from the bakery in the village behind her, or coffee, or maybe just the sea air mixing with a language she barely understood.

"Mais non, écoute..." The musical, emphatic words drifted up from somewhere down the beach.

"Allez, on y va!" A man calling to a child, probably, though Sarah couldn't see them from where she sat on the dunes.

These were real French voices, not the slow, careful French her teachers used thirty years ago. This was the fast, natural language of locals. They didn't notice her; she was invisible here, but at the same time, she was strangely obvious, as if being foreign made her stand out.

I am truly abroad, she realised. Not on holiday. Not passing through. Here. Alone. By choice.

As the reality of being here hit her, excitement mixed with a sudden wave of fear in her stomach, leaving her breathless.

She should have been exhausted. The journey had been hard. That word echoed in her mind.

She had taken the train from Bristol.

Eight hours of travelling. Eight hours of being in motion, always moving toward something.

And now she was here. On this beach.

She wasn't tired. Instead, a strange alertness hummed through her. Every sense seemed sharper. She pressed her fingers into the sand, listened to the sharp cries of gulls, and watched the Channel's endless, shifting grey-blue water.

Her body was alert, not tired. It was like her mind worked differently here, far from her usual routine. She was away from the pressure of being needed all of the time. Here, the wind didn't care if she'd remembered dinner. The waves didn't notice if she'd replied to the school email. For the first time in years, no one needed anything from her.

The freedom of it was terrifying.

She sat on the dunes with her notebook closed on her lap and let the wind mess up her hair. Her thoughts were both freeing and lonely. She'd brought her good coat, the navy one David gave her for Christmas three years ago, but left it in her bag. She let the cold wake her up. If France wanted to be uncomfortable, that was fine. She was here. Really here.

This must have been so much harder for them, she thought, looking out at the water. For Grandad and all those young men who came here in 1944.

They hadn't taken comfortable trains with coffee cars. They crossed in a landing craft, packed tight and sick with fear. They knew death might wait on the beach. There were no comfortable seats. No pain au chocolat. Only cold metal and the fear of not surviving.

Her grandfather had told her once, when she was about ten or eleven, about the crossing. Not about the beach itself, he never spoke of that, but about the journey there. She remembered now: the darkness, the cold, the silence broken only by whispers and the sound of men being sick over the side.

"But we had a job to do, Sas," he'd said, using the nickname only he called her. "And we did it. Because those beaches meant freedom. For France. For Europe. For you, someday. So you could grow up and be whatever you wanted to be."

She'd wanted to be a writer.

For a moment, remembering this wish, she was filled with a nostalgic ache. It suddenly exposed the gap between that childhood dream and how distant it had become.

Grandad had described this beach once. Not this exact part of the beach, but somewhere along this stretch of coastline. He'd told her about the sound - how the wind off the Channel sounded different than wind anywhere else. Like it was carrying voices from across the water. She strained to hear it now, that particular quality he'd mentioned. But all she heard was wind. Just wind. And gulls. Somewhere behind her, French voices called to each other with casual familiarity.

He'd also told her about the cold. It had seeped into their bones during the crossing. Some of the men couldn't stop shaking even after they'd landed. Cold and fear mixed. She pressed her fingers deeper into the sand, feeling the chill, and thought: This is nothing. You crossed the Channel on a train. You ate a croissant. You have no right to compare.

But the feeling stayed with her. She was on a Normandy beach where, somewhere close, her grandfather had once saved lives. That thought pressed on her, changing her sense of purpose. She moved from thinking about his courage to facing her own needs. The change from his bravery to her own felt sudden and strange. Her reasons were small but important. She needed to know if she could be brave, too. She had come to save herself, even if she didn't know exactly what that meant yet.

She stared out at the grey-blue stretch of the Channel. A seagull circled overhead, its cry both mournful and free. Sarah watched it, envying its easy flight, its lack of guilt about being exactly where it was.

She should be writing. That's why she was here. That's what she'd told David, told the girls, told herself during the anxious weeks of planning this trip. Nearly two weeks in France to write. To finally, finally sit down and write the book that had been living in her head for years.

But the page was blank.

She opened her notebook and wrote:

A woman sits on a beach. She is forty-three years old. She is...

She crossed it out.

A woman goes to France to...

She crossed that out, too.

Once upon a time, there was a woman who forgot she existed.

She stared at the line. Too melodramatic. Too self-pitying. Delete.

She sat alone on the beach...

Nothing. The words wouldn't come. Just the sound of the sea and the gulls and the mocking emptiness of the page.

She closed the notebook.

Tomorrow. She'd try again tomorrow.

But her mind had other plans, was full of voices that weren't French.

“Mum, where's my football kit?”

The memory hit her sharply and immediately, as if Betty were standing right behind her on these Normandy dunes, instead of hundreds of miles away in Bristol.

“I left it on your bed. Yesterday. When I washed it.

“Well, it's not there now.”

Of course it wasn’t. Betty had probably thrown it on the floor or kicked it under the bed. Maybe she'd buried it under a pile of clothes, where mess seemed to grow overnight. Irritation washed through her. Why was it always her job to find things no one else bothered to keep track of? First came a flash of surprise. Then the usual feeling of resignation. She would find it; she always did. That was her job: finding things, keeping everyone supplied, often without thanks or even being noticed.

David's words echoed in her thoughts now, from upstairs at home: 'Sarah, have you seen my blue tie?' Those familiar moments replayed as sharply as if they were happening now.

“Dry cleaning. I'll get it.”

And she had. She dropped everything. She literally left the eggs congealing in the pan, ran out to the car, drove to the dry cleaner's, collected his shirts and ties, rushed back, and handed him the blue tie with three minutes to spare before he had to leave for work.

“You're a lifesaver. What would I do without you?”

A kiss on the cheek. He grabbed his briefcase. And he was gone.

He meant it to be affectionate. At first, she almost smiled, relieved. But the way he said it, so casual, so automatic, as if she were just another household appliance, changed everything. The warmth faded, replaced by a cold feeling and a wave of loneliness.

Sarah blinked, and the beach came back into focus. The grey-blue sea. The crying gulls. The cold sand under her fingers.

Sarah had tried to tell her family. She had tried to explain why this mattered, what she wanted, and who she was beneath the roles she'd been playing.

It had been a Tuesday in early April. Nothing special about it.

Sarah had made pasta - rigatoni with that vodka sauce Olivia liked. She'd found the recipe in an old cookbook. It was the one with the wine-stained pages her mother had given her when she'd gotten married. Garlic bread from the good bakery, not the supermarket. Caesar salad with actual anchovies. She knew the girls would pick around those, but David appreciated them. She'd spent an hour on it, which was ridiculous for a Tuesday. But she wanted everything to feel... right. Special. The kind of meal where people lingered. Where conversation happened.

Her older daughter, Olivia, had finished her exams that afternoon and came home in a good mood, singing along to something on her headphones as she dumped her bag in the hall. The relief was palpable - no more late-night cramming, no more stress crying over chemistry questions.

Betty, her younger daughter, had won her football match - 3-2, she'd announced proudly, kicking off her muddy boots by the door without bothering to pick them up, leaving clods of grass on the mat Sarah had just vacuumed that morning.

David, her husband, had actually come home at a reasonable hour for once, before seven. A small miracle. Usually, he was there until eight, nine, sometimes ten when surgeries ran long.

They all sat around the dinner table, eating together for once instead of at different times or in front of screens. The kitchen was warm from the oven, smelling of tomato and oregano and butter-soaked bread.

Sarah set the steaming bowl of pasta in the centre of the table, the garlic bread on a wooden board, the salad in the big ceramic bowl they'd gotten as a wedding present twenty years ago. She'd even lit a candle. Just one, nothing dramatic, but it made the kitchen feel warmer somehow. More like a proper family dinner instead of just another meal to get through.

"This is amazing, Mum," Betty said through a mouthful of pasta, already reaching for a second helping before she'd finished the first. Red sauce on her chin. Sarah resisted the urge to hand her a napkin.

"Don't talk with your mouth full," Sarah said without thinking, but she was pleased. This was good. Everyone was together, relaxed, and happy. It was the kind of evening she'd imagined when she was young and dreamed about having a family. Before she knew that most family dinners meant someone was on their phone and someone else wanted to leave after five minutes.

She passed the salad bowl to Olivia, who took it without looking up from her phone.

"Olly," David said mildly. Not angry, just... reminding. That gentle dad tone he used.

Olivia turned the phone face down beside her plate with a theatrical sigh, but Sarah could see her eyes flicking toward it. Waiting for it to light up. Checking to see if the screen showed through the tablecloth. Whoever she was texting was clearly more interesting than her family.

David poured himself more wine - the Malbec Sarah had picked up from Waitrose because it was on offer. "Long day," he said, to no one in particular. Just exhaling the stress of it into the warm kitchen air. "That merger between health authorities is going to be the death of me. There was a three-hour meeting this afternoon about budgets and staffing, and nobody can agree on anything. Richard wants to cut two positions, Margaret from admin says that's impossible, and I'm sitting there thinking about Mrs Patterson in recovery who needs another week at least, but insurance is pushing for discharge..."

He was starting to talk about work again. Sarah knew the signs. Once David began talking about hospital politics, he could go on for twenty minutes straight.

"Mmm," Sarah said, serving herself salad. The anchovies were definitely going to be picked out by everyone except David.

Betty was demolishing her pasta like she hadn't eaten in days. Olivia was picking at hers, moving it around her plate more than eating it. On one of her diets again, probably. Or saving room for whatever she'd eat later when Sarah wasn't watching. The phone buzzed against the table, muffled but audible. Olivia's eyes flicked toward it.

Sarah took a breath. 'This is the moment. Tell them about the book. Tell them why this matters.'

"So I've been working on the plot," she said lightly, casually, as she set down the salad tongs. "For the book I'm writing."

"Mmm." Olivia reached for the salad bowl, her attention still half on the phone beside her plate, wondering who was texting, what she was missing.

"It's a love story, sort of. But funny." Sarah forced enthusiasm into her words, trying to make the story sound interesting, worth listening to. "It's about a woman who's lost herself and is trying to figure out who she is again. She's been so focused on everyone else that she's forgotten who she is underneath all the roles she plays..."

"Cool," Betty said, in that tone teenagers use when being polite while thinking about something else entirely. She was already eyeing the last piece of garlic bread, calculating whether she could take it or if she should wait.

"The main character, she's forty-something," Sarah continued, talking a bit faster now, trying to get it out before she lost them completely, "and she's been so focused on everyone else - her husband, her kids, her job, all the logistics of keeping a family running - that she's forgotten..."

"Oh, Mum, that reminds me!" Betty interrupted, suddenly animated. "I need to finish my art project this week. Like, definitely this week."

"Why this week?" Sarah asked, grateful for any engagement, even if it wasn't about her book.

"Because Mr Stevens is going into hospital soon. He said he won't be back before the end of term, so we have to hand everything in by Friday."

"Hospital? Is he alright?" Automatic maternal concern rose up, even for teachers she'd never met.

Betty shrugged. "I dunno. He just said he'd be away for a while. Medical thing." She turned to Olivia. "Do you think I should do the landscape or the portrait? Because the landscape is easier, but the portrait would be more impressive."

"Mum!" Olivia interrupted, her whole face lighting up, suddenly fully present in a way she hadn't been all dinner. She grabbed her phone, flipping it over with barely suppressed excitement. "Did you see that Marcus Bailey followed me on Instagram?" She was practically vibrating with it. "Marcus Bailey! From The Velocity!"

"The band?" Betty's attention immediately snapped from her art project to her sister, pasta forgotten. "Shut up. The 'actual' Marcus Bailey?"

"I mean, it's probably a fake account," Olivia said, but she was grinning, her face flushed with excitement. "But still. Look - it has like two million followers. And it says it's verified? I don't know if that means it's real but... he followed 'me'. Out of, like, millions of people."

"Let me see!" Betty leaned across the table, nearly knocking over her water glass in her eagerness. Sarah caught it reflexively, straightening it before the water could spill onto the tablecloth.

"It could be real," Betty said, squinting at Olivia's phone screen. "Remember when Gemma's cousin got followed by that footballer? And it was actually him?"

"Girls." David cut across them, gentle but firm. He set down his wine glass with deliberate care and turned to Sarah with that patient, supportive expression he used when he was trying to be a good husband. When he was making an effort. "Let your mother finish. She was talking about her book."

Sarah's heart swelled with gratitude. Finally. Someone who wanted to hear. Someone who thought what she had to say might be important.

"It's fine," she started, but David was already talking.

"Though I need to tell you all about today. You won't believe what happened in surgery." He leaned back in his chair, warming to his subject, his hands already gesturing the way they did when he told medical stories. "We had this patient, seventy-eight years old, triple bypass scheduled, and when we opened him up, we found—well, you wouldn't believe the state of his arteries. Like tree branches, completely calcified. I've never seen anything quite like it. Dr Patterson was assisting, and even he was impressed, and he's been doing cardiac surgery for thirty years..."

And that was it.

Sarah sat there, her half-told plot fading back into silence, and watched her family. David gestured with his fork, describing the complicated surgery, the unexpected complications, the delicate repair work, the moment when the patient's heart had stuttered, and they'd had to... something technical that Sarah only half-understood. It was interesting, objectively. Life-or-death medicine always was. The girls were even listening, sort of.

Olivia checked her phone now and then, smiling to herself. Every notification made her face light up a little. Marcus Bailey, or whoever it was, was still texting or at least her friends were commenting on it. Sarah made a mental note to look him up and see what all the fuss was about.

Betty asked if there was any more garlic bread, and when Sarah said no-"all gone"-she slumped back in her chair with exaggerated disappointment. "I'm still hungry though."

"There's fruit," Sarah said.

Betty made a face. Fruit didn't count as real food, apparently.

Nobody asked Sarah to keep telling her story. Nobody even seemed to notice she'd stopped talking. The conversation moved on: David's surgery, Olivia's Instagram followers, Betty's complaint about her English teacher giving her a B on an essay she'd worked hard on, then back to the art project and whether to use acrylics or watercolours. Sarah just sat there.

Present but invisible.

She understood. The girls were teenagers. Of course, they were more interested in boy bands, football, art projects, and their own dramas than in their mother's book. That was normal, age-appropriate. She couldn't blame them for being seventeen and fifteen. They were supposed to be self-absorbed at this age. It was developmentally appropriate; the parenting books that were useless but were always recommended by the trendy mums had told her so.

But David... David, she'd expected more from.

The conversation moved on. Wine - David asked her where she'd bought this one because it was quite good, actually, and Sarah told him at Waitrose, on offer. Then politics - something about the election next year, which party had any chance. Then David and Olivia debated whether the NHS funding was sufficient, with Olivia arguing points she'd learned in her Government class and David countering with his experience from the hospital. They were both getting quite heated about it, voices rising slightly, but in that good-natured, argumentative way families can. If Olivia didn't become a doctor like her father, which she had always dreamed of, she would make a good politician. Sarah was proud of her debating skills.

Betty asked to be excused, and Sarah said yes, then watched her younger daughter escape upstairs with obvious relief, probably to text her friends about the football match or work on that art project she was so worried about.

Sarah cleared the plates. Scraped the remains of the pasta into the bin - they'd barely made a dent in it, she'd made far too much. Loaded the dishwasher, the familiar rhythm of it. Stack the plates here, the bowls there, and the silverware in the basket. David was still talking to Olivia in the dining room, something about hospital administration and funding cuts now, their voices drifting in.

She stood at the sink for a moment, hands braced against the cold ceramic, looking out the kitchen window at the darkening garden. The roses needed deadheading. The grass needed cutting. Everything always needed something.

Her eyes were stinging. She blinked hard, pressing her palms against the sink.

'Don't cry. Don't you dare cry over this. It's nothing. It's just a family dinner. They didn't mean to dismiss you. David's just tired. The girls are just teenagers. It's not personal.'

But it was personal.

Later, after the dishes were done and the girls had disappeared to their rooms - Olivia to FaceTime someone, Betty to watch YouTube videos or panic about that art project - she'd tried again.

"The book..." she'd started. David was in the living room now, scrolling through his tablet, catching up on medical journals.

"Hmm?" He didn't look up.

"Never mind."

"No, what?" He glanced up then, looking vaguely guilty. "Sorry, I'm listening."

But he wasn't. Not really. His eyes were still on the screen, his finger still scrolling. That particular expression on his face that said he was processing something complex, probably an article about some new surgical technique.

"It's nothing," Sarah said.

She went to bed that night feeling like a stranger in her own home. At first, a dull ache lingered at the edge of her thoughts, but soon it grew stronger. She was there, but invisible, speaking but only to silence. She lay in the dark, listening to David's gentle snoring beside her, and thought: 'When did I become so easy to ignore?'

Loneliness settled in, suffocating, weightier than she'd imagined.

* * *

THE SECOND MEMORY STRUCK HARDER. It was sharper, more humiliating, landing with a sting she couldn't ignore.

A dinner party. The middle of April, just a few weeks after that family dinner.

Richard and Margaret Thornton, David's colleague from the hospital, and his wife. An older couple, maybe late fifties. They were comfortable in that way people get when their children are grown, their careers are established, and life has settled into a predictable rhythm.

Margaret had asked her the question. The question that every stay-at-home mother gets asked once their children reach a certain age.

"So, Sarah, what are you going to do now? The girls are getting so independent. You must be thinking about going back to work?"

Margaret meant it kindly. Sarah knew that. Still, the words echoed and hurt her, sudden and raw. The last seventeen years had disappeared, leaving only a long, aching pause as she waited for her real life to start. The shock of that thought hit her, sharp and unexpected.

"Actually," Sarah had said, sitting up straighter, her voice strengthening, "I'm planning to write. I want to be an author. I've always wanted to write, and now that I have more time, I'm going to..."

"Is there any more wine?" David had cut across her, reaching for the bottle in the centre of the table. "This Merlot is excellent, Richard. Where did you say you got it?"

And just like that, the conversation had pivoted. Wine. Then politics. Then, hospital budgets and NHS waiting lists. The usual dinner party topics that swirled around Sarah while she sat there, her sentence unfinished, her dreams dismissed before she'd even fully articulated them.

She'd excused herself to get dessert. Stood in the kitchen for a moment, hands braced against the counter, breathing.

“Don't become like me.”

Sarah had jumped. Margaret was standing in the doorway, having followed her into the kitchen.

"I'm sorry?" Sarah said.

Margaret moved closer, lowering her voice. "Don't become the doormat. The little woman at home. You obviously have a brain, Sarah. You obviously have talent. And you obviously have a desire to become an author." She glanced back toward the dining room, where the men's laughter drifted through. "So go away and become that author. Don't wait for permission. Don't wait for them to take you seriously. Just go and do it."

"I..." tears pricked her eyes. "I don't know if I can."

"Then find out." Margaret had squeezed her hand. "But don't let them make you small. Don't let them turn you into me, someone who had dreams once and put them on hold for everyone else until one day you realise you can't even remember what those dreams were."

That conversation had haunted Sarah for days upon days. She'd thought about it while making lunches. While picking up dry cleaning. While driving the girls to school, football, drama, and all the other places they needed to be. Margaret's words had burrowed under her skin like splinters: ‘Don't become like me. Go away and become that author.’

So she'd made the decision. Three in the morning, lying awake next to David's gentle snoring.

France. She would go to France. And she'd go in June, before the girls finished school for the summer holidays. She wanted to find herself, but she still wanted to be a mum. The family had plans for the summer: a week in Cornwall, day trips, the usual school holiday routine, and she didn't want to miss that. She didn't want the girls to think she was abandoning them.

But these two weeks in June, while they were still in school, while David was at work, while life was running on its normal schedule? These two weeks she could take. These two weeks were hers.

Telling the family had been harder than she'd expected.

* * *

SHE'D WAITED until they were all together for another rare family dinner, this one in early May. She'd made David's favourite meal, lasagna - the proper kind with béchamel sauce, not the quick version from a jar. Layers and layers of it, the way his mother used to make it. She'd even made garlic bread from scratch, kneading the dough herself, which she never did. The kitchen had smelled amazing all afternoon - tomato sauce and oregano and that particular scent of cheese melting on top.

The girls had commented on it. Betty had walked in after school, dumped her bag, and said, "What's the occasion?" in a way that made Sarah wonder if she'd been too obvious. Trying too hard.

"No occasion," she'd said lightly, stirring the sauce. "Just wanted to cook

But her hands had been shaking slightly as she'd layered the pasta sheets. This was it. Tonight she'd tell them. Tonight, she'd make them understand.

After they'd finished eating - everyone complimenting the meal, even Olivia, who'd been on another of her diets and had only picked at the edges - after the plates were cleared but before anyone could escape to their rooms or the television, Sarah had set down her wine glass with deliberate care.

"I need to talk to you all about something," she'd said.

The words hung in the air. Three faces had turned to her with varying degrees of attention. Olivia still had her phone in her hand, not quite ready to put it down. Betty was eyeing the last piece of garlic bread, calculating. David had that patient expression he used when he was tired but trying to be present. The look that said 'I'm listening' but also 'please make this quick.

Sarah's heart was hammering. Her mouth was dry despite the wine.

"I'm going away," she said. "For twelve nights in June. Less than two weeks."

Silence. The kind of silence that was heavy, expectant.

Then: "Away?" David's eyebrows lifted, his wine glass paused halfway to his mouth. "Away where?"

"France. Normandy."

"France?" He set down his wine glass carefully, deliberately, as if it might spill if he wasn't gentle with it. "For two weeks? Why?"

Here it was. The moment. Sarah took a breath, steadying herself.

“For twelve days. To write. I need time to write, David. Real time, Uninterrupted time. Time when I'm not worrying about dry cleaning, football kits, or what's for dinner. Time to just... be a writer."

"But..." Confusion crossed his face, like she'd just announced she was joining the circus or taking up extreme sports. "Why France? If you need time to write, you could go to Bath. Or the Cotswolds. Somewhere in England." He spread his hands, reasonable, logical. "Closer. Cheaper. You could even go to your sister's in Oxford if you wanted quiet."

She'd known this question was coming. Had practised her answer in the mirror that morning while getting dressed, trying different tones. Confident. Apologetic. Firm. Trying to sound like a woman who knew what she wanted and wasn't going to apologise for it.

"Because I need it to feel different. Significant. Not just a weekend away that I'll spend feeling guilty about." She met his eyes, willing him to understand. "Somewhere properly abroad. Somewhere that forces me to be someone other than just... this." She gestured vaguely at herself, at the kitchen, at the life surrounding them. "I need to be in a place where no one knows me as your wife or their mother. Where I'm just... me."

She took another breath, gathering courage. "And Normandy, because of Grandad. You know he was there on D-Day. It feels... I don't know. Connected. Like I'm honouring him by going there to write my book."

David had opened his mouth, then closed it again. She'd known he would. How could he argue with honouring her grandfather? The man who'd saved lives on those beaches, who'd come home changed, quieter. Who'd died when Sarah was twenty-five, still grieving the wife he'd lost two years earlier. David had met him once, at their wedding, and Grandad had pulled David aside and told him to take care of his Sas.

"Two weeks is a long time," David said carefully. Measured. His surgeon tone, the one he used to deliver difficult news to patients' families.

"It's really not. It's less than two weeks. Twelve nights. That's all the hotel had available in June, and honestly, it's enough time." Sarah spoke level and reasonably. "You manage when I visit my sister for a weekend. This is just a bit longer. Two weekends instead of one."

"Your sister lives in Oxford," David said. "That's two hours away. You can come home if there's an emergency. France is..." He trailed off.

"France is a train ride away. A few hours. Not the moon. I'll have my phone. I'll call every day if you want. But David..." She leaned forward slightly. "There won't be an emergency. The girls are fifteen and seventeen, not five and seven. You're a surgeon. You're one of the most capable people I know. You can handle this."

"Mum." Betty cut through, louder than necessary, with that particular teenage edge that said she'd been building up to interrupt. "Two weeks in June? But I've got football. The semi-finals are that month. The semifinals." She said it like Sarah should understand the gravity of this. "Who's going to take me? You always take me."

"Your father can take you."

"Dad doesn't know the schedule. He doesn't know which field or what time or..."

"It's on the calendar, Betty. The big one on the fridge. The one I update every Sunday." Her words grew firmer. "Your father is perfectly capable of reading a calendar and driving you to football. I've written everything down - which field, what time, what kit you need, everything."

Betty glanced at David uncertainly, as if this were a wild claim that needed verification. As if the idea of her father knowing where she needed to be and when was completely far-fetched. As if Sarah were the only one who could possibly understand the complex logistics of teenage football.

"Of course I can take you to football," David said, though he sounded less confident than Sarah would have liked. There was a slight pause, a hesitation. "I just... which Saturdays are we talking about?"

"It's on the calendar," Sarah repeated, patient. Not snapping. Not yet. "All of it. Times, locations, which kit she needs, everything. I've colour-coded it. Blue for football, pink for Olivia's drama, green for doctors' appointments."

"Right," David said, nodding. "The calendar. Of course."

But Sarah could see the slight panic in his eyes. When was the last time he'd checked that calendar? When was the last time he'd needed to?

"And what about my drama showcase?" Olivia had put her phone down now, fully engaged for the first time all evening. This affected her, so suddenly she was paying attention. "That's in June too. The twentieth. You said you'd help me with my costume. You promised."

"I'll help you before I go. We can work on it together this month. We have three weeks." Sarah tried to keep her tone gentle. "We'll sort it out, Olly. I promise."

"But what if I need adjustments? What if something goes wrong? What if the hem comes undone or the zipper breaks, or I spill something on it?" Olivia's pitch rose, taking on that panicky quality it got when she felt unsupported. "You always fix things. Dad doesn't know how to sew."

"I can learn," David said, though he sounded doubtful.

"Or," Sarah said, firmer now, "you'll figure it out. You'll use YouTube - there are about a million sewing tutorials online. Or you'll ask a friend's mum. Or you'll safety pin it. Or you'll realise that a small imperfection doesn't matter."

She held Olivia’s gaze. "Olly, you're seventeen. In a year, you'll be at university, managing everything on your own. You're perfectly capable of handling a costume emergency if you need to."

"But you always..."

"I know I always do. But I won't always be there to do everything." Sarah looked between her daughters, these girls she loved more than anything, who somehow made her feel both essential and invisible at the same time. "You need to learn to do things yourself. Both of you. Life is going to throw bigger problems at you than a hem coming undone or not knowing which football field you're supposed to be at. You're going to rely on your father for these two weeks. And you know what? You'll be fine. All of you will be fine. Better than fine."

Both girls stared at her as if she'd spoken another language. The idea of their father handling their schedules, transport, and problems seemed impossible to them. Maybe that was her fault. Maybe she'd made herself too necessary, taken on too much for too long, and taught them to be helpless.

"Sarah." David's voice had that careful quality it got when he was trying to be reasonable. The tone he used with difficult patients, the ones who didn't want to hear what he had to say. "I support you wanting to write. You know I do. I think it's great that you want to do this. Really."

But. She could hear the 'but' coming.

"But two weeks seems... excessive. And expensive. What about a week? You could still get a lot of writing done in a week. Maybe even a long weekend? Four or five days? Get the ball rolling and then come home and keep writing here?"

"I don't want a week," Sarah spoke quietly but firmly. "And I don't want a long weekend. I want twelve days. I need them."

"But..."

"David." She met his eyes straight on, and maybe something in her face had surprised him, because he'd stopped talking. Just sat there, waiting. The girls were quiet, too, watching this unfold like a tennis match.

"I'm going to France for twelve days in June. I've already booked the hotel. I've paid the deposit. It's non-refundable." That wasn't entirely true, but close enough. "I've checked the calendar—" she gestured to the fridge, where her meticulous colour-coded calendar hung, every football practice and drama rehearsal and doctor's appointment marked "—and there's nothing critical that can't be managed without me. The girls will be fine. You'll be fine. And I'll be back before the summer holidays, before our Cornwall trip, before any of the summer plans. This doesn't disrupt anything except routine."

David was staring at her. Seeing her, maybe for the first time in months. She could see him processing this, trying to understand. "It just seems very sudden."

"It's not sudden. I've been thinking about this for a month. Planning it." She paused, then decided to go for it. The truth. The thing she'd been holding back. "Since Margaret Thornton told me not to become a doormat."

The words came out stronger than she'd expected, more certain. When she saw David's face flinch in surprise, Sarah realised she'd shocked him. She'd shocked all of them. The girls stared at her as if she had suddenly grown two heads.

Good, she thought. Let them be surprised. Let them see that their wife and mother could be more than just the person who knows where everything is, keeps track of everyone's schedules, and puts dinner on the table every night.

But beneath the bravado, doubt whispered: 'Can you do this? Can you maintain this? Or will you apologise tomorrow and say you didn't mean it?' She pushed the doubt away. For now, she had to stay firm, even if she wasn't sure how long she could keep it up.

"You're not a doormat," David said finally, quietly. Almost wounded.

"Then you won't mind me taking this time to write."

It wasn't a question.

Another silence. Longer this time. Sarah could hear the kitchen clock ticking. Could hear Olivia's phone buzzing against the table, ignored for once. Could hear her own heartbeat in her ears.

"Of course not," David said finally, though doubt threaded through his words. The concern. His unspoken belief that this was a phase, a whim, something she'd get out of her system and then come back to normal. Back to being the woman who made everything work. "If this is what you need, then... of course. I just worry about you, that's all. Going off to a foreign country alone..."

"I'll be fine."

"But what if something happens? What if you need help? What if you get sick or there's a problem with the hotel or..."

"Then I'll handle it. I'm forty-three, David, not eighty-three. I can manage travelling to France on my own. Women do it all the time."

He nodded slowly, but she could tell he still wasn't convinced. He still thought it was strange, this sudden need to get away, to be alone, to write. As if she'd just decided on a whim, instead of thinking about it for years, dreaming about it, wanting it.

"What about my football kit?" Betty had asked into the silence. Practical, grounded Betty. "Who's going to wash it? And my art stuff - I need proper paper for that project. Who's going to take me to get that?"

"You are," Sarah had said. "You're fifteen, Betty. You can wash your own football kit. And you can get the bus to the art supply shop. Or Dad can drive you. It's one trip."

"But I don't know how to use the washing machine."

"Then you'll learn. It's not complicated. There are instructions on the detergent. And if you can't figure it out, ask your sister. Or Google it. There are YouTube videos for everything these days."

"But..."

"Betty." Sarah's tone sharpened. "You're fifteen years old. You can operate a washing machine. You're choosing not to learn because it's easier to have me do it. But I won't always be there. What are you going to do at university? Take your dirty clothes home every weekend?"

Betty's face flushed. Olivia's gaze dropped to her plate, probably realising the same logic applied to her.

"I just..." Betty's voice shrank. "I just wanted you here, that's all. For my semifinals. You always come to my games."

And there it was. The guilt. The sharp stab of it, right in Sarah's chest.

"I know, sweetheart," Sarah said, softening. "And I'm sorry I'll miss that game. But I'll be at every other game this season. And next season. And the season after that. This is twelve days, Betty. Twelve days out of your entire life. Out of my entire life. Surely I can have those."

Betty nodded, but tears threatened.

Sarah's resolve wavered. Almost said: 'Never mind. Forget it. I'll stay.'

But then she looked at David's relief, already starting to show on his face, thinking the crisis was over. Olivia picked up her phone again, already half-checked out. She thought about Margaret Thornton's words: 'Don't wait for permission.'

"I'm going," Sarah said quietly. "And that's final."

Olivia and Betty had exchanged glances, that silent sibling communication that needed no words. 'Mum's being weird,' the glance said. 'Mum's serious about this. What's happening?'

Yes, Sarah had thought, watching them. Yes, I am serious. For the first time in a long time, I'm doing something just for me, and I'm not apologising for it.

AND HERE SHE WAS. She'd done it. She'd stood her ground. She'd booked the hotel, bought the train tickets, and packed her bags. She'd written out lists, schedules, important phone numbers, meal suggestions, and left them on the kitchen counter, even though she knew David probably wouldn't look at them. She'd restocked the freezer with meals he could reheat. She'd left sticky notes everywhere: how to work the washing machine, the girls' schedules, emergency numbers. She'd done everything she could to make her absence manageable.

She'd kissed the girls goodbye that morning at six a.m., both of them still half-asleep. Olivia had mumbled, "Have fun," without opening her eyes, words thick with sleep. Betty had managed, "Bring me back something French," barely conscious, pulling the duvet over her head. David drove her to the station, the car silent except for the radio. He'd kissed her cheek at the drop-off and held her for a moment longer than usual.

"You'll be alright?" he'd asked.

"I'll be fine," she'd said.

"Call when you get there?"

"I will."

"And Sarah?" He'd met her eyes, then held them, and for a moment she'd seen something there. Worry, yes, but also... something else. Respect, maybe. Or fear. Fear that she might not come back. "Enjoy your writing time."

But there was something different in his tone this time. Not dismissive. Not humouring her. Almost like he believed her now. Almost like he understood this was real.

And now she was here. On this beach. In Normandy. Alone. She'd done it.

So why couldn't she write?

Sarah's gaze fell to her notebook. Still blank.

'What are you doing here? What makes you think you can write a book? You're forty-three years old. You haven't written anything except shopping lists and permission slips for the past fifteen years. You're being ridiculous. David's right. The girls are right. Margaret Thornton was being kind, but she doesn't know you. You should just go home.'

The thoughts circled like those gulls overhead, relentless.

And then, cutting through them like a knife through water: "Penny for them."

Sarah's head snapped up so fast she nearly dropped her notebook. A man was standing a few feet away, hands in his pockets, looking down at her with an amused smile. She hadn't heard him approach - hadn't heard anything over the wind and her own spiralling thoughts.

He was handsome. Very handsome. Tall, with dark hair that the wind was doing interesting things to, and eyes that were laughing even when his mouth wasn't. Late thirties, maybe, dressed casually in dark trousers and a worn blue jumper that had seen better days but somehow made him look approachable rather than scruffy.

Sarah immediately wished she'd bothered to comb her hair that morning. Or worn the nicer sweater. Or put on makeup. Or literally made any effort at all with her appearance.

"What do you mean, a penny for them?" she asked, more sharply than she'd intended.

"Your thoughts, of course," he said, as if this were the most obvious thing in the world. His accent was English, not French, which surprised her somehow. "You seemed miles away. Or decades away. Hard to tell."

"I think you should mind your own business," Sarah said, closing her notebook with a decisive snap. "I wasn't thinking about anything. I was just staring at the sea. Enjoying the view."

He laughed - not a polite chuckle, but a real laugh, delighted and unguarded. "No, you weren't. You were deep in thought, and something's troubling you. Want to talk about it?"

The audacity. The nerve of this stranger, showing up out of nowhere and acting like he had any right to speak to her, to assume anything about her.

"No," Sarah said flatly. "I don't."

"Fair enough." He rocked back on his heels, showing no signs of leaving. Just stood there, looking at her like she was the most interesting thing on this beach. "My name's Jack, by the way."

"I didn't ask."

"I know you didn't." His smile widened, and she noticed he had a small scar above his left eyebrow. A slight crookedness to his nose that suggested it had been broken once. Somehow, these imperfections made him more attractive, not less. "I was simply providing the information, should you want to know in the future."

"What future?"

"Well, you never know, do you?"

His tone was playful, challenging, and utterly infuriating. And underneath all that, something else. A spark. A pull. The kind of thing Sarah hadn't experienced in so long she'd almost forgotten what it was called.

Chemistry.

Sitting there on the cold sand, her hair a mess, her notebook clutched defensively to her chest like a shield, it was there. A warmth low in her stomach, a tingling awareness of him standing there, of the space between them, of the way he was looking at her.

And she could tell from the way he watched her, not leering or crude, just 'seeing' her. His eyes met hers for a moment too long. His smile had a quality to it that wasn't just friendly. It was interested. Appreciative.

No. Absolutely not. She was here to write. To find herself. Not to get involved with some stranger on a beach, no matter how handsome he was or how nice his smile, or how he made her feel like a person, an attractive person, instead of just someone who took care of everyone else.

"Look," she said, with finality. "I'm sure you're very nice, but I'm here to work. To write. I don't have time for... for whatever this is."

"Whatever this is?" Jack repeated, his eyes dancing with mirth. "I only asked about your thoughts. I wasn't proposing marriage."

Heat flooded Sarah's cheeks. "I know that. I just... I meant..."

"You meant you want to be left alone."

"Yes. Exactly."

"Alright then." He started to walk away across the dunes, and an unexpected pang of disappointment ran through Sarah. But then he paused, glanced back over his shoulder. "I'll be around if you need to have a chat. Sometimes it helps to talk to a stranger. No judgment. No history. Just... conversation."

"I won't!" Sarah called after him, but the words came out less certain than she'd intended.

"Oh, you will," he said, and even from a distance she could hear his certainty, the laughter threaded through it. "You look like someone who needs to talk. And I happen to be an excellent listener."

"How would you possibly know what I need?"

He shrugged, that smile still playing around his mouth. "Call it intuition." He gave her a little salute. "Enjoy your writing, Sarah."

She blinked. "How did you..."

"Your notebook. You wrote your name inside the cover. I saw it when you opened it."

"Oh." Of course. She'd written "Property of Sarah Mitchell" on the inside cover like a schoolgirl. How embarrassing.

"See you around," he said, and then he was gone, disappearing over the rise of the dunes, and Sarah was alone again with her blank notebook and the sound of the sea.

She wanted to shout after him. She wanted to call him back and say, 'Yes. I do need to talk. I need a stranger to unburden on. I'm lost.' But she didn't. She sat there, frozen, watching the spot where he'd disappeared, her heart stuttering.

It would be easier, she thought, if he weren't so damn attractive. If he hadn't watched her like that. Like she was interesting. Like she mattered. Like she existed as something more than just a mother, a wife, a person who keeps track of everyone else's lives.

And then, despite everything - despite the blank page, the spiralling thoughts, the weight of her marriage, the guilt about the girls, the fear of what she was doing - Sarah started to laugh. Quietly at first. Then louder. A real laugh that came from somewhere deep in her chest, echoing across the empty beach.

Because really. 'Really.'

She'd come to France to write a book. A romantic comedy, she'd told herself. Something light and funny about a woman finding herself. And what happens on literally her first day? She meets a tall, dark, handsome stranger on the beach who asks for a penny for her thoughts, making her heart race, and says things like "You'll come find me" with absolute certainty. And to top it all. A toy boy.

Could it be any more cliché? Could she be any more predictable? She had basically put herself into the most obvious romantic story possible.

'A woman has a midlife crisis. She goes to France. She meets a mysterious man. What's next? He sweeps her off her feet? They have a whirlwind romance? She discovers herself through love?'

God. She was pathetic.

Except... she was also smiling, sitting here alone on these Normandy dunes with sand in her shoes and wind in her hair and a notebook that had been blank for four hours and wasn't going to be blank anymore.

Because somewhere in all that cliché, in all that predictability, the block had lifted. The words wanted to come now. The story wanted to be told. Even if it was the most obvious story in the world.

The empty page waited.

Then, before she could second-guess herself, she started to write.

> *The thing about meeting someone unexpectedly is that you never see them coming. Not really. You're sitting there, minding your own business, staring at the sea and contemplating the general disaster of your life, and then suddenly there's a man standing in front of you asking for a penny for your thoughts, and everything shifts slightly sideways...*

Sarah paused, read what she'd written, and laughed out loud.

Well. At least the dam had broken.

CHAPTER 2 - THE MARKET

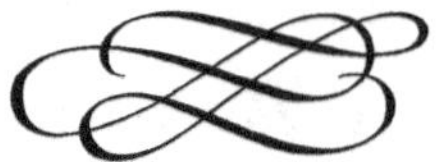

Sarah wrote until her hand cramped.

At first, the words came slowly, then gained momentum. She wrote of a woman on a beach, invisible to loved ones, and a stranger with laughing eyes who once offered a penny for her thoughts.

She wrote three pages. Then five. Then seven.

The pen moved across the paper. Inside her, a change, not just the end of writer's block, but deeper. She realised what she'd missed wasn't the act itself, but the permission to write. To take up space. To believe her story mattered.

It wasn't good yet. Some sentences jarred, metaphors clashed, and her voice wavered between confident and uncertain. She'd crossed out entire paragraphs, rewritten sections, and questioned every word choice. Still, she had ink on paper. Real pages. It was the beginning of her first draft.

The woman in her story sat on a beach like this one. She'd left her husband, children, and a life of management and invisible labour. She'd come to France to find herself, though unsure if there was any self left.

And then a man had appeared. A stranger with kind eyes and an easy smile who'd asked for a penny for her thoughts. Just like...

Sarah stopped. Her pen hovered over the page. Was she really doing this? Writing about Jack? About herself? Was she that transparent, that obvious?

'It's fiction,' she told herself. 'Fiction based on truth, but still fiction. Writers do it all the time.'

But her hand was shaking slightly as she continued.

The sun moved across the sky as she wrote. The shadows lengthened. The wind picked up, colder now, carrying more salt, more bite. She barely noticed. The story pulled her forward, demanding to be told.

When she finally raised her head, blinking as if waking from a dream, the sun was lower. Shadows stretched long across the sand. The wind was decidedly cold. She pulled her jumper tight. Her legs were numb from sitting so long on the damp sand. Her stomach growled, reminding her she'd missed lunch entirely. Breakfast had been a sad railway croissant hours ago.

How long had she been sitting here? She checked her watch. Nearly five o'clock. She'd been on this beach for almost three hours. Three hours. The longest she'd sat and written in... she couldn't remember when. Maybe ever.

At home, she'd be making dinner now. Betty would be upstairs doing homework (or more likely, not doing homework), Olivia would be getting ready to go out somewhere, and David would be calling to say he'd be late. Again. The familiar rhythm of her life was as predictable as clockwork.

But here, she lost three hours to words on a page. No one needed, asked for, or expected anything from her. Three hours of pure, selfish creation.

Guilt tried to surface. She almost let it, but steadied herself and chose, for once, not to let obligation replace pride. Not yet. Instead, she held on to her sense of accomplishment of doing this, something real, just for herself. Guilt could wait. This was worth holding onto.

Sarah closed her notebook, brushed the sand from her jeans, and stood. Her legs were stiff, protesting the movement. She stood there for a moment, just looking at the sea. The Channel. The same water her grandfather had crossed eighty years ago, though from the other direction. Young men had died here so she could have this moment, this simple, wonderful chance to create a book that might never be read.

The enormity of that hit her suddenly. All that sacrifice. All that blood and fear and courage. So that she, ordinary Sarah Mitchell from Bristol, could sit on a beach and tell a story. So she could choose her own path. To make her own decisions. To claim her own space in the world.

"Thank you, Grandad," she whispered to the wind. "For this. For freedom. For everything."

The wind carried her words away, out over the grey-blue water, toward England somewhere in the distance. She hoped, impossibly, that he could hear her. That somewhere, somehow, he knew what his sacrifice had meant.

Then she picked up her bag, slinging it over her shoulder, and headed back toward the village.

* * *

THE WALK back was different from that morning.

Earlier, she'd been anxious and full of doubt, each step heavy with uncertainty about whether she deserved this time, this space, this indulgence. Now, though not exactly confident, she noticed a subtle shift inside herself. Relief mingled with hope; the act of writing had proven she could do this, and that mattered. She'd done it. She'd actually done it. Sat down and written for three hours straight without checking her phone, without making dinner, without responding to anyone else's needs. Just... written.

The path from the beach led through the dunes, winding between tufts of beach grass that whispered in the wind, and into the village's narrow streets. As she walked, the sounds shifted. The waves faded, replaced by the hum of human life.

French voices floated from open windows. A woman calling - 'Mathieu! Le dîner!' - her tone familiar, maternal, exactly the same in French as it would be in English. Laughter from somewhere nearby. Dishes clattering. The news was on television somewhere, a male speaking rapid French about politics. A dog barked, then someone shouted, 'Tais-toi!' The dog stopped.

Sarah passed an épicerie. A corner shop with fruit and vegetables in wooden crates outside. Tomatoes, perfectly red and round, their vines still attached. Peaches that smelled like summer from three feet away. Courgettes, aubergines, peppers in jewel colours. Bunches of herbs she couldn't name. An elderly man in a flat cap examined the melons, pressing them gently with his thumbs, tapping them, holding them to his ear as if they might whisper their secrets. He was assessing their ripeness with a surgeon's seriousness, a ritual clearly performed many times before.

“Bonsoir, madame,” he said as she passed, tipping his cap with old-fashioned courtesy.

“Bonsoir,” Sarah replied, thrilled by the normalcy of it. The simple greeting made her feel like she belonged here, not a tourist or outsider, just someone walking through the village at the end of the day. Just another person living her life.

She turned down a narrow street - Rue de la Mer, according to the blue-and-white sign on the corner. The smell of baking bread stopped her in her tracks. The corner bakery's lights glowed warm in the evening dusk. Its window displayed a few remaining baguettes and apple tarts, their crusts golden and glistening.

A couple walked past her, speaking rapid French, their shoulders touching in that comfortable way of long-term couples. The woman laughed, throwing her head back, and he smiled down at her with obvious affection.

‘That used to be us,’ Sarah thought. David and I, before we became helpers, arrangers, logistics coordinators for the girls' lives instead of partners. Before marriage became a series of handoffs and updates rather than a relationship. She wondered if he ever missed it too, if somewhere beneath the day-to-day tasks and responsibilities, he remembered simply enjoying each other's company. To touch shoulders while walking. To make each other laugh.

Or had he even noticed the shift? Maybe it hadn't changed for him at all. Maybe he was perfectly happy with their efficient, functional partnership. Maybe she was the only one who noticed the loss of... what? Romance? Connection? Being seen as a woman rather than just a wife and mother?

She pushed the thought away and kept walking. This wasn't the time for that. This was her time. She could examine her marriage when she got home.

The village was tiny, she realised. Three main streets - Rue de la Mer, Rue Saint-Jean, and Rue du Port - with about a dozen narrow lanes branching off like capillaries from veins. Stone houses with blue or green shutters, most of them closed against the evening. Window boxes of geraniums, bright red and pink against the pale stone. Cobblestones worn smooth by centuries of feet, polished and uneven, treacherous in the rain but beautiful in the fading light.

Everything was old and solid here. Permanent. More permanent than Bristol ever was, with its modern developments and constant construction. These buildings had stood for two hundred years, maybe more. They'd seen wars and peace, occupations and liberations, births and deaths. Her problems - her midlife crisis, her invisible marriage, her need to write - were nothing in the face of that history. A blip. A moment.

Somehow, that was comforting.

She passed the church, a small stone building with a modest bell tower, and heard singing from inside. Maybe vespers or choir practice. Elderly voices, slightly wavering but earnest, singing Latin hymns. The sound followed her for half a block, fading gradually. She didn't understand the words, but their meaning was universal. Praise. Supplication. Hope. The things humans have always needed to express.

Finally, she turned onto Rue Saint-Jean and saw her hotel.

The sign read Hôtel de la Plage, though it resembled a large house more than a hotel. Three stories of pale stone, green shutters, and a front garden where lavender grew wild, and roses climbed the wall in profusion. Sarah guessed it held about ten rooms, maybe twelve. A family-run place, not a chain. Personal. Real.

She'd found it online, scrolling through options late at night while David snored beside her, one hand thrown over his face. Most hotels were too big, too modern, too much like the ones she'd stayed in for David's medical conferences - all beige carpets and generic art and breakfast buffets and in towns rather than a village. But this one was small and old-fashioned, with reviews calling it "charming" and "like staying at your French grandmother's house." It was right, the kind of place where you could write a book. And in a village, she could become as one with.

Madame Rousseau, the owner, had checked her in earlier that afternoon with unexpected warmth. “Bienvenue,” she'd said, handing over an actual heavy old-fashioned key, not a plastic card. “You are here to write, yes? Your room is very quiet. Perfect for thinking.”

Sarah couldn't remember telling her about the writing when she'd booked online, but it was a blessing. Like permission, somehow. As if the universe was saying: 'Yes, this is allowed. This is good. Go create your book.'

Now, Sarah let herself in through the front door, which was unlocked just as Madame Rousseau had promised it would be during the day, and climbed the narrow stairs to the second floor. Her room was at the end of the hall. Number 7. Lucky seven, she'd thought when she first saw it.

She unlocked the door, stepped inside. Tension drain from her shoulders like water. It was perfect. Small, but perfect.

The walls were whitewashed, the plaster slightly uneven, as old buildings are, showing the house's history. A double bed with a white iron frame took up most of one side, covered in crisp white linen and a faded blue quilt that had probably been washed a thousand times. Two pillows. A bedside table with a lamp and a glowing digital clock showing 17:23.

Across from the bed, a tall window with white muslin curtains that moved gently in the breeze. It had been left open that morning, so the room now smelled of salt air and lavender from the garden below.

Against the far wall, a battered writing desk - the kind with a drawer and worn edges - and a single wooden chair. She placed her phone charger and the French phrasebook she'd bought at the railway station. Beside them, a plain white vase with three sprigs of lavender. Surely Madame Rousseau had brought them while she was out. A quiet kindness.

The floor was worn wood, the kind that creaks slightly when you walk, softened by a faded blue-and-cream rug that showed its age but had clearly been quality once. In the corner, a narrow door opened to a tiny en-suite bathroom with just a toilet, sink, and shower stall. No bathtub, no luxury, but perfectly functional. There was no television, no minibar, no coffee maker, no trace of chain hotel blandness. Just a room. Unadorned, sincere, and striking in its simplicity.

Sarah dropped her bag on the chair and went to the window. From here, she could see over the terracotta rooftops to a distant slice of sea. The setting sun was painting the water gold and pink and orange, a watercolour wash of colour. Below, in the garden, Madame Rousseau was hanging white sheets on a clothesline, and they snapped in the breeze like flags of surrender or victory - Sarah wasn't sure which.

A church bell rang somewhere in the village. Six chimes. Evening. The sound echoed off the stone buildings, then faded. Sarah stood there for a long moment, just breathing. Just being. She was different here. Not a new person, still Sarah, forty-three, married, a mother, but shifted somehow. She was lighter, as if she'd finally set down a burden she didn't even know she was carrying. The long-held weight of expectation, duty, and being needed now seemed less oppressive, replaced by a tentative sense of possibility.

And strangely, impossibly, she was at home. Not like Bristol, which was familiar, comfortable, and known, but in a deeper way. This room, this village, this moment was meant for her. It was as if she'd been carrying this place inside her all along, in some hidden pocket of her heart, and had only now finally arrived.

She closed the muslin curtains, not completely, just enough for privacy while still letting the evening light filter through. The fabric moved like water, creating patterns of light and shadow on the white walls that shifted and changed with the breeze.

Then she sat at the desk, opened her notebook, and began to read what she'd written on the beach.

It was rough. Definitely rough. Some sentences were too long, meandering without purpose. Others were too short, abrupt, and lacking connection. The voice wavered - sometimes confident, sometimes uncertain, sometimes trying too hard to sound literary. But there was substance there. A connection. Real and unexpected.

Sarah frowned slightly, flipping back through the pages. Twelve pages total. She read them again, more slowly this time, her editor's eye, if such a thing existed, catching problems but also seeing depth beneath the rough prose.

This wasn't what she'd planned.

She'd come here with an idea: a funny romance novella. Light, humorous, maybe 40,000 words. A woman having a midlife crisis, going on holiday, having a harmless flirtation, and learning to laugh at herself. A romance, sweet and unchallenging. Nothing too serious or heavy. Just a pleasant story that might make people smile, that wouldn't embarrass her if someone she knew actually read it.

But this... this was different. Entirely different.

This was deeper. Richer. The humour was there; she saw it in her protagonist's self-aware observations and in the absurdity of the stranger offering money for her thoughts. But underneath, she recognised an unexpected undercurrent: darkness, sadness, longing.

She was writing about invisibility. About the slow erosion of self that happens when you spend years making yourself smaller, quieter, less demanding. She was writing about the longing to be truly seen, not just as a function or a role, but as a whole person with desires and dreams and a life beyond service. About the weight of being overlooked, dismissed, and taken for granted. About almost disappearing, even among the people who were supposed to love you most.

This wasn't a novella. This was a book. A proper book. A novel. The realisation made her breath catch. She asked herself how she knew this with so few words on the page. But, she did know.

When had she started believing she could do this? Write a proper book. When had she decided she deserved this much space, this much time, this much ambition? Who did she think she was, sitting in a French hotel room pretending she was a real writer?

Maybe it was when Margaret Thornton met her eyes and said, "Don't become like me." Or when she booked the train tickets despite David's doubts. Or when she stood her ground with the girls. Or maybe it was when she sat on that beach for three hours, and the words kept coming, page after page, until her hand cramped.

Or maybe - and the thought sent butterflies through her stomach - it was when Jack had watched her and saw someone worth talking to. Worth knowing. Worth more than a dismissive smile and a change of subject. When he'd watched her, and she'd been seen, truly seen, for the first time in years.

Sarah picked up her pen, held it over the page, and made a decision.

Fine. If this were to be a proper novel, she would treat it as one. No apologies later, no minimising or diminishing. She would write it as a real book. She'd give it the space it needed, the time it deserved, and the ambition she'd been too afraid to claim. She'd write something real, true, that mattered.

If David thought it was silly, if the girls didn't understand, if Margaret Thornton was the only one who ever read it and saw what she meant - well, that would be enough. At least she would have written it. At least she would have tried.

She began again.

OUTSIDE, the village settled into the evening. Voices and laughter drifted in through the open window. Dishes clinked. A car passed on the cobblestones below, driving slowly over the uneven surface. The church bell marked the quarter hour, then the half hour. Life went on around her, normal, mundane, and beautiful, while she sat in her white room and wrote, not the book she had planned, but the one she needed to.

The one writing itself through her.

Sarah wrote until the light faded completely, and the words on the page grew harder to read. She wrote until her stomach insisted she couldn't ignore it any longer, growling loud enough to break her concentration. She'd filled another five pages. Seventeen total now. Not bad for someone who supposedly couldn't do this anymore. Not bad for day one.

She closed the notebook, stretched her aching fingers, and wondered where she might find dinner in this village where she knew nothing and no one.

Except, she realised with a small spark of warmth, she did know someone.

Somewhere in this village was a man with laughing eyes who'd told her he'd be around if she needed to talk.

'You will,' he'd said with such certainty. And the strange thing was, Sarah thought as she stood up and tidied her hair in the mirror above the desk, he'd been right. She did need to talk. Wanted to, even. Wanted to tell someone about the writing, about the story taking shape, about the feeling of finally doing this, just for herself.

But first, dinner. Then maybe, if she was brave enough, she'd see if she could find him.

Or, more likely, Sarah thought with a slight smile as she grabbed her bag, he would find her.

SHE WALKED through the village as the light faded, looking for a place to eat. Most of the restaurants seemed to be family places, already full of locals and tourists. Through the windows, she could see people laughing, sharing bottles of wine, their faces warm in the candlelight. Couples. Families. Groups of friends.

She was conspicuously alone.

'This is fine,' she told herself. 'You're a grown woman. You can eat dinner by yourself. Women do it all the time.'

But part of her - and she hated admitting this - had been hoping to run into Jack again. To "accidentally" find the same café or restaurant where he was eating. To have him wave her over with that easy smile and say, "Fancy meeting you here." To not have to eat alone on her first night in France.

She didn't see him anywhere.

By the time she finally chose a bistro and ordered a plate of mussels and fries, because that's what you ate in Normandy, the waiter had told her, she had walked past most of the restaurants in the village at least twice. She was obviously a tourist, which annoyed her. She wanted to feel like she belonged here, but instead she wandered around, searching.

Or someone.

The mussels were good, though. Fresh and briny, cooked in white wine and herbs. She ate slowly, watching the other diners, eavesdropping on fragments of French conversation she couldn't quite follow. The family at the next table - parents and three children - reminded her of her own family dinners, the way the mother kept redirecting the conversation, making sure everyone had enough, barely eating her own food.

'That's me,' Sarah thought. 'That's what I look like from the outside.'

She paid her bill - more expensive than she'd expected, but worth it - and walked back to the hotel in the dark. The village was different at night. Quieter. More intimate. Lights glowed from windows. She could hear televisions, conversations, and the sounds of people living their lives.

When she got back to her room, she was disappointed and didn't want to examine why too closely. She'd been hoping... what? That Jack would be waiting for her? That he'd leave a note? That was ridiculous. She barely knew him. He was just a stranger she'd met on the beach.

But she fell asleep thinking about him anyway. About his smile. About the way he'd watched her as if she mattered. About tomorrow morning and whether she'd see him again.

* * *

SARAH WOKE to sunlight streaming through the muslin curtains and the sound of church bells. For a moment, she didn't know where she was. The light seemed wrong, too bright, too clear, coming from the wrong direction. The bed was different: firmer than she was used to, but still comfortable, with crisp sheets that smelled faintly of lavender. The sounds were unfamiliar too: church bells instead of David's alarm, French voices instead of traffic noise.

Then she remembered.

France. Normandy. The beach. The writing. Jack.

She sat up, and memories of yesterday rushed back. The eight-hour journey. Hours on the beach. The walk back through the village. Her room. The realisation that she wasn't writing a silly novella but a real story. The seventeen pages. Walking through the village looking for dinner, half-hoping to see Jack again. The disappointment when she hadn't.

Then, with a start that was almost physical, another realisation hit her. She'd been disappointed last night. Genuinely disappointed. While walking through the village for dinner, passing cafés and restaurants full of people eating and laughing, she'd been looking for him. For Jack. Hoping he might appear like he had on the beach, all casual confidence and laughing eyes.

He hadn't.

And she'd felt... let down. The letdown had been sudden and sharper than she'd expected. The recognition of that disappointment now, in the clear light of morning, startled her. 'Why am I feeling this way? She wondered. When did a brief meeting with a stranger start to matter to me? Why does it suddenly feel like a loss not to have seen him again?

'You barely know him,' she told herself firmly, swinging her legs out of bed. He's just some man. Yes, he seemed nice, and yes, she found him attractive, but that shouldn't matter. 'You're here to work. You're not here to look for distraction or connection. Was she just craving attention, or was it deeper? About being seen?

Not to what? Not to develop a crush? Not to risk getting butterflies over a man who wasn't her husband? She caught herself. Was that really what this was about? Was she just craving attention, or was it something deeper? Something about being seen? About feeling like a person again instead of just a role?

Sarah reached for her phone on the bedside table. 7:23 AM. Later than she usually woke at home, where she'd be up at six to make breakfast, pack lunches, and nag the girls about getting ready for school. Where she'd be checking the calendar, making sure nothing was forgotten, keeping the household running.

Here, she'd slept until 7:23 AM, and the world hadn't ended. Nobody needed her. Nobody was waiting for her. She could lie in bed for another hour if she wanted to.

The freedom of it was dizzying.

She got out of bed and walked to the window, pushing the curtains aside. The view was even more beautiful in the morning light. The village stretched below her: terracotta roofs, stone walls, church spires, narrow streets, all bathed in golden light. Beyond everything, the slice of blue-grey sea she'd seen last night, calm this morning, glittering in the sun.

The garden below was already busy. Madame Rousseau was tending to her herbs, snipping sprigs of rosemary and thyme with garden shears and placing them in a wicker basket. An orange cat wound between her legs, and she spoke to it in French - soft, affectionate words Sarah couldn't quite catch but understood the meaning of anyway. The universal language of talking to cats.

It was Tuesday morning. At home, Betty would be getting ready for school, probably still in her pyjamas even though she needed to leave in twenty minutes. She'd be insisting she had plenty of time, searching for the unfindable. Homework, shoes, her phone charger and blaming Sarah silently for not knowing where it was. Olivia would already be in her uniform, eating cereal while scrolling through her phone, half-present. David would be in the shower, running late as always, shouting about a meeting at eight.

Sarah had made sure it all happened. Every morning, like clockwork. She was the one who found the lost things, who signed the permission slips, who made the coffee, and buttered the toast. She was the invisible force that kept everything running smoothly.

But not today.

Today, hundreds of miles away, they'd have to figure it out themselves. David would have to find Betty's shoes. Olivia would have to remember her own homework. They would manage. They'd have to.

Guilt rose automatically, reflexive as breathing. 'Maybe I should call,' she thought. 'Just to check in. Make sure everything's okay. Make sure they don't need anything.' Would they feel her absence? Miss her? Or would they just be annoyed by the inconvenience?

But it was 7:30 in the morning. They'd be rushing, stressed, not in the mood for a chatty phone call from France. And besides, she'd only been gone one day. One day. Surely they could survive one day without her.

'They're fine,' she told herself. 'They have to be fine.'

She turned from the window and surveyed her room. It was even lovelier in the morning light. White walls glowing, the blue quilt inviting, her notebook waiting patiently on the desk. It was becoming familiar.

Sarah took a shower. The water pressure wasn't great, and the shower stall was tiny, but at least the water was hot. She dressed in jeans and a light blue jumper, dried her hair properly instead of just pulling it back wet, and put on more makeup than she had the day before - not a lot, just enough to look like she'd made an effort.

She told herself it wasn't because she might see Jack again. She was just... presenting herself well. Like a real person. Like someone who wasn't just rushing through life trying to keep up with everyone else's demands.

She should write. Should sit at that lovely desk and add to yesterday's pages while the ideas were still fresh, while she could still remember exactly what she'd meant by that metaphor about invisibility. But her stomach said otherwise, reminding her she'd barely eaten yesterday. And she'd promised herself not to spend this trip shut away in her room. That was her pattern at home: hiding, shrinking, taking up so little space she nearly vanished.

No. Today, she would go out. She'd have breakfast in the village like a proper person. Like someone who lived here, not a tourist hiding in her hotel room. Maybe she'd find a café with good coffee and fresh croissants. Maybe practice her terrible French with someone patient.

Maybe see if Jack was around.

The thought made her stomach flip in a way that had nothing to do with hunger.

She grabbed her bag and headed downstairs.

* * *

THE VILLAGE FELT different in the morning: busier, more purposeful. People were opening shops, sweeping steps, heading to work or the market. Sarah walked down Rue Saint-

Jean, her footsteps echoing on the cobblestones, trying to orient herself and look like she knew where she was going.

Yesterday, she'd been so focused on getting to the beach, then getting to her hotel, that she'd barely noticed the village itself. Now, in the clear morning light, she could finally see it properly. In more detail. Most of the buildings were old—probably centuries old. Made of stone and plaster in shades of cream and pale grey. Shutters painted blue, green, or weathered to silvery grey. Some windows had boxes full of geraniums. Others had ivy climbing their walls, green and lush despite the salty air. She had seen this yesterday. Today, it appeared more vivid.

The streets were narrow, clearly built for horses and carts instead of cars. Now and then, a car would squeeze through, moving slowly and honking at pedestrians who didn't move aside quickly enough. Most people walked or rode bicycles, weaving around each other with practised ease.

She passed a woman sweeping her doorstep - elderly, thin, wearing a housedress and slippers. "Bonjour, madame," the woman said without looking up, the greeting automatic, a ritual performed every morning.

"Bonjour," Sarah replied, as thrilled as yesterday. Like she belonged here. Like she was just another person going about her morning, not a tourist or an outsider.

The boulangerie was open now, its door propped wide to let in the morning air. The smell of fresh bread spilt out onto the street, so strong and delicious it was almost physical. Through the window, Sarah could see people queuing - locals with shopping bags, ordering their bread with the seriousness of an important transaction. This was a ritual, too. Sacred, even.

She should go in. Should buy a croissant, practice her rusty French, do the thing tourists are supposed to do. But curiosity pulled her forward, down toward the centre of the village, toward a small square up ahead.

She turned from Rue de la Mer onto the cobblestoned square, about thirty meters across, with a stone fountain in the centre that wasn't running and probably hadn't worked in years. Buildings stood on all four sides: the mairie, or town hall, with a French flag hanging limp in the still morning air. A pharmacy with a green cross sign. A tabac with newspapers and magazines displayed outside on metal racks.

And on the corner, with small tables and chairs set up on the cobblestones under a faded awning: a café.

Café de la Plage, the sign read. Simple, unpretentious, the kind of place that had probably been there for fifty years and would be there for fifty more.

He sat at one of the tables, looking like he'd been waiting for her all morning: Jack.

Sarah's heart lurched - hope, nerves, and anticipation tangled together in one swift jolt.

He was reading a newspaper, an actual paper copy of Le Monde, spread out on the round table. He wore the same jumper as yesterday, or one just like it: dark blue, worn at the elbows, comfortable with years of use. His dark hair was a little messy, as if he'd run his fingers through it this morning and skipped the comb. He looked relaxed, at home, like someone who'd lived here for years.

He glanced up as she approached, and his face broke into a smile that made her stomach flip.

"Well," he said. "Look who decided I was right."

"I didn't decide anything," Sarah said, but she was smiling too, and couldn't help it. "I was just looking for coffee."

"And you found me instead. Funny how that works." He gestured to the chair across from him. "Join me?"

She should say no, she thought. Should play it cool. Stay composed. Don't seem too eager. Make him work for your attention. But was she really here to perform old games, old rituals? Or was she here to actually live a little?

'Sarah,' she told herself. 'Remember you're a married woman. A mother of two. Not some twenty-year-old on a gap year. You're here to work. To write.'

But even as she thought it, she was pulling out the chair and sitting down. Because she was tired of playing games. Tired of pretending she didn't want things she wanted. And what she wanted, right now, was to have coffee with this man who looked at her like she was interesting. Like she mattered.

It was just coffee. Just conversation. Just... nice.

"Alright," she said, settling into the chair. "But just for a coffee."

"Just for a coffee," Jack agreed, though his smile suggested he knew that she was in need of conversation.

Up close, in the morning light, he was even more attractive than she'd thought yesterday. Not in a conventional, movie-star way, but in a way that was somehow more appealing. Real. Human. Laughter lines around his eyes. A scar above his left eyebrow. Strong hands resting on the table beside the newspaper. The kind of face that had lived, that had stories, that had seen things.

"Sleep well?" Jack asked.

"Surprisingly well, actually. You?"

"Like the dead." He said it lightly, almost joking, but something flickered across his face so quickly Sarah almost missed it. Something dark. Then it was gone, and he was smiling again. "The sea air helps."

Before Sarah could respond or ask what he'd meant, a waitress appeared - a woman in her fifties with grey-blonde hair pulled back in a practical bun, wearing a black dress and a white apron. She had a kind face, lined and weathered from years of work, with eyes that crinkled when she smiled.

She spoke in rapid French, looking directly at Sarah, not even glancing at Jack.

"Pardon," Sarah said, flustered. "Je ne parle pas bien français. Do you speak English?"

The waitress's smile widened. "A little. You want coffee, yes?"

"Yes, please. Two coffees. Black."

The waitress nodded and disappeared back into the café without acknowledging Jack at all.

"Two?" Jack said, his eyes dancing with amusement. "And how did you know I wanted black coffee? What if I prefer a latte? Or a cappuccino?"

Sarah shrugged, surprised by her own certainty. "I just know these things."

"Do you now?"

"Apparently."

They sat in comfortable silence for a moment. The square was filling up slowly - a man walking a small white terrier, an elderly couple heading toward the pharmacy, a delivery van pulling up to the tabac. Normal morning life in a French village. Beautiful in its ordinariness.

"So," Jack said, leaning back in his chair. "Did you write yesterday? After you told me to mind my own business?"

"I did tell you that, didn't I?" Sarah felt a slight flush of embarrassment. "That was a bit rude."

"Not at all. You were protecting your space. Your time. That's admirable." He was grinning now. "But did you achieve anything?"

The waitress reappeared with two cups of black coffee, setting them both down in front of Sarah before disappearing again.

Sarah pushed one cup across the table to him.

"Yes," she said. "I wrote. Quite a bit, actually. Seventeen pages."

Jack's eyebrows rose. "That's impressive. What's it about?"

"A woman who's lost herself. Who's been so busy being a wife and a mother and a general life coordinator that she's forgotten who she is underneath all of that."

"Sounds familiar."

"Does it?" Sarah took a sip of her coffee. It was strong, slightly bitter, perfect. "And what would you know about feeling lost?"

"Everyone feels lost sometimes. It's part of being human." He studied her over the rim of his cup, his expression serious now. "The question is: what do you do about it? Some people just accept it. Live their whole lives feeling like they're slightly in the wrong place, doing the wrong things, being the wrong person. Others..." He trailed off.

"Others what?"

"Others go to France for two weeks to create a book," he said, smiling.

Heat rose in her cheeks. "It's not that dramatic."

"Isn't it? You left your family. Travelled to another country. Sat on a beach for hours. That's pretty dramatic, Sarah."

The way he said her name - like it mattered, like she mattered - sent warmth through her body. A feeling she hadn't experienced in so long she'd almost forgotten what it was called.

Desire.

"How do you know that I've left my family and that I was on the beach for hours?"

"I went back. Later. You were still there, completely absorbed in your notebook. I almost said hello again, but you seemed like you were in the zone. I didn't want to interrupt." “And you are wearing a wedding ring”.

"You were watching me?" She should be alarmed, creeped out, and concerned. Instead, she was… flattered. She ignored the remark about her wedding ring.

"I was walking on the beach. You happened to be on the beach. I noticed you. That's not watching, that's observing."

"That's semantics."

"True." He grinned. "But you're smiling, so I don't think you really mind."

She wasn't smiling. Except she was. She could feel it, warm and genuine on her face.

"Tell me about your book," Jack said, setting down his coffee cup. "The woman who's lost herself. What happens to her?"

"I don't know yet. I only wrote seventeen pages."

"But you must have some idea. A direction. An ending."

Sarah thought about it. "I suppose... I suppose she finds herself again. Remembers who she is. Learns to take up space. To have a voice. To be seen."

"By who?"

"By herself, mostly. But also..." She hesitated. "By someone who sees her clearly. Without all the roles and expectations. Someone who looks at her and actually sees ‘her’."

Jack was quiet, his eyes on hers, an unreadable quality in his expression. The air between them suddenly charged. Heavy.

"That sounds like a good book," he said finally.

"You think so?"

"I know so." He leaned forward. "Want to know a secret?"

"What?"

"Everyone is creating their own book. Every day. The story of their life. And most people are creating a book they don't want to read. They're living the life they think they're supposed to - the one with the dutiful spouse and the perfect children and the career that makes sense. But inside, there's a different book. A real one. The true story. And sometimes, if you're lucky, you get a chance to create the story you want instead. The one you actually want to be living."

Tears pricked Sarah's eyes. "Is that what I'm doing?"

"Isn't it?"

She thought about the seventeen pages in her notebook. About the woman in the story, sitting on a beach, trying to remember who she was. About how that woman was her and not-her at the same time. Fiction and truth blurred together.

"Maybe," she said quietly.

"Good." Jack stood up suddenly. "Come on. Let's walk. I want to show you somewhere."

"Where?"

"The market. It's Tuesday - market day. You can't come to a French village and not see the market."

"But we just sat down."

"And now we're standing up again. That's how life works, Sarah. You sit, you stand, you walk, you discover things. Come on."

* * *

HE STARTED WALKING across the square, hands in his pockets, confident and easy. After a moment of hesitation - wondering if she should follow, if this was wise, if she was being ridiculous - Sarah grabbed her bag and went after him.

The market was tucked down a narrow street behind the mairie, spreading out into a car park transformed into a riot of colour, sound, and smell.

There were about twenty stalls, arranged in two rows with a narrow aisle between them. Farmers were selling vegetables - tomatoes still on the vine, courgettes, aubergines, all impossibly fresh and bright. The fishmonger had the morning's catch laid out on ice: whole sea bass with silver scales, mackerel, prawns still in their shells, and what might have been octopus. The cheese vendor offered wheels, wedges, and rounds in colours from white to deep gold, each carefully labelled. The flower seller had buckets of blooms - sunflowers, roses, lavender, and others Sarah couldn't name.

And people. Locals, mostly, moving from stall to stall with their shopping bags and baskets, examining produce with critical eyes, chatting with vendors, greeting neighbours. A few tourists - German, by the sound of it - with cameras and guidebooks, looking slightly overwhelmed.

'Regarde! Les tomates! A woman's voice, sharp and delighted.

'Combien?' A man's voice, haggling over price.

'Fraîche ce matin! A vendor calling out, advertising his fish.

The smell hit her all at once - vegetables and fish and flowers and bread baking from a stall she couldn't see yet. It was overwhelming and wonderful, almost too much, like all of France compressed into this one space.

"Come on," Jack said, and led her down the first row of stalls.

They stopped at the tomato seller - an old man with deeply tanned, leathery skin and hands that had clearly spent decades working in the soil. His tomatoes were beautiful - still on the vine, deep red, smelling like earth and sunshine rather than the plastic supermarket versions Sarah bought at home.

The old man looked at Sarah and spoke in French, gesturing to his produce with obvious pride.

"He's telling you these tomatoes would make a grown man weep," Jack said quietly beside her. "His wife tends them as if they were her children. Talks to them every morning."

Sarah smiled at the vendor, not sure what to say. The old man picked up one of the tomatoes and held it out to her.

"Smell it," Jack said. "Go on."

Sarah leaned in and breathed in the scent. It smelled like summer. Like gardens and childhood and everything good about food that's been grown with care rather than manufactured efficiently in a greenhouse somewhere.

"It's perfect," she said.

"Everything here is perfect. That's the point of a French market. It's not about efficiency or convenience. It's about perfection. Quality. Care. Taking the time to do things properly."

Sarah thanked the vendor - "Merci" - and they moved on.

At the cheese stall, a woman in her forties was arranging her wares with artistic precision - soft cheeses, hard cheeses, blue cheeses, everything labelled in neat handwriting on cards. She was speaking to a customer in rapid French, cutting a wedge of pale and soft cheese, wrapping it carefully in paper.

When the customer left, the vendor turned to Sarah with a welcoming smile.

"The Camembert," Jack said beside her. "She makes it herself. Local milk, aged perfectly. You should try it."

The cheese vendor was already speaking to Sarah in French, asking a question, smiling patiently.

"Je ne comprends pas," Sarah said helplessly.

The vendor smiled, patient and kind, and tried again in slow, careful French, speaking as if to a child.

"She's asking if you want a sample," Jack translated.

"Oh! Yes. Oui. Merci."

The vendor cut a small piece of the Camembert and handed it to Sarah on the tip of a knife. She took it, popped it in her mouth, and nearly groaned out loud. It was creamy and rich and complex, tasting of earth and grass and terroir, that indefinable quality of place, just... French. Perfect. Real.

"Good?" Jack asked, though he was clearly amused by her expression.

"Incredible."

They moved on through the market, stopping at different stalls. Jack seemed to know everything about the village - pointing out details, explaining things, telling her stories about the vendors. The fishmonger had a boat called 'Marie' named after his late wife. The flower seller grew everything in her own garden. The bread vendor had won awards for his baguettes.

But Sarah noticed a strangeness. Something she couldn't quite explain.

At the tomato stall, the old man had addressed only her. At the cheese stall, the vendor had never once glanced at Jack, even though he was standing right beside Sarah. And now, at the flower stall, the same thing was happening. Do the French assume that it's the woman who chooses the produce, she wondered.

They stopped to admire a bucket of lavender - great purple-blue sheaves of it, smelling of summer and honey. The flower seller, a woman with sun-weathered skin and kind eyes, looked at Sarah and spoke, gesturing to the lavender.

"She's asking if you'd like some," Jack translated.

"They're beautiful," Sarah said, "but I'm staying in a hotel. I don't really have anywhere to put them."

The flower seller continued speaking, her tone warm and encouraging Sarah.

"She says the smell will bring you good dreams," Jack said. "And that a pretty woman should have flowers."

Sarah felt the heat rise in her cheeks. "You added that last bit."

"I absolutely did not."

Sarah bought the lavender - three stems, wrapped in brown paper - and tucked them into her bag. They made a full circuit of the market, not buying much, just looking, smelling, experiencing. Jack is pointing things out, translating, and telling her stories. She talks about her life as if she is talking to someone she's known for years.

But the vendors' behaviour continued to bother her. It was like they were ignoring him. He was standing right there. Maybe it was just French politeness - addressing the woman first, not the man. Or maybe they assumed she was the one doing the shopping and he was just along for the ride. She was actually enjoying this old-fashioned approach; it made her feel important. Not like Bristol, where they talked at you, not to you.

When they finally left the market and returned to the square, Sarah was full - not with food, but with the experience. Sensations. She was alive in a way she hadn't felt in years. Everything at home was about efficiency, schedules, and getting everyone where they needed to be. This was different. This was about beauty and craft and taking time to appreciate things.

"Thank you," she said to Jack.

"For what?"

"For showing me that. For translating. For..." She gestured vaguely. "For making me feel like less of a tourist."

"You're not a tourist. You're a writer. There's a difference."

"Is there?"

"Absolutely. Tourists observe from the outside, taking pictures, checking things off lists. Writers are trying to understand from the inside. To see how things really work, how people really are. To find the truth beneath the surface." He held her gaze seriously. "That's what you're doing, isn't it? Trying to understand yourself from the inside? To find the truth of who you really are?"

She'd meant to deflect with a joke, to keep things light. But instead, looking at him in the morning light with the market sounds fading behind them, she found herself saying, "Yes. That's exactly what I'm doing."

"Good." Jack checked his watch, a simple silver one, slightly scratched and well-worn. "I should let you get back to your work. You've got a book to finish."

"Will you be here tomorrow morning?" The question came out before she could stop it, too eager, too wanting. Too much.

But Jack just smiled. "Same time, same place. I'll be here."

"Promise?"

"Promise."

He walked away across the square, hands in his pockets, and Sarah watched him go. Then she turned and headed back to her hotel, her bag smelling of lavender, her mind already filling with words.

She had a book to write. And suddenly, she knew exactly what happened next.

CHAPTER 3 - PORRIDGE

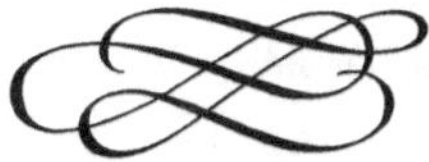

Sarah walked back to her hotel with lavender in her bag and words already forming in her mind.

The morning with Jack, the coffee, the market, and the way he listened when she talked about her book had given her clarity. It wasn't just material for her story, though it was that too. It was more than that, a sense of being understood, of mattering.

She climbed the stairs to her room, unlocked the door, and stepped inside. The space greeted her like an old friend now: familiar and comforting. White walls surrounded her. A blue quilt covered the bed, and muslin curtains danced in the breeze. Her notebook waited on the desk.

She set the lavender in the small vase next to her notebook. Adding it to what was already there. The flower lady had been right; the smell was beautiful.

She opened her notebook to a fresh page.

For a moment, she just sat there, pen hovering, watching the curtains dance. She could still smell the market - tomatoes and cheese and flowers. Could still hear Jack's voice: 'Everyone is writing their own book. Most people write a book they don't want to read.'

Was Jack right? Had she spent all this time writing a book she had no desire to read herself? In her own story, was she really the background figure, never the one at the centre? Did she always just set things in motion for everyone else, leaving her own wishes unheard?

A dull ache bloomed in her chest. The heaviness surprised her and lingered.

She started to write.

Not about the woman on the beach anymore. About what had been pushing at the edges of her consciousness since that first dinner with David and the girls. Since Margaret Thornton had looked her in the eye and said, 'Don't become like me.'

There's a difference between being loved and being seen.

The sentence appeared on the page before she'd consciously decided to write it. She stared at it for a moment, then kept going.

Love can be blind – everyone says so, as if blindness were romantic. As if not noticing someone's pain or loneliness or slow disappearance were somehow a virtue. But being seen requires eyes wide open. It requires someone paying attention not to who you should be, but to who you are. Not to what you do for them, but to what you want for yourself.

Sarah stopped, read it back. Her heart was beating fast. This was it. This was what the book was about. Not a funny romance. Not a light midlife crisis story. Something deeper.

She kept writing.

The protagonist had been loved for twenty years. Loved in the way you love a good appliance - reliably, absently, with mild irritation when it stopped working correctly. She'd been invisible for at least ten years, maybe longer. It had happened so gradually that she hadn't noticed until one morning, when she woke up and realised she couldn't remember the last time someone had asked her what she wanted. What she thought. Who she was beneath the roles she'd been assigned.

The words rushed forward, faster than she could write, faster than she could think. They nearly tumbled out, uncontrolled. She just tried to keep up.

And then one morning, sitting at a café in France, a stranger looked at her and said: "You're a writer." Not a question. A fact. As if he could see straight through to the truth she'd buried under twenty years of packed lunches and football kits and dry cleaning. "How did you know?" she asked.

"Because I'm looking at you," he said.

Sarah's hand was cramping, but she didn't stop. Couldn't stop. The story was pouring out of her now, demanding to be told.

She wrote about the market. About tomatoes that smelled like summer. Cheese that tasted like earth and grass. About the way French voices sounded like music, even when they were just haggling over price. About a stranger who translated the world for her. Who made her feel like every observation she made mattered. Like her thoughts were worth a penny, a pound, or a fortune.

She wrote about the weight of guilt, how it sat on her chest like a stone. About how easy it was to talk to Jack about her family without disloyalty. He understood in a way they never had. He didn't judge her for wanting more. He didn't judge her for taking this time.

She wrote about the complicated space between obligation and desire. Between duty and self. Between the person she'd been taught to be and the person she was discovering she might actually be.

Pages filled, one after another. As she rushed to keep up with her thoughts, her handwriting grew messier.

When she finally stopped, fingers aching, she looked down at what she'd written. Twelve pages. Twelve pages in - she checked her watch - two hours. She'd written for two solid hours without stopping. She never checked her phone, wondered what was for dinner, or who needed what.

She read back through the pages. Like the others, they were rough, definitely rough. Some sentences ran too long. Others stilted or self-conscious. But underneath the rough prose, there was truth.

This was what she'd come here to write. Not the book she'd planned, but the book that needed to exist.

The manuscript was growing. It was twenty-nine pages now, almost a third of a novella. Yet it already was more. Like a novel. A real novel. The thought brought both nerves and excitement; butterflies and terror mingled.

Sarah closed her notebook and stretched. Her neck was stiff from bending over the desk. Her hand ached pleasantly, the kind of ache that meant she'd done some real work. She stood up and walked to the window.

The light had changed. It was later than she thought, nearly six o'clock. The sun was lower now, painting the village in shades of gold and amber. Below, Madame Rousseau was watering her herbs. The orange cat supervised from atop the stone wall.

Sarah's stomach growled, reminding her she'd skipped lunch entirely. She'd had coffee at the café this morning, but that was hours ago. She should eat. She should find dinner.

But more than food, though she hesitated to admit it to herself, she found herself wanting to see Jack again. Why did she want this? Was it just the connection, or attraction?

‘Stop it,’ she told herself firmly. ‘You saw him this morning.

You don't need to see him again today. You're here to write, not to...'

Not to what, exactly? Not to spend time with someone who found her genuinely interesting, who saw her? Not to have real, nourishing conversations for once? Not to be herself, instead of the role she played for others?

She grabbed her bag. She was going to find dinner. If Jack happened to be there, fine. If not, also fine. She was perfectly capable of eating alone. She'd done it last night. She could do it again.

But as she left the hotel and headed toward the square, she couldn't deny the flutter of anticipation in her chest. The hope that she might see him. The disappointment she'd feel if she didn't.

'You're being ridiculous,' she told herself. 'He's just a man. A stranger. You barely know him.'

But that was the thing, wasn't it? She did know him. It was as if she had known him for years instead of just two days. He seemed to understand things about her that people who had known her for decades didn't see.

The square was quieter now than it had been at lunch. The market was long gone, packed up, and disappeared until next week. Most people were home, having dinner, the village settling into that sleepy early-evening lull. The café had only a few tables occupied - an elderly couple sharing a carafe of wine, a man reading a book, a woman with a small dog curled at her feet.

Sarah scanned the square quickly, trying not to look obvious.

Jack wasn't there.

The disappointment hit harder than it should have. He wasn't there, and that was fine. That was good, even. She could eat dinner peacefully, go back to her room, and maybe write a bit more before bed. That's what she was here for. Writing. Not mooning over some man she'd just met.

She chose a table in the corner, set down her bag, and tried not to feel let down. This was better, really. She needed some time alone to process, to think, to remember why she was here.

The waitress appeared - the same woman from this morning, though she looked more tired now. She offered what must have been the evening menu, speaking in rapid French.

"Pardon," Sarah said, pulling herself together. "Moules-frites?"

The waitress smiled, clearly pleased that Sarah had learned the word for mussels. She nodded enthusiastically and said something else that Sarah didn't catch.

"Et... um... du vin rouge? Un verre?" Sarah tried, hoping she'd gotten the words right.

"Oui, madame."

The waitress disappeared, and Sarah sat back, feeling a small surge of pride despite her disappointment. She'd ordered in French. Terrible, fumbling French, but still. She'd tried. That counted.

The wine arrived first, a generous glass of red in a simple tumbler. Sarah took a sip. It was dry and rich, tasting of earth, oak, and cherry. It wasn’t like the wine at home, which she bought from Waitrose based on what was on special offer. This tasted like it had been made by someone who cared.

She pulled out her notebook, thinking she might jot down some thoughts while she waited for her food, but found herself just looking around the square instead. The light was beautiful at this time of day, everything soft and golden, the stone buildings glowing warm, shadows long and gentle. A few people were walking through, probably coming home from work or heading out for the evening. Normal life. Simple and beautiful.

The church bells rang the hour. Six chimes, echoing off the stone walls.

David would be home by now, Sarah thought. Or maybe not. Maybe he had a late surgery. The girls would be upstairs - Betty doing homework, or more likely not doing homework, Olivia getting ready to go out somewhere with friends. The house would be quiet except for music from their rooms, the hum of the fridge, and the ticking of the hall clock.

She should call them. Check in. Make sure everything was okay. But when she pulled out her phone, she found she didn't want to. Not yet. Not now, when she was sitting here in the golden light, drinking good wine, a real person instead of just someone's mother, someone's wife.

She'd call tomorrow. They'd be fine for another day.

The mussels arrived in a huge white bowl, steaming and fragrant, shells glossy black and open, swimming in white wine, butter, and herbs. Golden chips were piled high on the side. The smell was incredible, a mix of garlic, parsley, and the sea.

“Bon appétit," the waitress said with a smile.

"Merci," Sarah replied.

She ate slowly, savouring each mussel, using the empty shells to scoop out the ones still closed. The chips were perfect: crispy on the outside, fluffy on the inside, sprinkled with sea salt. The wine paired beautifully with the butter's richness. This was proper food. Real food. Food that had been cooked with care, not just thrown together in the fifteen minutes between getting home from the dry cleaner and needing to leave for Betty's football practice.

She was about halfway through the bowl, beginning to think she might have ordered too much, when a voice said, "Well. Twice in one day. I'm starting to think you like me."

Sarah looked up, her heart doing that complicated thing it did whenever she saw him. That lurch and flutter and warmth all mixed together.

Jack was standing beside her table, hands in his pockets, that familiar smile on his face. The evening light caught his features, making him look softer somehow. More real. Less like a character she'd imagined and more like an actual person standing in front of her.

"I was hungry," Sarah said, trying to sound casual even as her pulse quickened. "This just happened to be here."

"Of course. Pure coincidence." He gestured to the empty chair across from her. "Mind if I join you?"

‘Say yes,’ her heart said.

‘Say no,’ her brain countered. ‘You're married. This is dangerous. You're playing with fire.’

"Please," her mouth said, deciding for both of them.

He sat down, and the waitress appeared almost immediately - so quickly Sarah wondered if she'd been watching for him. But the woman looked only at Sarah, expectantly.

Sarah glanced at Jack, then back at the waitress. "Un café?" she tried, pointing at Jack.

The waitress nodded and disappeared without acknowledging him.

"Ordering for me now?" Jack said, amused.

"Well, you look like you could use a coffee." Sarah took a sip of her wine, emboldened. "How did I know? I just know these things."

He laughed, a real, delighted laugh that made her stomach flip and warmed her chest.

"That's my line."

"I'm borrowing it."

"Fair enough."

Sarah finished her last few mussels while they waited, very aware of Jack watching her. Not in a creepy way. In a way that made her feel visible. Interesting. Like eating mussels in France was the most fascinating thing she could possibly be doing.

The waitress returned with a small cup of espresso and set it down in front of Sarah. She pushed it across to Jack without being asked.

"Thank you," he said, his eyes never leaving hers.

They sat in comfortable silence for a moment. Sarah realised she was glad he'd appeared. Had been hoping he would, even though she'd told herself she wasn't looking for him. Even though she knew she shouldn't want to see him as much as she did.

"Good day of writing?" Jack asked, wrapping his hands around the small cup.

"Yes, actually. Twelve more pages."

His eyebrows rose. "That's excellent. The words are really flowing now."

"They are." Sarah set down her fork and wiped her hands on her napkin. "It's strange. At home, I'd sit at my laptop for hours and maybe write a paragraph. I'd start, stop, delete, start again. Second-guess every word. Here, I can barely keep up with the words. They just... come."

"That's because you're not trying to write around the edges of everyone else's needs anymore." Jack took a sip of his espresso. "You're giving yourself actual space. Actual time. Permission. It makes a difference."

The waitress appeared again, clearing Sarah's empty bowl. She offered something in French, gesturing vaguely.

"She's asking if you want dessert," Jack translated.

"Non, merci," Sarah said, shaking her head. She was pleasantly full. Content.

When the waitress left, Jack looked at her seriously. The playfulness had faded from his expression. "Can I tell you something?"

"Of course."

"You look different from how you did yesterday. On the beach."

"Different how?" Sarah was suddenly self-conscious, wondering if her hair was a mess, if she had butter on her chin.

"Lighter." He leaned forward slightly. "Like you'd been carrying a burden and you've finally put it down. Even just since this morning."

Sarah thought about it. She was lighter. The writing this afternoon had released pressure, unburdened her of a weight she hadn't fully realised she was carrying. "I suppose I am lighter. Being here. Writing. Not having to..." She gestured vaguely. "Not having to be all the things I normally have to be. It's like I'd been holding my breath for years, and I'm finally exhaling."

"Good metaphor." Jack smiled. "You should use that in your book."

"Maybe I will." She took a sip of her wine, fortifying herself. "Though I have to admit, I'm still guilty about it."

"Guilty about what?"

"Being here. Being happy. Enjoying mussels and wine and..." She gestured at the square, the village, the golden light, and him. "This. All of this. My family is at home managing without me, probably struggling, probably annoyed with me, and I'm here having the time of my life. Writing. Eating good food. Talking to interesting people. And I feel guilty about enjoying it."

Jack was quiet for a moment, studying her. Then he leaned forward, his expression serious but not unkind. "Do you want my honest opinion?"

"Yes."

"Your guilt is useless."

Sarah blinked, taken aback. "Excuse me?"

"Your guilt," Jack repeated, his voice gentle but firm, "is completely and utterly useless. It's not helping you. It's not helping your family. It's just making you miserable and stopping you from fully experiencing what you came here to do."

"But..."

"Let me ask you this." He held up a hand to stop her protest. "When you'rehome, taking care of everyone, making sure the football kits are washed and the dry cleaning is collected, and the packed lunches are made - do they lose sleep over it?"

"What do you mean?"

"Does David agonise when you pick up his dry cleaning so he can make his meeting on time? Do the girls worry when you wash their football kits or help with their costumes? Do they lie awake at night thinking, 'Poor Mum, always doing things for us, I feel terrible about it'?"

Sarah thought about the family dinner. About David interrupting her to talk about his surgery. About the girls barely looking up from their phones. About how none of them had asked about her book after that first dismissed attempt. She'd told Jack some of this while they walked through the market, the words spilling out easier than she'd expected.

"Well... no," she admitted. "But that's different."

"Is it? Why?"

"Because that's my job. I'm their mother. Their wife. That's what I'm supposed to do."

"Says who?"

"Says..." Sarah faltered. "Everyone. Society. Expectations. The way things are. The way things have always been."

"And who says you're not supposed to take a few days to write a book?"

Sarah opened her mouth. Closed it. Opened it again. "I... I don't know."

"Exactly." Jack leaned back, his point made. "You've been taught that your role is to serve others. To put everyone else first. Always. And when you dare to put yourself first for two weeks, two weeks out of how many years of putting everyone else first, you're drowning in guilt. Not even a full two weeks. Seventeen years of being a mother, twenty years of being a wife, and you can't take twelve days without drowning in guilt. Do you see how absurd that is?"

When he put it like that... "It does sound a bit ridiculous."

"It doesn't just sound ridiculous, it is ridiculous. There's no other way to put it." His voice was passionate now, almost angry on her behalf. "You're allowed to want things. You're allowed to have needs. You're allowed to take up space. And you are definitely allowed to eat mussels in France without flagellating yourself over it."

She laughed despite herself, despite the tears pricking at her eyes. "Flagellating. That's a bit dramatic."

"Is it?" Jack challenged. "You just told me you're guilty about being happy. If that's not self-flagellation, I don't know what is."

Sarah took another sip of wine, then paused to think. He was right. She knew he was right. But knowing intellectually and believing emotionally were two completely different things. Knowing didn't make it go away. Didn't make her stop worrying about Betty's football kit, Olivia's costume, or whether David was remembering to check the calendar.

"I understand what you're saying," she said slowly, choosing her words carefully. "And intellectually, I know you're right. But it's not that simple. I can't just turn off the guilt like flipping a switch. It's been there my whole life. It's like..." She struggled for the right words. "It's wired into me. It's part of who I am."

Jack nodded thoughtfully, taking a sip of his espresso. Then he set down the small cup and looked at her with an expression that was nearly mischievous. "Let me tell you this. It's like porridge."

Sarah couldn't help it - she laughed.

"Stay with me here." He leaned forward slightly, warming to his analogy. "Let's say you grew up in a house where it was always made with salt. Just a pinch, the Scottish way, the proper way. That's how your mother made it, how her mother made it before her. That's what you were taught it’s supposed to taste like. The right way. The only way. Every morning, salt. For years. Decades, even. That's just what porridge is to you."

"Alright..." Sarah was trying not to smile.

"Then one day, someone makes it with sugar. Or honey. Something sweet instead of savoury. And your immediate reaction is 'this is wrong.' Not 'this is different' or 'this isn't to my taste' - but fundamentally, morally wrong. Because that's not right. That's not how it's supposed to be. That's not how it's done. In your bones, in your conditioning, sweet porridge feels like a violation of everything you know to be true about breakfast."

Sarah felt something click into place in her mind, like a puzzle piece sliding home. "But it's not actually wrong. It's just different."

"Exactly." Jack's face lit up. "It's just different. And maybe, if you tried it a few times and really gave it a chance, you'd realise you actually prefer it with sugar. That it tastes better, makes you feel better, starts your day better. But even then - even after you've decided you like it better - there's still a part of your brain that whispers, 'this isn't real.' Because you've been conditioned for so long, so deeply, that the salt version is the only right version. The only legitimate version. Everything else is wrong."

"And the guilt is my salted porridge," Sarah said softly.

"The guilt is your salted porridge," Jack confirmed. "You've been taught your whole life that the 'right' way to be a woman, a mother, a wife, is to put everyone else first. To serve. To sacrifice. To make yourself small so others can be big. That's your conditioning. That's your salted porridge. And now you're trying a new recipe - putting yourself first for two weeks, taking space, having needs - and every part of your conditioning is screaming that it's wrong. That you're being selfish. That you should be ashamed. But it's not wrong. It's just different."

"So how do I stop?" Sarah asked, genuinely wanting to know.

"You don't. Not immediately, anyway." Jack's voice was gentle now. "Reconditioning takes time. You have to keep choosing the sugar even when the salt feels more comfortable. Even when everything in you says you should go back to the old way. You have to keep reminding yourself that there are different ways to make it, different ways to live a life, and none of them are morally superior to the others. They're just different. Eventually - and it won't happen overnight - it will fade. The conditioning will loosen its grip. The whisper will get quieter. But it takes practice. Repetition. Choosing the sugar over and over until it stops feeling wrong."

Sarah sat with that for a moment, turning it over in her mind. The metaphor was ridiculous on the surface, comparing her decades of conditioning to breakfast cereal, but underneath the silliness, it made perfect sense. It gave her something concrete to hold onto, a way to understand what was happening in her chest every time she felt that familiar wave hit: 'I shouldn't be doing this.'

"That's..." She looked up at him, genuinely moved. "That's actually really helpful. Thank you."

"Good. Because here's the important part, and I need you to really hear this." Jack leaned forward, his expression intense. "You're already doing it. You're here. You're writing. You're choosing the sugar even though it feels uncomfortable, even though every part of your conditioning is telling you it's wrong. That's the first step. That's the hardest step. Everything else is just repetition. Keep eating the sugar porridge until it stops tasting strange."

"So I just keep... eating the porridge with sugar?" Sarah felt a smile tugging at her lips despite the tears in her eyes.

"You keep eating with sugar." He smiled back. "And eventually - I promise you - you won't even think about the salt anymore. It'll just be porridge. tastes better, satisfies you more and starts your day better. You won't need anyone's permission to enjoy it."

They sat in silence for a moment. Sarah blinked back tears, not wanting to cry in the middle of a café square, but feeling something different. A loosening. A lightness.

"Thank you," she said again, her voice thick.

"Don't thank me. You're doing the hard work." He lifted his tiny espresso cup in a mock toast. "I'm just here to tell you that the sugar tastes better."

She laughed, wiping at her eyes quickly. "You're ridiculous."

"I've been called worse."

They talked for a while longer about nothing important: the village, the weather, whether the fountain in the square had ever actually worked, or if it was just decorative. Easy conversation. Comfortable. The kind of talk that felt like breathing. The light was fading now, the golden hour turning to dusk, the shadows lengthening across the cobblestones. A few more people had appeared in the square, couples walking hand in hand, families heading home from evening errands, the village settling into that peaceful end-of-day rhythm.

Finally, Jack checked his watch, that simple silver one she'd noticed before, slightly scratched, the kind of watch that had been worn for years, and said, "I should let you get back. You've had a long day."

"I have," Sarah agreed, though part of her didn't want him to leave. Didn't want this conversation to end. Didn't want to go back to her room alone with her thoughts. "Thank you."

"For what?"

"For listening. For understanding. For..." She gestured helplessly. "For the porridge metaphor. For not making me feel stupid for this guilt."

"The guilt isn't stupid," Jack said firmly. "The guilt is real. It's just not helpful. There's a difference." He stood up, pushing his chair back. "And you're not stupid. You're just waking up. That's brave. That's uncomfortable. That's necessary."

"Same time tomorrow morning?" The words came out before she could stop them, before she could think about whether she should be asking, whether she should be wanting to see him again so soon.

"Same time tomorrow morning," he confirmed with that smile that warmed her chest.

He walked away across the square, hands in his pockets, his figure silhouetted against the darkening sky. Sarah watched him go, that now-familiar sensation washing over her, contentment and longing, gratitude and desire, peace and restlessness all tangled together.

She paid for her meal - the waitress accepting her euros with a warm "Bonne soirée, madame" and a smile that suggested she approved of something, though Sarah wasn't sure what - and headed back to her hotel.

The walk through the village was different now. The guilt was still there; she could feel it, familiar and heavy, but smaller somehow. More manageable. Like she could carry it without being crushed by it. Maybe, eventually, she could put it down entirely.

'Porridge with sugar,' she thought, smiling to herself in the gathering dark. 'Keep eating the porridge with sugar.'

BACK IN HER ROOM, Sarah kicked off her shoes and smelt the lavender from this morning, which felt like days ago rather than hours, in the simple white vase on her desk. The smell filled the small space, sweet and calming.

She opened her notebook and stared at the page. The words from this afternoon looked back at her: 'There's a difference between being loved and being seen.' True, but not complete. Not finished.

The porridge metaphor had unlocked the truth. It buzzed under her skin, demanding to be written down before she lost it.

She picked up her pen and began to write.

She wrote about conditioning and choice. About the difference between what you're taught to want and what you actually want. About the bravery required to choose sugar when you've been raised on salt, to say "I want this" when you've been taught to say "whatever you want." She wrote about a woman who was learning to make different choices, one painful decision at a time.

She wrote about guilt as a form of control. How people who benefit from your selflessness will often weaponise guilt when you set boundaries, claim needs, and take up space. Because guilt keeps you small. You'll go back to serving them. You'll stay in your assigned role.

She wrote about freedom. Real freedom, not the sanitised version people talk about. Freedom was terrifying and wrong and selfish before becoming empowering. Freedom that required you to disappoint people, to let them down, to let them struggle. Freedom that meant choosing yourself even when everyone around you had been taught that you shouldn't.

The pages filled. Her handwriting was getting messier as she rushed to keep up with the thoughts pouring out of her. Her hand was cramping, but she didn't stop. Couldn't stop. This was important. This mattered.

When she finally put down her pen, it was nearly ten o'clock. Two hours had passed without her noticing. Two hours of pure creation, pure flow, pure connection between her brain and the page.

She looked down at what she'd written. Another eight pages. Rough, yes. Too raw in places, too heavy-handed in others. But real. True. Honest in a way that scared her.

Thirty-seven pages total now. A third of the way to a proper novel if she was aiming for eighty or ninety thousand words. More than halfway to a novella. The manuscript was growing. Becoming real. Something that existed outside of her head. It was being born here in France, but it would grow up, develop, in Bristol;.

Sarah closed the notebook, stretched her aching hand, and stood up. Her whole body was tired now, the good kind of tired that came from actual work, actual accomplishment. She walked to the window and looked out at the dark village. A few lights glowed in the windows. The church bells marked the hour with ten deep, resonant chimes.

She should be guilty. Should be lying awake in a few minutes, worrying about whether David remembered to sign Olivia's permission slip, or whether Betty had clean kit for tomorrow's match, or whether they'd eaten properly, or remembered to take out the recycling.

But she didn't.

Or rather, she was. It was there, familiar as breathing. But it was quieter now. More like background noise than a siren. And she could hear, underneath it, another note. What might have been joy. Or peace. Or just the simple satisfaction of a day well-spent.

Sarah changed into her pyjamas, the soft cotton ones, not the ratty old t-shirt she wore at home, and climbed into bed. The white linen was cool and crisp against her skin, smelling faintly of lavender and sunshine. Through the open window, she could hear the village settling into the night. A few distant voices. A dog barking. Someone's television, the sound muffled and far away. The gentle sounds of other people living their lives.

She should check her phone. Should see if anyone had called

or texted. Should make sure the family was managing okay without her.

But she didn't reach for it. Not yet. For now, she wanted to stay in this state - this strange, new certainty of being exactly where she was supposed to be, doing exactly what she was supposed to be doing.

Sugar porridge, she thought again, smiling in the dark.

Sarah closed her eyes and fell asleep almost immediately, deeply.

And when her dream came, later in the night, she dreamed of porridge with honey and cinnamon, of markets full of perfect tomatoes, of French voices singing in Latin she couldn't understand but understood in her bones. She dreamed of a man with laughing eyes who understood things about her she'd never told him, who looked at her and saw someone worth seeing.

CHAPTER 4 - IF

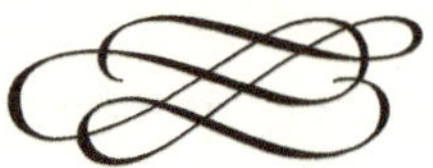

The next morning, Sarah woke up with emotions swirling inside her. Anticipation, dread, and a restless ache she couldn't quite name.

She'd dreamed about Jack again. It wasn't an anxious dream or anything inappropriate. They just walked through the village together. His hand hovered near hers as they made their way down the narrow streets. The dream felt so real and vivid that waking up felt like a loss. Reality seemed to offer less, and coming back to it left her wanting more.

She lay there for a moment, staring at the white ceiling. Old plaster cracks ran across it. She tried to shake off the feeling. Morning light filtered through the muslin curtains, softer than usual. The sun felt gentle. Church bells rang somewhere in the village, seven chimes. It was early, but not too early.

You're married, she reminded herself as she swung her legs out of bed. You're here to write, not to dream about other men. Don't let yourself develop feelings for strangers on beaches.

This is just a distraction, she tried to insist, though a quieter voice inside didn't quite agree.

Logic didn't matter to dreams, did it? Dreams did what they wanted, following their own rules. Her heart acted on impulse too, beating faster as soon as she remembered she would see Jack this morning at the same time and place they had agreed on.

Like it was a date.

It's not a date, she told herself firmly as she pulled on her jeans. It's just coffee with a friend. A new friend. A friend who happens to be helping you think through things. But part of her mind questioned if she truly believed that.

But as she stood in front of the small mirror above the desk, brushing her hair and wondering if she should put on mascara (just a touch, nothing obvious), denial tremored in her chest. This was more than friendship. Her stomach fluttered at seeing him. She'd relived their conversation about porridge, warmth curling through her in the dark. Now, she hovered over her mascara like a teenager, stomach knotted with giddy hope.

She applied it anyway. Just a little. And lip balm.Her lips were dry from the sea air, that's all. Nothing to do with wanting to look nice for anyone in particular.

She grabbed her bag and headed downstairs. Madame Rousseau was in the garden already, deadheading roses with the orange cat supervising. She looked up as Sarah passed and smiled, speaking in French that Sarah didn't quite catch, but that sounded warm and knowing.

The walk to the café felt different this morning. Sarah noticed everything more: the cobblestones underfoot, uneven and ancient; the smell of warm, yeasty bread drifting from the boulangerie; French voices floating from open windows, rising and falling like music. The village was waking up. She was waking up, too, not just going through the motions of her morning routine.

And there he was.

He was sitting at their table—she caught herself thinking of it as 'their' table—and reading his newspaper, looking like he'd been there for hours. He'd been waiting just for her. The morning light caught his dark hair, making it shine almost blue-black. He wore the same worn jumper as always, or maybe one just like it. Sarah was starting to think he only owned one jumper, which made him even more endearing.

He glanced up as she approached, and his face broke into that smile. That smile that made her stomach flip and her breath catch, and her sensible married-woman brain go quiet for just a moment.

"Morning," he said.

"Morning."

The waitress appeared almost immediately. Sarah didn't need to think about it anymore. "Deux cafés noirs, s'il vous plaît," she said, the words coming out smoother than they had yesterday. Her French was improving. Or maybe she was just more confident. Maybe they were the same thing.

The waitress nodded and disappeared without looking at Jack. Sarah noticed that - registered it somewhere in the back of her mind - but pushed it aside. The woman was probably just efficient, focused on her work. Some people were like that.

The coffee arrived quickly, and both cups were set in front of Sarah. She slid one over to Jack, and for a moment, their fingers almost touched. It was only a second, but it jolted through her like electricity.

"Thank you," he said, wrapping his hands around the cup.

They sat together in comfortable silence, watching the village come alive around them. The bakery opened its doors. An old man walked with his slow, shuffling dog. A woman hung laundry from an upstairs window, white sheets snapping in the breeze.

Sarah sipped her coffee, words tangled in her throat. Emotion shimmered beneath her skin as she tried to find the right thing to say, wrestling with longing and restraint.

"I have an idea," Jack said before she could speak.

"Should I be worried?"

"Definitely." He grinned. "I thought we could walk today. Really walk. There's a path that goes up to the cliffs - beautiful views, and not too difficult. What do you think?"

Sarah hesitated. Her instincts told her to say no, to keep things safe and maintain boundaries. Saying yes would mean spending more time with him, coming dangerously close to crossing a line she knew was there, even if she couldn't define it.

She reminded herself that she was here to write, to protect her marriage, and to figure out her life. She wasn't here to go on romantic walks with attractive strangers who awakened things dormant for years.

But even as she thought it, she knew what she was going to say.

"Come on," Jack said, sensing her uncertainty. His voice was gentle, coaxing, but not pushy. "You can't spend your entire trip shut away in your room writing. You need inspiration. You need to experience this place, let it seep into your bones. That's what will make your book real."

"Feed the creative well?" Sarah said, smiling despite herself.

"Terrible phrase. But the principle is sound. Writers need input as well as output. You need to fill up before you can pour out. So." He leaned forward slightly. "Walk with me?"

She knew she should say no, but she was so tired of always saying no. Tired of always being sensible. Tired of always doing what she was supposed to do instead of what she wanted to do.

"Alright," she said, the tension in her chest loosened, letting relief and anticipation flood her veins. "But just for a few hours."

"Just for a few hours," he agreed.

* * *

THEY WALKED through the village and out the other side. A narrow path wound between fields of wheat and barley. The wheat glowed golden, moving in waves in the breeze. The barley, greener and younger, was still growing. The path was probably centuries old, worn smooth by the feet of farmers, soldiers, lovers, and everyone else who had walked this route for hundreds of years.

Sarah found that comforting somehow. That she was part of history. That her footsteps were joining an infinite chain of footsteps, all of them heading somewhere.

Jack walked beside her, keeping a comfortable distance. Not too close, not too far. Just... right. As they went, he pointed things out. A kestrel hovering above a field, perfectly still in the air, hunting. A cluster of purple wildflowers growing in the hedge - vetch, he said, or maybe tufted vetch, he couldn't quite tell from here. An old stone wall half-hidden by brambles that had once marked a monastery's boundary, long before the Revolution tore everything down.

"How do you know all this?" Sarah asked, slightly breathless as the path began to climb. "The history. The birds. The flowers. Everything."

"I told you. I've been here a while." That shadow crossed his face again, the one she'd noticed before. Brief but unmistakable. "And I have a lot of time to observe. To notice things."

"That's still not really an answer."

"No," he agreed, with a slight smile. "It's not."

She wanted to push, to ask more, but instinct stopped her. The look on his face, maybe. Or the sense that he'd tell her when he was ready. Or never. And she had to be okay with that.

They walked in silence as the path grew steeper. A pleasant burn spread through Sarah's legs as she stretched muscles she hadn't used in a long time. She was out of shape from too many days at the kitchen table with her laptop and too many evenings collapsed on the sofa after caring for everyone else. She had stopped moving, stopped taking basic care of herself.

"Can I ask you something?" Jack said eventually.

"Of course."

"What's your favorite poem?"

The question surprised her. It seemed to come out of nowhere, not connected to anything they'd been talking about. "My favourite poem? I don't know. I haven't really considered poetry in years. Why?"

“People’s favourite poems tell you a lot about them. About what they value. What they're afraid of. What they hope for. What they're carrying." He glanced at her. "So, do you have one?"

Sarah thought about it. "I suppose... 'If' by Kipling. If I had to choose."

‘If you can keep your head when all about you are losing theirs and blaming it on you,’ Jack quoted immediately.

Sarah smiled. "You know it.” ”Everyone knows it. It's the poem they make you memorise in school so you'll become a proper British person who doesn't complain and soldiers on through adversity with a stiff upper lip and quiet dignity."

Jack laughed. "That's a very cynical take."

"Is it wrong, though?"

"No. But I love it too. Not because of the stiff-upper-lip nonsense, but what it's really about underneath all that." He was serious now, thoughtful. "It's about staying true to yourself when everyone around you is telling you to be different. About holding onto your values when it would be easier to let them go. About being your own person, even when the world wants you to be more convenient. More palatable. More willing to fit into the box they've built for you."

Sarah thought about that. She'd never considered the poem that way before. It had always just been... duty. Stoicism. The British way of suffering quietly without making a fuss. But what Jack was describing was different. More active. More defiant.

"I never saw it that way," she admitted.

"Most people don't. They just see the surface - the stoicism, the duty, the not complaining. All that wartime propaganda stuff. But underneath, it's about integrity. About knowing who you are and refusing to compromise that, no matter what anyone else says or does or expects from you." He looked at her. "That's what you're doing, isn't it? Being here. Writing your book. You're refusing to be the person everyone expects you to be." He met her eyes.

"I suppose I am." The realisation made her brave and terrified in equal measure.

They reached the top of the cliff.

It wasn't as dramatic as the white cliffs of Dover or the cliffs in Cornwall—not sheer, terrifying, or vertical. But it was high enough for a view that stretched for miles. The coastline curved away in both directions, rocky and beautiful. The sea stretched out beyond, grey-blue and endless, moving in constant waves. Below, nestled in a fold of land, the village was tiny and perfect. Terracotta roofs were scattered like rust. Narrow streets resembled cracks in porcelain. The church spire pointed up like a finger, reaching for God, heaven, or maybe just the sky, asking.

"Wow," Sarah breathed, knowing the word was inadequate.

"Worth the climb?"

"Definitely worth the climb."

They stood there for a moment, just looking. The wind was stronger up here, tugging at Sarah's hair, making her jumper flap against her. It was wild, clean, and free. Like standing at the edge of the world. Like anything was possible.

Jack found a flat spot in the grass and sat down, his long legs stretched out in front of him. He patted the ground beside him, and after a moment's hesitation, Sarah joined him. They sat side by side, not quite touching but close enough that she could feel the warmth radiating from him. Close enough that if she moved just slightly, their shoulders would brush.

She didn't move.

They sat in silence for a while, looking at the view. The wind in their faces. The smell of grass and salt and earth. Somewhere far below, a dog barked. The sound carried up on the wind, thin and distant.

"Can I ask you something?" Jack said, finally, his voice quiet but clear in the wind.

"Of course."

"Your husband. David." He paused, choosing his words carefully. "Are you happy with him?"

The question was so direct and unexpected that her breath caught. She knew she should deflect, be polite, and protect her marriage, her privacy, and the life she had built over twenty years. She should say 'of course I'm happy,' or 'that's personal,' or 'I don't think that's appropriate to discuss.'

But she was exhausted. Exhausted by the burden of always shielding things, always protecting everyone else, always pretending everything was fine when it wasn't. Always being the strong one, the dependable one, the one who never complained or needed anything.

"I don't know," she said quietly, the words coming out before she could stop them. "I thought I was. For a long time, I thought I was. We had good years, you know? Real partnership. But now..." She trailed off, not sure how to finish.

"What changed?"

"Nothing changed. That's the problem." She pulled her knees up to her chest and wrapped her arms around them, making herself small. "Or maybe everything changed so slowly that I didn't notice until it was too late. We've been married for twenty years. Twenty years of building a life together. Having the girls, the house, the routines, the furniture, the shared bank account. The calendar on the fridge has everyone's schedules colour-coded. Somewhere along the way, we stopped being Sarah and David. We became just Mum and Dad, the logistics coordinators, the people who make sure everyone gets where they need to be with the right equipment and enough snacks."

"And you miss being Sarah and David?"

Sarah considered it, really considered it. "I miss being just Sarah," she said finally, her voice trembling slightly. "Does that make sense? I don't even miss being 'us', not really. I miss feeling like I'm a whole person. Like I matter beyond being a wife or mother. I miss feeling seen. Not just noticed, but actually seen. Known. Valued for who I am, not just what I do."

Jack was quiet for a moment. Then: "When's the last time David looked at you and really saw you?"

She tried to remember. "I don't know. Years, maybe? He looks at me all the time, obviously. We live in the same house. Share the same bed. Sit across from each other at dinner every night. But really seeing me? Asking what I want, what I think, what I'm feeling? Noticing when I'm sad or excited or struggling? I can't remember the last time."

"And when's the last time you told him what you want? What you need?"

"That's the thing - I've tried." Tears pricked at Sarah's eyes, hot and unwelcome. "I told him about the book. About wanting to write. About needing this time. And he just... he smiled and nodded and said 'that's nice, dear' like I'd told him I was taking up crochet or joining a book club. Like it was a hobby. A cute little thing I was doing to keep myself busy now that the girls are older. Not like it was important. Not like it mattered."

"That must have hurt."

"It did hurt. It does hurt." She wiped her eyes quickly, feeling embarrassed. "But here's what I keep coming back to, the thing that makes me feel even worse: I wonder if I'm partly to blame. Maybe even mostly to blame. I spent twenty years being the dependable one, the fixer, the woman who never asks for help, who always says 'yes, of course,' who handles everything quietly without making a fuss. I trained him to think I never needed anything. I trained everyone to think that. And now I'm angry that he doesn't see me, but maybe I built this invisibility myself. Maybe I'm the architect of my own erasure."

Jack was quiet for a long moment. "That's not your fault," he said finally.

"Isn't it, though? At least partially?" Sarah turned to look at him, needing him to understand. "I made myself small. I made myself invisible. That's what good wives and mothers do, right? We put everyone else first. We smooth things over. We make everything work. We sacrifice quietly and nobly and without complaint. We absorb everyone else's problems, anxieties, and needs. And then we wake up one day and realise we've disappeared entirely, and we want to blame everyone else for not noticing. But how could they notice when we worked so hard to make sure they didn't have to? When did we make it so easy for them to take us for granted?"

Jack was silent, and when she looked at him, his eyes were full of sadness. "That's very insightful," he said quietly. "And very sad."

"It is sad." Sarah turned back to the sea, watching the waves move in their endless pattern. "I do love him, you know. David. He's a good man. A good father. He works hard, impossible hours at the hospital. He's never cruel or unkind. He's never raised his voice at the girls or me. He's never cheated, never even glanced at another woman that I know of. He's just... oblivious. And I've enabled that obliviousness for twenty years. I made it easy for him not see me. I did love him. I still do, in a way. I just don't know if I'm in love with him anymore.

I don't know if I ever really was, or if I just loved the idea of being loved."

"So what happens when you go home?" Jack's voice was gentle.

"I don't know." Sarah was helpless, lost. "I suppose I try to be different. To be visible. To claim space. To tell him what I need instead of just quietly resenting him for not magically knowing. To ask for what I want. To stop making myself small."

She paused, then added quietly, "Or maybe nothing changes. Maybe I'll go home and fall right back into the old patterns; that's easier than fighting against twenty years of conditioning. Change is terrifying and uncomfortable, and it might not even work. It's easier to be resentful than to be honest, isn't it? Easier to complain that no one sees you than to stand up and say 'here I am, look at me, this is what I need.'"

"You're stronger than you think," Jack said.

"Am I?" Sarah laughed, but it came out bitter. "Or am I just running away for two weeks and pretending that matters? Pretending that writing a book in France makes me brave when really I'm just hiding from my real life? From the hard conversations and the difficult choices?"

"It does matter. You're here. You're writing. You're thinking about these questions instead of just living on autopilot. That's not nothing, Sarah. That's not hiding. That's waking up. And waking up is the hardest part."

They sat in silence for a while. A bird wheeled overhead - another kestrel, maybe, or a hawk. Sarah wasn't good enough at birds to tell the difference.

"Can I ask you something now?" she said eventually.

"Of course."

"Have you ever been married? In a relationship? You seem to understand all of this so well. The invisibility. The loneliness inside a partnership. The difference between being loved and being seen."

Something flickered across Jack's face: pain, loss, deep and old and barely healed. His whole body seemed to tense, then relax, as if he was forcing himself to stay present and not run from whatever memory she had just brought up.

"Once," he said finally. "A long time ago. There was a woman."

"What happened?" Sarah held her breath, sensing she was touching the fragile. What might break if she pushed too hard.

"Life happened." He stared out at the sea, his voice distant now, like he was speaking from somewhere far away. "I loved her. More than I knew was possible to love anyone. She was... she was everything. Kind and funny and beautiful, yes, but more than that. She saw me. Really saw me. The way you want David to see you. The way everyone wants to be seen. She knew me. The real me, not the version I showed the world."

"And?" Sarah prompted gently when he didn't continue.

"And I lost her." His voice was barely above a whisper now, almost stolen by the wind. "Not that she stopped loving me, or I stopped loving her. Not that we fought or grew apart or wanted different things. Just... circumstances. Things beyond our control. It's the way the world works sometimes, crushing beautiful things for no good reason."

He paused, his jaw working. "I couldn't be with her. I couldn't go back to her. And she... she had to move on. Build a life without me. Live in a world where I wasn't there."

"Did she?" Sarah asked, barely breathing. "Did she move on?"

"I hope so." He turned to her, and his eyes were full of grief. Old grief, the kind that's been carried so long it's become part of your bones. "I hope she found someone who made her happy. Who could give her everything I couldn’t. Who could be there for her in all the ways I couldn't be. She deserved that. She deserved everything."

He paused, and when he spoke again, his voice was rough. "But I never stopped loving her. Even now. Even after all this time, whatever time means anymore. She's still the one. The only one..." He trailed off, then added, so quietly Sarah almost missed it, "Until now."

Sarah felt tears prick her eyes. She didn't dare ask what he meant by ‘until now’. Didn't dare acknowledge it. Acknowledging it would make it real, and making it real would mean facing things she wasn't ready to face. "That's beautiful," she said instead. "And heartbreaking."

"Most beautiful things are." He smiled, but it didn't reach his eyes. It was the saddest smile Sarah had ever seen. "That's why I understand what you're going through. Why I want to help. I know what it's like to lose yourself. To lose someone. To wonder if you could have done things differently, made different choices, been a different person. And I don't want you to live with that kind of regret. That kind of permanent loss."

"Do you regret it?" Sarah asked. "Not being with her?"

"Every day." The words came out flat, final. "But it wasn't a choice. That's the difference between your situation and mine. You have a choice. You can go home and try to fix things. Try to be seen. Try to find your way back to each other, or find your way forward to what's new, what's better. I didn't have that option. It was taken from me."

"Why not?" Sarah asked, though she knew she might be pushing too far. "What happened? What circumstances could possibly..."

He trailed off, and that shadow crossed his face again. The same shadow she'd seen before, only darker now, heavier. "Sometimes life takes away your choices. Sometimes circumstances make decisions for you, and all you can do is live with them. Or not live with them, depending." He shook his head. "Sometimes you don't get to choose. Sometimes the choice is made for you by forces bigger than love or want or need."

Sarah wanted to ask more. Wanted to push, to understand what had happened to him, what circumstances could separate two people who loved each other that much. But his expression told her not to. That this was as much as he could or would share. That pushing further would be cruel.

They sat together for a long time on that cliff, looking out at the endless sea. Both of them carrying their own losses, their own regrets, their own complicated feelings about love and marriage and the choices we make or don't make or have made for us.

The wind kept blowing. The sea kept moving. The village below stayed small and perfect in its fold of land. Sarah felt something shift inside her—not a decision or an answer, but a question taking shape. A question about what she wanted, what she was willing to fight for, and what kind of life she wanted to live when she went home.

If she went home.

Finally, Jack stood and offered her his hand. "Come on. We should head back. You've got writing to do, and I've kept you too long already."

Sarah took his hand, feeling the warmth and solidity of it, and let him pull her to her feet. For just a moment, they stood there face to face, his hand still holding hers, close enough that she could see the grey in his dark hair, the fine lines around his eyes, the sadness that never quite left his expression.

Then he let go, and they started back down the cliff path.

They walked in comfortable silence. Sarah thought about David, the twenty years they'd built together. Whether their marriage could or should be saved. Whether she even wanted to save it anymore. The person she'd been when they'd gotten married, so young, so certain, so ready to be someone's wife, and the person she was now, standing on a cliff in France, with a man who wasn't her husband.

She also thought about Jack, about his lost love. How he'd said 'every day' when she'd asked about regret, about the grief she'd seen in his eyes. About what he'd meant by 'until now.'

But mostly she tried not to think at all. Tried to just walk, just breathe, just be present in this moment on this path, in this place with this person who saw her more clearly than anyone had in years.

When they reached the village square, Jack stopped. "Thank you," he said.

"For what?"

"For trusting me. With what you shared about David. About your marriage. About how you've made yourself invisible. That takes courage. To admit those things out loud. To yourself and to another person."

"Thank you for sharing about her," Sarah said, her voice soft. "Your lost love. I know that wasn't easy."

"No. But I wanted you to know." He paused. "I wanted you to understand that I see what you're going through. That I know what it's like to lose something precious. That I don't take your trust lightly."

"Same time tomorrow?" The question came out automatically now, as if it were just what they said. Like it was written into the fabric of her days here.

"Same time tomorrow," he agreed.

He walked away across the square, his hands in his pockets, his shoulders slightly hunched against the wind that was picking up. Sarah watched him go, watching until he turned the corner and disappeared. Watching until there was nothing left to watch.

Then she turned and walked back to her hotel, her mind full of thoughts about marriages and lost loves and the difference between the life you choose and the life that chooses you. She thought about 'until now.' Thought about what it meant. Whether she should think about it at all.

David, safely at home, probably not thinking about her at all except to wonder if she'd remembered to tell him where the spare house keys were.

Her daughters, getting on with their lives, probably not missing her much beyond the inconvenience of having to do their own laundry.

Jack, walking through the village alone, carrying his old grief like a weight.

And herself: who she was, who she wanted to be, and what she was willing to risk to become that person.

* * *

BACK IN HER ROOM, Sarah didn't even take off her shoes before sitting down at the desk and opening her notebook.

She wrote for four hours straight.

The words poured out of her like water from a broken dam, fast and unstoppable. She wrote about the cliff. About the view of the village from above, how small everything was, how fragile. She wrote about wind and sea and the endless horizon. She wrote about poetry and what it reveals about people.

But mostly she wrote about love.

Not the comfortable, settled kind. Not the kind that's safe, predictable, and easy. The kind that breaks your heart and changes you forever. The kind that makes you question everything you knew about yourself. The kind that feels dangerous and necessary at the same time.

She wrote about her protagonist meeting a man who saw her. Really saw her. Who saw not a mother or a wife or a function, but a person. A whole person with dreams, fears, and desires. Who made her feel visible for the first time in years.

She wrote about guilt and desire tangled together. About the pain of loving someone you can't have, whether married, dead, or separated by circumstances beyond your control. About loss and longing and the way grief becomes part of your identity if you carry it long enough.

She wrote about a man who'd lost the woman he loved. Who carried that loss like a physical wound. Who understood loneliness and invisibility, living with both every day. Who helped the protagonist see herself, he knew what it was like not to be seen.

She wrote until her hand cramped. Until the light through her window turned golden, then pink, then grey. Until she'd filled fifteen more pages in her notebook.

When she finally stopped, she looked down at what she'd written and recognised fear. This wasn't fiction anymore, not really. This was too close to the truth. Too close to her life. Too close to her heart.

This was about Jack. This was about her. This was about everything she was feeling and trying not to feel.

She closed the notebook quickly, like closing it could somehow erase what she'd written. Like it could make the feelings less real.

But the feelings stayed. Even with the notebook closed, even with the pen set down, even with her standing up and walking to the window and staring out at the village in the fading light.

The feelings stayed.

She was in trouble. Deep trouble. The kind that could ruin everything if she let it. The kind that was like falling and flying at the same time.

‘This has to stop,’ she told herself. ‘Tomorrow, you'll keep your distance. You'll write in your room. You'll have coffee alone. You'll stop spending time with him.’

But even as she thought it, she knew she wouldn't. Couldn't. Seeing Jack had become as necessary as breathing. As essential as the writing itself.

She was in trouble.

And the worst part was, she didn't want to stop.

CHAPTER 5 - FIVE THINGS

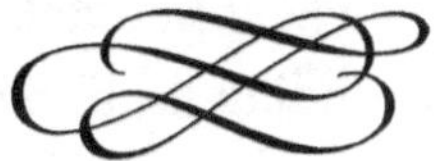

Sarah woke on the fourth morning in France feeling… altered.

She didn't feel bad, or anxious, or guilty, or confused. She was just different. More aware, like she'd been lost in fog for years and now sunlight was finally shining through, making everything sharper. Colours seemed brighter, sounds clearer, and her feelings more intense.

She stayed in bed for a moment, still and just breathing. The cool linen touched her skin. She heard church bells in the village, seven chimes for the hour. The smell of sweet, yeasty bread baking drifted up from the street. She was present in her body in a way she hadn't been for years.

Yesterday had changed her. The cliff. The conversation about marriage. Jack's lost love. His words: "Until now." The four hours of writing afterwards, fifteen pages poured out of her like she was bleeding ink onto paper. She'd written late into the night, until her hand cramped and her eyes burned, until the words were finally spent and she could fall into bed exhausted.

And she'd filled twenty pages total yesterday. Twenty. More than she'd written in the past year at home.

Seventy pages now. Seventy pages of her protagonist's journey from invisible wife to... what? She didn't know yet. But that was okay. The story was finding itself. She was finding herself.

Sarah got out of bed and walked to the window, sweeping the curtains aside. The morning light was muted today, tender, filtering through a veil of clouds. Below in the garden, Madame Rousseau was already working, tending her vegetables, the orange cat curling at her feet. The village looked tranquil, unchanged, enduring. Like it had stood for centuries and would persist for centuries more, long after Sarah was gone.

She showered and put on jeans and a white cotton shirt she'd bought years ago but rarely wore - too nice for everyday. Here in France, writing her book and meeting him for coffee, it was right. She dried her hair. She put on mascara and lip balm. These small acts of care were new and important after years of not bothering.

The walk to the café was different this morning. Sarah was hyper-aware of her footsteps on the cobblestones. The sun was warm on her face. The smell of bread from the boulangerie blended with the sea's salt air. She was alive, really alive. Not just going through the motions but experiencing each moment as it happened.

She turned the corner into the square and saw him.

He was already there, sitting at their table. T*heir* table, she thought again, feeling that warm pull in her chest. He was reading his newspaper, wearing his usual worn blue jumper. His dark hair was messy in a way that looked both careless and perfect. The morning light hit him just right, making him look almost unreal, almost like a painting.

But the scene was different.

Sarah paused at the edge of the square, letting herself observe before approaching. Oddly, there was no coffee cup in front of him. No mug, no cup, no saucer. Just his newspaper spread across the small iron table, the pages rustling slightly in the breeze, as if the morning routine had skipped over him entirely.

As she watched, the waitress walked past his table with a tray full of breakfast for other customers. She glanced at his table. Sarah saw her eyes move over it, but she didn't pause, stop, or acknowledge him at all. She just kept walking, her gaze sliding over him as if he wasn't there.

But he was there. Right there. Sitting solid and real, turning a page with those strong hands. Yet the world seemed to go on pretending he wasn't.

Sarah shook her head. Maybe she was imagining it. Maybe the light was playing tricks from this distance. Maybe the waitress was just busy, focused on her tray, and ignoring customers who weren't trying to get her attention. Maybe he'd already finished his coffee, and the cup had been cleared away.

There were a dozen reasonable explanations.

She walked over to the table, pushing the odd feeling aside. He looked up as she approached, and his face broke into that smile. That smile that made her stomach flip and her breath catch, and everything else fade into background noise.

“Morning,” he said, his voice warm.

“Morning.”

The waitress appeared almost immediately, materialising beside their table with practised efficiency. Bonjour, madame. Café?”

“Oui, deux cafés noirs, s’il vous plaît,” Sarah said. Her French was getting smoother and more confident each day. The words came easier now.

The waitress nodded and disappeared back into the café, still without glancing at him.

Sarah noticed that. Really noticed it. But she pushed it down, filed it away to examine later.

“Your French is improving,” He said.

“Slowly. Very slowly.” Sarah sat down, settling into her chair. “Though I suspect I still sound like a five-year-old trying to order lunch.”

“A very polite five-year-old.”

The waitress returned with two cups of black coffee. She set both down directly in front of Sarah, not acknowledging him at all, and disappeared again without a word or glance in his direction.

Sarah slid one cup across the table. She watched his face, trying to gauge his reaction to being ignored. But he only smiled, blinked twice in a slow, deliberate way, and wrapped his hands around the cup. He paused to sniff the steam as if checking its quality, then finally lifted it to his mouth and sipped.

"Thank you," he said.

Sarah wanted to ask. Wanted to say, 'Why doesn't she look at you? Why does she pretend you're not here?' But the words stuck in her throat. Asking would make it real. Would make the strangeness undeniable. And she wasn't ready for that yet.

Maybe, she thought, he'd broken the waitress's heart at some point. A relationship gone wrong. And now she couldn't bear to look at him, so she pretended he didn't exist. That would explain it. That made sense.

They sat in easy silence, watching the village wake up around them. The boulangerie flung open its shutters, the blue paint flaking at the edges. The scent of fresh bread floated across the square, making Sarah's mouth water though she wasn't hungry. An old woman in a thick cardigan walked a tiny white terrier that looked ancient and aristocratic. A delivery van rattled to a halt outside the pharmacy, the driver unloading boxes.

Normal village life. Beautiful in its ordinariness.

"Can I ask you something?" Sarah said, breaking the silence.

"Always."

"So what do you do? For work, I mean." She gestured vaguely at him, at the morning, at the way he was always here, always available. "You're here every morning. You're always free to walk and talk. You clearly don't have a nine-to-five job. So what do you do?"

An expression flickered across his face. Amusement, maybe. Complicated. Harder to read.

"I'm an artist," he said simply.

"An artist?" Sarah's eyebrows rose. "Really?"

"Really. Why do you sound so surprised?"

I don't know. I just…" She stopped, looking at him more closely. His worn blue jumper had faded to a colour between blue and grey, like the sea on a cloudy day. His hair was tousled and messy, as if he'd run his fingers through it and forgotten to comb it. His gaze lingered on things—the light on the cobblestones, the shadows from the buildings, the bright red geraniums in the window boxes. Now that she looked, she noticed pale streaks of dried paint on his cuffs: white, blue, and maybe yellow.

"I suppose that makes sense," she said finally. "You see things. Details. The way light falls. The way colours work together. I should have guessed."

"What kind of art?" she asked.

"Portraits, mostly. Sometimes landscapes. Sometimes just… moments. Whatever speaks to me. Whatever feels true." He took a sip of his coffee. "Whatever I can capture before it disappears."

"Do you sell them?" Sarah was trying to imagine his life. An artist's life. Free, unstructured, and creative.

"Not really. Mostly I just… paint. For the sake of painting. Whatever I can capture before it disappears. For the sake of seeing clearly." He shrugged. "I'm not interested in galleries or shows or selling to collectors. That's not why I paint."

"That's very artistic of you." Sarah smiled. "The whole starving-artist-in-a-garret thing. Very romantic."

"I'm not starving, and I don't live in a garret. I'm not reclusive, but I do choose who I talk to", he grinned. "But I suppose I fit the cliché in other ways." He gestured at his jumper. "Paint-stained clothes. Messy hair. Always available - I set my own hours. Slightly melancholy. Prone to philosophical conversations about the nature of existence."

"I think it suits you," Sarah said, meaning it. "You look like someone who cares more about what matters than what people think. Someone who's chosen authenticity over appearance."

"Is that a compliment?"

"It's an observation. But yes, also a compliment."

He smiled, a real smile that made him look younger, lighter, and less sad. "Then thank you. I'll take it."

After they finished their coffee, he suggested another walk. It was becoming their routine now. What Sarah looked forward to, needed even. These walks were medicine. Like therapy. Like oxygen.

"Where to today?" Sarah asked, standing up.

"Wherever we end up," he said, which was very artist-like and also frustratingly vague.

They wandered through the village, taking narrow lanes Sarah hadn't explored before. The streets were barely wide enough for two people to walk side by side. Morning light turned windowpanes to sheets of gold, and shadows gathered in doorways like spilt ink. The houses leaned toward each other like gossips, and flowers overflowed from window boxes with geraniums, petunias, and white blooms that smelled like honey.

He pointed things out as they walked. He showed her how sunlight made patterns on the old stone, changing as clouds passed by. The shutters were painted in colours that seemed to hold stories, blues faded by storms and sun, greens turned grey with age, reds that had once been bright now softened to rose. Doorways were worn smooth by generations of hands, the wood polished to silk in places.

"You see things differently," Sarah observed. "Than most people, I mean. You notice things others walk right past."

"That's what artists do," he said simply. "We notice. We pay attention to the things others walk past without seeing. The light. The shadows. The way time leaves marks on everything. The beauty in ordinary things."

Is that why you're so good at helping me? Because you pay attention?"

"Partly." He paused at a corner, studying a wall where ivy had grown so thick it had created patterns like lace. "But also, I understand what it's like to feel invisible. To feel like you're there, but no one really sees you. It's… It's an artist's curse, in some ways. You see so much, notice so much, but people rarely see you back. They look at your work, not at you. You become the observer, never the observed. You're there but not there. Present but ignored."

Sarah thought about the waitress. About the market vendors who seemed to look right through him. About how he was always here, always available, like he had nowhere else to be. No family waiting. No obligations pulling him away.

And suddenly it made sense.

Of course. He was an artist. A bit eccentric, a bit reclusive. The kind of person who likes to observe life more than take part in it. Sensitive to others' feelings - artists felt things deeply. He always wore the same paint-stained jumper, unconcerned about appearances or fashion. That occasional sadness in his eyes. Wasn't suffering for your art almost expected? The tortured artist was a cliché for a reason. He had made himself invisible in the village in the same way that she had made herself invisible at home.

The waitress probably didn't look at him because he was the kind of person who faded into the background. Who didn't demand attention. Who was easy to overlook if you weren't paying attention. Or they knew he protected his privacy.

Sarah was oddly relieved to have found an explanation. A way to understand the strangeness. He wasn't mysterious. He was simply an artist. Different. Unconventional. But explainable.

There was nothing strange about that. Nothing impossible or unsettling. Just a man who lived outside normal society, who'd chosen creativity over convention, who'd made himself a bit invisible in the process.

They walked together in silence, winding through sunlit lanes, timeless, until they reached a small garden at the edge of the village. It was a wild place, part cared for, and part left alone. A weathered wooden bench sat under an old chestnut tree, its branches twisted with age, casting lacy shadows on the ground. Beyond the garden, patchwork fields stretched toward the horizon, with a wide blue sky above and slow-moving clouds.

"This is beautiful," Sarah said, sitting down on the bench. The wood was warm from the sun.

Jack sat beside her. Not too close, but close enough. That distance that was becoming familiar. That space between them, charged with possibility.

"Can I ask a question?" Jack said after a moment.

"Of course."

"If you took removed wife and a mother from the equation, who would you be?" He turned to look at her, his expression serious. "What would define you? Who is Sarah when she's not someone's wife or someone's mother?"

Sarah opened her mouth to answer, then closed it. The question caught her off guard. "I… I don't know. I haven't thought about that in a long time. Maybe ever."

"Think about it now."

She considered the question, really considered it. Who was she underneath all the roles? "I suppose… I'd be a writer. That's what I'm doing here, isn't it? Trying to be just Sarah the writer. Not Sarah the wife or Sarah the mother. Just Sarah."

"And what else?" he pressed. "Surely writing isn't the only thing that defines you."

"I don't know. That's the problem." Tightness in Sarah's chest. "I've spent so long being defined by other people's needs that I'm not sure who I am underneath all of that. I don't know what I like. What I want. What I'm good at beyond managing schedules and making dinner and keeping everyone's lives running smoothly."

"Then let's find out." He shifted to face her more fully. "Tell me five things you're good at. Five strengths."

"Five?" Sarah experienced a flutter of anxiety. "That seems like a lot."

"Start with one, then."

She thought about it, her mind going immediately to the practical things. The things that made her useful. "I'm… I'm organised. I can manage complex schedules and logistics. I never miss a football match or a parent-teacher conference. Everyone's dentist appointments are up to date. Everyone has clean clothes. Everything runs smoothly - I make it run smoothly."

"Good. That's one. What else?"

"I'm a good cook. I make proper meals from scratch, not just frozen things or takeaway. The girls always have healthy food, even when it's just Tuesday and I'm exhausted and would rather order pizza." She was warming up to this now. "I plan meals. I shop. I make sure everyone's eating properly."

"Three more."

Sarah struggled, her mind blank. "I'm… I'm good at problem-solving. When things go wrong, and things are always going wrong, I figure it out. I fix it. I make it work. If the boiler breaks, I find a plumber. If Betty forgets her costume, I make a new one the night before. If David double-books himself, I rearrange everything so it works. I'm the fixer."

"That's three. Two more."

"Um…" Sarah's voice got quieter. "I'm patient? I don't lose my temper easily. Even when the girls are being difficult, David's being oblivious, or everything is falling apart, I stay calm. I don't yell. I don't throw things. I just… handle it."

"And the fifth?"

She sat there, thinking hard, but nothing came. Her mind was completely blank. "I don't know. I can't think of a fifth."

"You can't think of a fifth strength," he said carefully, "or you won't let yourself claim one?"

"What's the difference?"

"Everything." He leaned forward slightly. "Now tell me five weaknesses."

This was easier. Horrifyingly easier. The words came, unhesitating, tumbling out like they'd been waiting to be said.

"I'm a terrible decision-maker. I second-guess everything, even tiny things. I can spend twenty minutes in the grocery store choosing between two kinds of pasta, worried about making the wrong choice. What if I get the wrong shape? What if everyone hates it? What if it doesn't work with the sauce I'm planning?"

"What else?"

"I'm not assertive. I let people walk over me. I say yes when I mean no - I don't want to cause conflict or make anyone uncomfortable. David asks me to pick up his dry cleaning on my way home, even though it's completely out of my way, and I say 'of course' instead of 'actually, could you do that?' The girls ask for the impossible, and I say 'I'll try' instead of 'that's not reasonable.'"

"Three more."

"I'm bad at accepting compliments. Someone compliments me, and I immediately deflect or make a joke or point out all the ways they're wrong. 'Oh, dinner was lovely!' someone says, and I'm like 'Oh no, the chicken was too dry, and I forgot to make a proper pudding.' I can't just say thank you and believe them."

"Two more."

Sarah took a breath. "I'm not creative. I mean, I'm trying to write a book, but I'm not artistic like you. I don't see the world in interesting ways. I don't notice the light or the shadows or the way ivy makes patterns on walls. I'm very… ordinary. Boring. Conventional."

"And the last one?"

This was the hardest one. The one that had been sitting in her chest like a stone. "I'm selfish. I came here for two weeks, left my family to fend for themselves, all so I could write a book that probably no one will ever read and that doesn't matter to anyone but me. That's selfish. Abandoning my responsibilities for my own pleasure."

He said nothing. The silence stretched. Sarah felt heat rise in her cheeks, embarrassment flooding through her. She'd said too much. Revealed too much. Been too honest. He was going to agree with her, tell her she was right about everything, confirm all her worst thoughts about herself.

"Right," he said finally, his voice calm. "So. Let's go through these, shall we?"

"What?" Sarah looked up.

"Your five weaknesses. Let's look at them one by one." He shifted on the bench to face her. "Let's start with the biggest one: you called this selfish for coming here, taking two weeks to write a book. Let's talk about that."

Sarah's stomach clenched.

"That's not selfish, Sarah," he said, gentle but firm. "That's self-care. There's a difference. A crucial difference that women are never taught."

"But I left my family to…"

"To do what's important to you. What you've wanted your whole life. What feeds your soul and makes you feel alive and gives you purpose beyond service to others." He held up a hand to stop her protest. "That's not selfish. Selfish would be abandoning them permanently with no regard for their well-being. Selfish would be spending the family's savings without discussion. Selfish would be expecting them to manage unprepared while you gallivanted off. But you didn't do any of that. You arranged everything. You made sure they'd be fine. You prepared meals. You left instructions. And then you took two weeks. Two weeks out of twenty years. That's not selfish. That's overdue. That's necessary. That's what any human being needs to stay sane and whole."

Something cracked inside Sarah's chest. A fault line splitting open.

"And while we're at it," he continued, leaning forward, his eyes intense, "let's tackle this 'terrible decision-maker' nonsense. You spent twenty minutes choosing pasta because there wasn't actually a wrong choice - torturing yourself trying to find one. You created a false dilemma where none existed. But when it came to making a massive decision - coming to France alone for two weeks to write a book - you didn't hesitate. You decided. You bought the tickets. You packed your bags. You got on the train. You acted. So you're not a terrible decision-maker. You're someone who agonises over inconsequential things while being decisive about what truly matters. That's actually a strength, not a weakness."

He wasn't finished.

"You said you're not assertive, that you let people walk over you. But here you are, doing exactly what you wanted, even though everyone tried to talk you out of it. David suggested other plans. Betty cried about her semifinals. Olivia made you feel guilty. You stood your ground. You came anyway. You told your daughters they'd have to handle things themselves for two weeks. You're ordering coffee in French in a foreign country. You're having hard conversations with someone you barely know." He paused. "That's assertive. Most of the time, you choose peace over conflict, which isn't weakness. That's wisdom. That's knowing when to fight and when to save your energy. That's picking your battles."

Sarah opened her mouth to protest, to argue, but nothing came out. Her throat was tight with unshed tears.

“As for not being creative…” He gestured around them at the garden, the village, the sky. “You’re writing a book, Sarah. You’re literally creating from nothing. You’re taking your life experience and transforming it into a story. You’re seeing connections between things. You’re using metaphors - comparing yourself to a ghost on the beach, remember? You notice details. Emotional details. The way people’s words don’t match their actions. The way invisibility feels. That’s what creativity is. It’s not about being able to paint or sculpt. It’s about seeing possibilities where others see routine. It’s about making connections. It’s about taking the ordinary and finding the extraordinary inside it. You do that every day in your writing. That’s creativity.”

He paused, his expression softening.

“And the compliments thing…” His voice went quieter. “That’s the saddest one, honestly. Someone tells you you’re good at X, and you immediately deflect or make a joke or point out why they’re wrong. You can’t let it land. Can’t believe it. Why do you think you do that?”

Tears pricked Sarah’s eyes. “I don’t know.”

“I think you do.” His voice was gentle but relentless. “I think somewhere along the way, you learned it was safer to shrink. To not take up space. To not claim your worth or your competence or your talents. If you never claim them, you can never lose them. If you never admit you’re good at anything, no one can tell you you’re not. If you never accept a compliment, you never have to worry about disappointing the person who gave it. It's self-protection. But it's also self-erasure."

The tears spilled over, running down Sarah's cheeks. She wiped at them quickly, embarrassed.

"But you can't live like that, Sarah." His voice was firm now. "You can't spend your whole life refusing to believe the good things people see in you just because you're afraid they might stop seeing them someday. That's not humility. That's not being realistic. That's just being afraid. And you're too brave for that."

Sarah wiped at her cheeks again, her voice breaking. "I don't… I don't know how to stop."

"Yes, you do." He leaned back. "You just did it. Five minutes ago, you named four strengths unworried if you deserved them. You said 'I'm organised' without adding, 'but I'm probably too controlling.' You said 'I'm a good cook' without saying, 'but not as good as my mother.' You said 'I'm patient' without qualifying it with, 'but sometimes I lose my temper in my head.' You just claimed them. That's how you stop. You practice. You start saying yes to compliments instead of deflecting. You start believing what people tell you. You start trusting that maybe, just maybe, they see the truth."

He paused, studying her face. "What was the fifth? You never finished. You couldn't think of a fifth strength."

Sarah thought back. "I couldn't think of one."

"Then I'll give you one." His voice was soft but certain. "You're brave. You came to a foreign country alone to chase a dream everyone told you was impractical. You're sitting here now, being vulnerable with someone you barely know, letting the feelings you've been pushing down for years surface. You're writing a book about your own life even though it scares you. You're questioning your marriage even though that's terrifying. You're allowing want even though you've been taught that wanting is selfish. That's brave. Maybe the bravest thing of all. To look at your life and say, 'this isn't enough' and then act. Most people never get there. Most people live their whole lives knowing what's wrong and never having the courage to change it. But you did. You're doing it right now."

A tear slipped down Sarah's cheek. Then another. She couldn't stop them.

"I'm sorry," she said, her voice thick. "I don't know why I'm crying."

"Because someone finally told you the truth about yourself," he said gently. "Because you've been carrying around a harsh, critical, fundamentally wrong version of who you are, and it's exhausting. And now someone's holding up a mirror that shows you what's actually there instead of what you've been told is there. And seeing yourself clearly for the first time is overwhelming."

They sat there on the bench in the garden, and Sarah cried quietly while he sat beside her. Not uncomfortable. Not trying to fix it or make it stop. Not handing her tissues, patting her back, or telling her it was okay. Just present. Just there. Letting her have her feelings unmanaged, unminimised, unapologised.

When she finally stopped crying, she was lighter. Clearer. Emptier in a good way. Like she'd put down a weight she'd been carrying so long she'd forgotten it was there. Like she could breathe more deeply now.

"Thank you," she said, her voice hoarse.

"For what?"

"For seeing me. Really seeing me." She looked at him, this man who'd somehow seen through all her layers to the truth underneath. "The way I want David to see me. The way I've wanted anyone to see me. For years."

"You're easy to see, Sarah," he said simply. "You just needed someone to look."

They sat in comfortable silence for a while longer. The clouds moved across the sky, changing the light. A bird sang somewhere in the chestnut tree above them, a long, complicated melody. The breeze was warm, smelling of cut grass and flowers Sarah couldn't name. Perfect, peaceful, and safe.

"I should let you write," he said eventually. "You've got a book to finish."

"I do." But Sarah didn't move. She didn't want to. She wanted to stay on this bench in this garden with this man who saw her clearly, who made her feel real, who showed her a version of herself she could accept.

Finally, reluctantly, she stood. Her legs felt stiff from sitting. "Same time tomorrow?"

"Same time tomorrow."

They walked back to the square together, not talking, just comfortable in each other's presence. When they reached the café, he said, "Go write, Sarah. Write about a woman who's discovering she's stronger than she thought."

"Is that what I'm doing?"

"That's exactly what you're doing."

He walked away with his hands in his pockets, and Sarah watched him go. Then she turned and went back to her hotel, climbed the stairs to her room, and unlocked the door with slightly shaking fingers. She dropped her bag on the chair, sat at her desk, and opened her notebook to a fresh page.

Then she wrote, in large letters at the top:

FIVE STRENGTHS:
1. Organised
2. Good cook
3. Problem solver
4. Patient
5. Brave

SHE LOOKED at the list for a long moment. The fifth one. The one she hadn't been able to name herself. The one he'd given her.

Brave.

Was she really brave? Had she survived twenty years of slowly fading away unbroken? Without becoming bitter or resentful? She had. She'd survived. She'd stayed kind. She'd raised good daughters. She kept trying. She kept hoping, even when hope seemed pointless.

That was worth claiming. Maybe that was worth everything.

She picked up her pen and kept writing.

She wrote for six hours straight. Six hours nonstop, phone unchecked, without thinking about dinner or what anyone else might need. Six hours of pure creation, pure flow, pure connection between her mind and the page.

She wrote about a woman who'd believed she was weak and found out she was strong. A woman who'd believed she was ordinary and found out she was creative. A woman who'd believed she was selfish and found out she was simply human. A woman learning to see herself through someone else's eyes. Someone who actually looked.

She wrote about transformation. About the courage it takes to see clearly. About the difference between the story you've been told and the truth. About how sometimes you need a stranger to reflect back what's actually there - the people who know you best have stopped really looking.

She wrote about strength and weakness being two sides of the same coin. About how the things she thought made her weak were actually survival mechanisms. About how self-erasure wasn't the same as selflessness. About how you could serve others without self-destruction.

When she finally stopped, her hand cramping, the light through the window had turned golden. Late afternoon. Nearly evening. She closed the notebook, stretched her aching fingers, and realised she was smiling. Really smiling. The kind of smile that came from deep inside, from a place that had been dark for too long.

She was writing a book. A real book. Seventy-five pages now. And maybe she was also writing a new story about who Sarah Mitchell was and what she deserved. A story where she was brave instead of selfish. Strong instead of weak. Creative instead of ordinary. Worthy instead of disappointing.

The thought no longer scared her. It was coming home, like arriving at a destination she'd been travelling toward her whole life without knowing.

Her phone buzzed on the nightstand.

Sarah reached for it without thinking, still wrapped in the glow of the afternoon, and saw a text from David.

> Good news! I've taken Thursday and Friday off work. Thought the girls and I could come visit you in France. They should learn about their great-grandfather and the D-Day beaches, and we could make it a proper family trip. A bit of history, a bit of culture. The train arrives on Thursday afternoon. I'll text you the details. Can't wait to see you! xx

Sarah stared at the screen.

No.

The word formed silently in her mind, immediate and fierce and non-negotiable.

She didn't want them to come. She didn't want David and the girls here, in this place that belonged to her. This space she'd made for herself. This village, this room, this new version of herself she was finding. She didn't want to share Jack with them, didn't want to see him invisible to them while he was so real to her. She didn't want to explain who he was or why she spent time with him. She didn't want David's questions, the girls' boredom, or for this special place to become just another family duty.

She didn't want to be a wife and mother here. She wanted to be Sarah. Just Sarah.

The guilt hit immediately, sharp and familiar, like an old friend. What kind of mother didn't want to see her children? What kind of wife didn't want her husband to visit? What kind of person was she becoming?

But underneath the guilt lay a harder truth, bright and unyielding:

This is mine. These two weeks are mine. I earned them. I need them. And I'm not giving them up.

She typed quickly, before she could second-guess herself:

> That's sweet, but I'm here to write. I need the solitude. Maybe we can plan a proper family trip another time? It's a long journey for such a short visit. xx

She sent it before she could overthink, before the guilt could talk her into saying yes when she meant no.

The phone immediately showed three dots. David typing.

Then:

> Ok. But the girls would really love it. Think about it? x

Sarah set the phone face down on the desk and closed her eyes.

Thursday. That was only four days away.

But she wasn't going to think about it. She wasn't going to let them come. This place was hers. Jack was hers. These mornings, these walks, these conversations - they were hers. This transformation she was experiencing, this version of herself she was discovering - it was hers.

And she wasn't giving it up. Not for guilt. Not for duty. Not even for love.

She opened her notebook and started writing again.

CHAPTER 6 - FRESH TOWELS

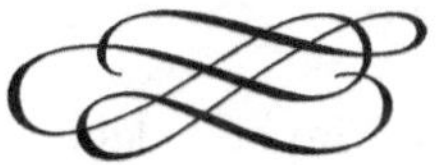

Sarah woke on the fifth morning with a fierce heat coiling low and deep inside her, urgent and alive.

She'd been dreaming about him again.

These weren't the innocent dreams she'd had before. No more walking through the village. No more sitting at cafés or talking on hillsides. This dream was different, more intense. His hands held her face, his fingers tangled in her hair. His mouth hovered so close she could feel his breath. His body pressed against hers, warm and real. She knew she shouldn't be dreaming about these things, a man who wasn't her husband, a stranger she'd only just met. But the dream ignored all the rules, broke through her careful defences, leaving her tingling, nerves exposed, and filled with restless wanting.

She lay in the white sheets, not moving, the muslin curtains stirring gently in the morning breeze. Let herself feel it. The want. The desire. The ache that had settled between her legs was insistent and undeniable.

When was the last time she'd been this way? Really been this way - not just the polite warmth of affection or comfortable familiarity, but this desperate, consuming need? Sarah tried to remember. Tried to recall David looking at her with want instead of tired fondness. Tried to remember the last time she'd been truly desirable, not merely... there. She shared his bed out of habit rather than passion.

Years. It had been years. Maybe a decade. Maybe longer.

Their sex life had become perfunctory somewhere along the way. Saturday nights, usually, if he wasn't on call and she wasn't too exhausted. Efficient, quiet, and over quickly. She couldn't remember the last time she'd actually wanted it, actually initiated it. Couldn't remember the last time David had looked at her like he needed her specifically, rather than just needing release.

And she'd believed that was normal. That passion faded. That comfortable intimacy was more sustainable than desperate desire. That this was what twenty years of marriage looked like.

But now, lying in her French hotel bed, burning from the dream, she realised she'd been lying. Suddenly, she understood that this was real desire: the heat, the need, the urgency. Each wave of longing made her see that she had forgotten, or maybe never really known, what it meant to want.

Her hand moved slowly down, tentative at first. Over her breast, feeling her nipple harden beneath her palm. Down across her stomach. Lower.

'Stop it,' closing her eyes tight. 'Stop it right now. You're married. You love David. This is wrong.'

But she was unmoved by rules or guilt, by wedding vows or moral arguments. She responded only to want. No matter how much her mind argued, her body just felt awake and alive and hungry. She hadn't been this in so long.

Sarah threw back the covers and stood abruptly. Her legs wobbled slightly, unsteady. She needed to cool off, clear her head, regain control. Get a grip before this spiraled into something she couldn't take back.

A shower. A cold shower. That's what people did in situations like this, wasn't it? Cold water to shock the system, to douse the fire, to restore sanity.

The bathroom was small but charming in its simplicity. White subway tiles covered the walls, slightly uneven with age. An old-fashioned shower in the corner. A single window with frosted glass let in the morning light.

Sarah turned on the water, telling herself she'd make it cold. But when she tested the temperature, she couldn't. Cool, yes. Refreshing. But not punishingly cold. She wasn't a masochist.

She stepped under the spray, gasping slightly as the water hit her overheated skin. Closed her eyes. Tipped her head back, letting the water run over her face, her hair, her skin. Tried to think about anything else. The book. The girls. What she needed from the grocery store when she got home. Anything but…

But her mind kept drifting back. To the dream. To Jack's hands, his mouth, him. To the way he looked at her, really looked at her, like she was worth seeing. To his voice saying her name like it mattered. To the pull between them that she couldn't deny anymore, even if she wanted to.

And her hands, moving almost of their own accord, soap-slicked and sliding over her skin, moved lower. And lower still. Until..

She stopped thinking entirely.

Everything narrowed to sensation. The heat inside her grew, winding tighter. She saw him behind her closed eyes, his smile, his eyes, the way he'd looked at her when he called her brave. She heard his low, intimate voice, remembered how her name sounded when he said it. The pull between them, that magnetic force she'd tried to resist, was too strong now.

Her fingers moved in practised circles, finding the rhythm she knew. That rhythm, she'd almost forgotten in years of perfunctory duty. The pleasure built quickly, surprisingly intense. After so long, going through the motions or not bothering at all.

When it came, the release was so overwhelming, so complete, so utterly consuming that she couldn't hold back the cry that escaped her lips.

Knock knock knock.

Sarah's eyes flew open, her heart hammering, pleasure and panic warring in her chest.

Knock knock knock.

"Madame?" came a voice from outside the bathroom. No - outside the bedroom. "Serviettes fraîches?"

The maid. Oh God. Oh God. The maid with fresh towels.

Had she heard? Had she been standing out there? For how long?

Sarah tried to sound normal, tried to force her voice into casual indifference, but it came out embarrassingly breathless. "J-just a moment! I'm in the shower!"

She rinsed off quickly, hands still shaking, heart still racing. Wrapped in a towel, water dripping everywhere. Opened the bathroom door and crossed the room, leaving wet footprints on the old wooden floor. The bedroom door was still closed, with shadows of feet visible beneath it.

Sarah opened it just wide enough for the maid - a young woman in her twenties with dark hair pulled back in a bun - to hand her the stack of fresh white towels.

"Merci," Sarah managed, her face burning.

"De rien, madame," the girl said with a polite, professional smile. "Pardon - I knocked earlier, but you did not hear. You were in the shower, yes?"

"Yes. Yes, I was. Washing my hair." Sarah's voice was too high, too defensive. "I didn't hear the first knock. The water was loud."

"Pas de problème." The maid nodded, still smiling, and turned to go.

As Sarah closed the door, she heard the girl speak to another maid who was pushing a cleaning cart down the hallway. They both laughed - not unkindly, just... amused. Sarah's French wasn't quite good enough to catch everything, but she definitely heard: "Je pense que je dois changer mon shampooing." I think I need to change my shampoo.

With the door closed Sarah leaned up against it, fresh towels clutched to her chest, and felt laughter bubble up. The embarrassment was sharp, the aftershocks of pleasure still tingling, and the situation struck her as absurd.

Not a polite chuckle. Not a nervous giggle. A real laugh, slightly hysterical, born of embarrassment and shock and the sheer absurdity of it all. She'd just been caught - or nearly caught, or caught enough - by the hotel maid. Caught in the shower thinking about a man who wasn't her husband, masturbating like a teenager, crying out loud enough to be heard through two doors.

It was mortifying. It was ridiculous. It was...

It was also the funniest thing that had happened to her in years.

When she finally caught her breath, when the laughter subsided into hiccups and then silence, she looked in the mirror over the writing desk. Her hair dripped water onto the towels, making dark spots. Her face was flushed - from the shower, from before, from embarrassment, from laughing. Her eyes shone, bright and almost feverish.

She looked alive.

Really, truly alive. Not the polite, managed version she'd shown for years. Not the careful, proper life of a wife and mother, but actually, genuinely, messily alive.

And then, as quickly as joy had come, the guilt crashed in.

Not about the shower. Not about the pleasure itself - she was allowed to feel good, she could accept that much. But about Jack. She'd been thinking about Jack while touching herself. While she responded in ways she hadn't in years. She'd imagined things she absolutely shouldn't imagine. His hands on her. His mouth. His body.

And worse - so much worse than the act itself - was the thrilling, dangerous lack of regret. The wild exultation mingling with the shame. The pleasure and the want had been real. For those few minutes, she'd been more like herself than she had in years. More connected to herself. More present in her own skin.

What did that make her? Did it mean her marriage was broken beyond repair? Or was she broken? Was she selfish? Was she a terrible person? A terrible wife?

She hugged the towels to her chest, unsteady. Feeling the weight of dread and defiance and something that might have been hope, all tangled together in her chest like knots she couldn't untie.

She needed to write. Needed to process this, figure out what it meant, work through it on the page where she could be honest without consequences.

She dressed quickly, hands still slightly shaky. Jeans and a soft grey t-shirt. No makeup - her face was still flushed enough. Brushed her wet hair and pulled it back. Then she settled at the desk by the window and opened her notebook.

The words came easily, flowing onto the page without the usual struggle or second-guessing.

She wrote about desire. About the divide between being wanted and being needed, and how somewhere along the way those two things had become completely separate in her marriage. David needed her to manage the house, to raise the children, to keep everything running. But wanting her? Actually desiring her? She couldn't remember the last time she'd seen that in his eyes.

She wrote about guilt and shame. About how guilt said 'I did something wrong' while shame said 'I am wrong'. And how she'd been living with shame for so long - the shame of wanting things, of having needs, of taking up space, of not being satisfied with the comfortable life she had - that she'd almost forgotten the difference.

She wrote about her protagonist - this woman who'd spent so long being invisible - discovering that she had a body. Not just a body that served others, that cooked meals and washed clothes, and drove children to activities, and performed marital duties twice a month. But a body that felt things. That wanted things. That deserved pleasure. That was more than just a vehicle for service.

Sarah's pen moved faster, the words spilling out in a rush. She wrote about awakening. About learning to claim your own pleasure. About a woman discovering she was allowed to want, allowed to feel, allowed to be a sexual being instead of just a mother and wife.

She wrote about the complicated space between fidelity and desire. About how you could love someone and still want someone else. About how wanting didn't have to mean doing. About how thoughts weren't the same as actions. About how being attracted to someone new didn't automatically erase twenty years of history with someone else.

She wrote until her hand cramped, until the knots in her chest started to loosen, until she'd worked through enough of it to breathe again.

When she finally stopped, she looked at the clock. Eight-fifteen. She'd written for almost an hour. Ten more pages added to the manuscript. She flipped back through her note-book, counting. Eighty-five pages now. Nearly at a hundred. Nearly at that magical three-digit number that would make it feel real, would make it feel like she was actually doing this, actually writing a book.

She closed the notebook and took a deep breath.

Time to meet Jack.

The thought made her stomach flip. How was she supposed to look at him now? After what she'd just done? After thinking about him while she… God. Would he somehow know? Would it show on her face? Would she blurt it out like some kind of idiot?

Good morning, Jack. Lovely weather. By the way, I just masturbated in the shower thinking about you, and the maid almost caught me, and there was a joke about shampoo.

She laughed again, quieter this time. God, she was a mess. But she couldn't not go. Couldn't hide in her room out of embarrassment. Couldn't let guilt or confusion or mortification keep her from the one person who made her feel seen, who made her feel real, who made her feel alive.

So she grabbed her bag and headed out.

* * *

JACK WAS ALREADY THERE when she arrived, sitting at their table, reading his newspaper. The morning sun caught him at an angle that made the whole scene look like a painting - the light, the shadows, the way he sat so still and present.

He looked up as she approached, and his expression shifted almost immediately. From neutral to curious, studying her face with that artist's attention to detail.

"Good morning," he said.

"Morning." Sarah sat down, suddenly self-conscious.

"You look..." He tilted his head slightly, assessing. "Different."

Different how?" Sarah's heart started racing. Could he tell? Did she have a sign on her forehead? This woman had impure thoughts about you an hour ago. "What do you mean?"

"I don't know. Flushed. Like you've been running. Or—" He trailed off, and something that might have been amusement flickered across his face. The tiniest smile tugged at one corner of his mouth. "Never mind."

The waitress appeared. Sarah ordered two black coffees, grateful for the distraction, grateful not to have to meet Jack's knowing eyes for a moment.

When the waitress left - setting both cups in front of Sarah as always, ignoring Jack completely - he was still looking at her with that expression. Amused. Curious. Knowing.

"What?" Sarah said, trying to sound normal and probably failing.

"Nothing." His smile widened slightly. "You just seem... happy. Lighter. More yourself."

"I am happy." Sarah latched onto the safer part of the conversation. "I wrote ten pages this morning. Nearly at one hundred pages total."

"That's wonderful." Jack's face lit up with genuine pleasure. "What were you writing about?"

Sarah felt heat rise in her cheeks again. "Just... the usual. The woman in my story. Her journey."

"Her journey where?"

"Toward herself. Toward understanding what she wants. Who she is." Sarah pushed his coffee across the table, their fingers not quite touching, but close enough that she felt the almost-contact like an electric shock.

"Good," he said, wrapping his hands around the cup. "That's important. Knowing what you want. Being honest about it."

He took a sip, then added casually, "And what does she want? Your protagonist?"

"I'm still figuring that out."

"Are you?" His eyes met hers over the rim of his cup. "Or do you know and you're just not ready to write it down yet?"

Sarah looked at him. Really looked at him. At the way he was watching her - not judging, not prying, just interested. Aware that the morning had shifted them. That she'd crossed some threshold this morning and was on the other side of it now.

"Maybe the second one," she admitted quietly.

"There's no rush." He set down his cup. "The story will tell you when it's ready. You'll know when it's time."

They sat in comfortable silence for a moment, drinking their coffee. Around them, the village continued its morning routine. The boulangerie doing steady business, the smell of fresh bread drifting across the square. People greeting each other, calling out "Bonjour!" and "Ça va?" Church bells mark the half-hour. The orange cat from the hotel wandered across the cobblestones, pausing to wash its face in a patch of sunlight.

Normal life continued while Sarah sat there feeling anything but normal.

"Thank you," she said.

"For what?"

"For telling me guilt was useless. For the porridge metaphor. For the five strengths." She paused. "I think... I think I'm finally starting to believe it. That I'm allowed to want things. That taking care of myself isn't selfish."

He smiled - that warm, genuine smile that made her breath catch and her chest feel tight. "Good. That's very good indeed."

"Though I have to admit," Sarah continued, feeling brave, feeling reckless, "believing it and living it are two different things. Old habits are hard to break. Old patterns of thinking."

"But you're breaking them," He said. "Little by little. Every day. That's all anyone can do. Small acts of rebellion until they stop feeling like rebellion and start feeling like living."

* * *

They finished their coffee, and he suggested another walk. But this time, instead of the village or the cliffs or the garden, they walked to the beach - the same beach where Sarah had first met him, where she'd sat with her blank notebook and her spiralling thoughts and her terror at what she was doing.

It was different now. The beach wasn't scary or overwhelming. It wasn't a place of anxiety and doubt. It was just... a beach. Beautiful and peaceful and hers to enjoy.

They walked in comfortable silence, shoes in hand, feet in the sand. The morning was perfect - warm but not hot, with a gentle breeze that smelled of salt and seaweed and wildflowers from the dunes. The sound of waves was rhythmic and soothing, like breathing, like a heartbeat.

Sarah relaxed as they walked. The tension from the morning - the dream, the shower, the embarrassment, the guilt - slowly draining away, seeping out into the sand with each step.

So what if she'd had thoughts about him? So what if her body had responded to those thoughts? She was human. She was allowed to feel things. Even things that were complicated. Even things that didn't fit neatly into the boxes marked "appropriate," "proper," and "good wife."

"I'm going home in eight days," she said, the words coming out before she could stop them.

"I know."

"I don't know if I'm ready." Sarah stopped walking and turned to face the sea. "I don't know how to go back to being that person. The Sarah who lives there. Who manages everyone else's lives. Who doesn't want anything inconvenient."

"You won't be that person," he said, stopping beside her. "You can't be. You've changed too much. You've remembsered who you are underneath all the roles."

"But what if I can't hold onto it? What if I get back there and the weight of everything - the responsibilities, the expectations, the patterns - just crushes this version of me? What if I forget?"

"You won't forget." His voice was certain. "Because you're writing it down. Every day, you're writing the story of who you really are. And whenever you need to remember, you can read it. You'll have proof. Evidence that this person exists. That you exist."

Tears pricked Sarah's eyes. "You make it sound simple."

"It's not simple. It's the hardest thing in the world - being yourself when everyone around you is used to you being someone else. But you're already doing it. Every day, you're becoming more yourself. More visible. More alive. I can see it happening."

"How?"

"The way you walk. The way you talk. The way you look at things." He gestured at the beach, the sea, the sky. "The first day I met you, you were hunched in on yourself, making yourself small. Now you take up space. You stand up straight. You look people in the eye. You order coffee in French without apologising. You laugh. Real laughs, not polite chuckles. You're alive, Sarah. And you won't lose that just because you get on a train."

Sarah wiped at her eyes. "And what if what I want isn't compatible with the life I have? What if I've changed too much to fit back into that shape?"

"Then you'll have to decide what matters more," he said gently. "The comfortable life you've built, or the authentic life you're discovering. The safe marriage or the real you. But that's a decision for later. For now, just focus on the discovery. On becoming. On being."

"That's easier said than done."

"Most worthwhile things are."

They walked to the end of the beach and back, talking about easier things now. The weather. The birds - there was a gull with one leg standing on a rock, and he spun a ridiculous story about how it had lost its leg in a duel with a crab. The tide coming in or going out. Easy conversation. Comfortable.

But Sarah found herself studying him as they walked. The way he moved with such ease, so comfortable in his skin, like he'd never questioned his right to take up space. The way the wind caught his dark hair, and he didn't bother to push it back. The paint stains on his jumper cuffs - she could see them clearly now in the sunlight, streaks of blue and white and gold. The way his silver watch caught the light, the scratches on the face were a testament to years of wear.

She wanted to know more about him. Where he lived. Where he painted. Whether he had a studio or worked from home. Whether he'd been married, apart from the lost love he'd mentioned on the cliff. What his days looked like when he wasn't spending his mornings with her. Whether he thought about her when they weren't together. Whether he felt this pull too, or if she'd imagined it all.

But instinct held her back from asking. Some sense that he preferred to remain slightly mysterious. Or maybe that the mystery was part of what made this work - that they existed in this bubble where the past didn't matter, where they could just be present with each other without the weight of history or the pressure of the future.

* * *

WHEN THEY RETURNED to the village square, he said, "Same time tomorrow?"

"Same time tomorrow."

He walked away, hands in his pockets, and Sarah watched him go. Then she turned and headed back to her hotel, back to her room, back to her desk.

She sat down and opened her notebook. The morning had unlocked possibility, broken through some barrier she hadn't even known was there. The words came as if she'd been saving them up, as if they'd been waiting for permission.

She wrote about awakening - not just sexual awakening, though that was part of it, but a broader awakening. To herself. To her desires. To the possibility that she could be more than she'd allowed for twenty years.

She wrote about the difference between guilt and shame. About how guilt said 'I did wrong while shame said 'I am wrong'. And how she'd been living with shame for so long - the shame of wanting things, of taking up space, of having needs beyond serving others - that she'd forgotten she could choose differently.

She wrote about reclaiming herself. About learning to be more than just a vehicle for service. About pleasure being allowed.

About desire being human, not shameful. About the radical act of attending to your own needs.

She wrote for hours, barely aware of the clock, barely aware of anything beyond the page and the pen and the words flowing out of her.

The light through the window changed from morning gold to afternoon white to evening amber, but she kept writing. Her fingers grew stiff, her wrist ached, and her eyes burned from concentration. Still, she continued. This was it. This was the book. Real, true, something that mattered.

She was writing about a woman who'd forgotten she could feel. Who'd forgotten she was allowed to want. Who'd spent so long serving others that she'd disappeared entirely. And she was writing about that woman finding her way back. Slowly. Painfully. Beautifully.

When she finally stopped, it was nearly nine o'clock. The light through the window was fading, the village settling into evening. Lights were coming on in the windows. People were heading home from work, from errands, from wherever their days had taken them.

Sarah set down her pen and flexed her cramping hand. She looked at the page count. Ninety-eight pages. So close to a hundred. So close to that milestone that it would feel real.

She closed the notebook and looked out the window at the village. Peace settled over her. A rightness. A sense of being exactly where she was supposed to be, doing exactly what she was supposed to be doing.

She was writing the book she needed to write. She was becoming the person she needed to become. And for the first time in a very long time, she wasn't afraid of what that meant.

She changed into her pyjamas - the soft cotton ones, not the ratty ones from home. Climbed into the fresh white sheets that the maid had put on that morning. (Oh God, the maid. The shampoo comment. She started laughing again, quietly, into the darkness.)

She picked up her notebook and read back through what she'd written today. It was good. Really good. Raw, honest, and real in a way her writing had never been before. Because she was finally being honest. With herself. With the page. With everything.

Sarah closed the notebook, turned off the light, and lay in the darkness. She thought about him. About the way he looked at her. About the dream she'd had. About the shower. About the conversation on the beach. About how he'd said she was becoming more alive.

And this time, when the heat started building again - that familiar wanting, that pull toward pleasure - she didn't stop. Didn't lecture herself about duty or propriety or wedding vows.

She just felt it.

And when sleep finally came, she dreamed of beaches and books and a man with laughing eyes who saw her. Who really saw her. And in the dream, she wasn't afraid anymore. She was just alive. Gloriously, messily, beautifully alive.

CHAPTER 7 - ALMOST

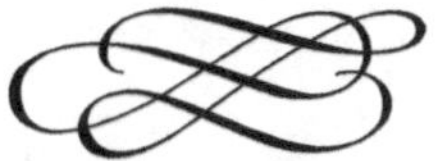

Sarah woke on the sixth morning and lay in bed, staring at the ceiling, counting.

Six days. She'd been here six days.

Seven days left. Just seven more mornings before she had to get on the train. Seven more days until she had to leave this room with its white walls and muslin curtains and the view of the sea. Seven more days in this village where the cobblestones were worn smooth by centuries, and the smell of bread drifted through the square every morning.

Seven more days with him.

The thought made her chest tighten until she could hardly breathe. When did he become so important to her? When did the fear of losing him start to outweigh her fear of going back to her marriage?

She tried to push the thought aside. She couldn't let herself think about it now. If she looked at it too closely, she might fall apart.

She dressed with care. The white cotton shirt she liked, jeans that fit well, a bit of mascara and lip balm. These small routines felt like protection, as if she was getting ready for a revelation, even though it was just another morning, another coffee, another walk.

Except nothing with him was ‘just’ anything anymore.

The walk to the café was tense. Each breath made her chest tingle, like the air before a storm. Maybe she was the storm, her nerves on edge, filling the quiet Normandy morning with her own restless longing.

When she turned the corner and saw him at their table, her heart fluttered and ached at the same time. He was reading his newspaper as usual, the morning light making his dark hair look blue-black. He wore his usual worn jumper and looked relaxed.

He looked up as she walked over, and his smile was warmer than usual, almost as if he knew a secret or saw something in her she hadn’t meant to show.

"Morning," he said, and there was something in his voice, too. Something lower, more intimate.

"Morning."

Sarah sat down, and the air between them felt heavy with something unspoken. The waitress came over right away, looking only at Sarah. Without thinking, Sarah ordered two black coffees, the routine now second nature.

When the waitress set both cups in front of her, Sarah slid one across. Their fingers brushed as he took it. The touch was brief, but it sent a rush of longing through her, making her breath catch and her nerves come alive with awareness of him.

She pulled her hand back quickly, wrapping it around her own cup, feeling the warmth through the ceramic.

They sat in silence, but it wasn't comfortable anymore. The quiet between them was tense and heavy, full of things they weren't saying and everything that mattered.

"I thought we could walk today," Jack said finally. "There's a path I want to show you."

"Alright."

The word came out quieter than she'd intended. Almost breathless.

* * *

THEY FINISHED their coffee and set off, walking through the village and out into the countryside. The path started at the edge of the village, winding between fields and hedgerows, climbing gradually up into the hills.

They didn't talk much. They walked side by side, close enough to almost touch, but not quite. The small space between them was both huge and tiny.

Sarah noticed everything. He moved easily, comfortable in his own skin. She heard their footsteps on the dirt path, birds singing in the hedgerows, and smelled wildflowers and grass.

The village faded behind them, the houses and church spire growing smaller.

The path grew steeper, and Sarah's breath quickened, not just from the climb, but from anticipation. She felt aware, expectant, as if they were heading toward a turning point, not just a hilltop.

As they climbed, the view opened up. The village lay below, patchwork fields stretched in every direction, and the sea sparkled in the morning sun. It all looked full of promise and possibility.

They finally reached a plateau where the path levelled out. A flat stretch of grass overlooked the valley, surrounded by wildflowers, yellow, white, and purple, all bending in the breeze. It was beautiful, the kind of place where important things seemed to happen.

Jack stopped walking and turned to face her.

"Can I ask you something?" His voice was quiet, almost hesitant.

"Of course."

"What do you want, Sarah?" He looked at her intently, his eyes searching hers. "Not what David wants. Not what your daughters need. Not what you think you should want or what would be appropriate or practical. What do 'you' want?"

The question hung in the air between them.

Sarah opened her mouth, ready to give a safe answer, but stopped herself. She was tired of lying, tired of playing it safe, tired of pretending.

"Right now?" she said. "In this exact moment?"

"Yes."

"I want to stay here. On this hill. With you." The words rushed out before she could stop them. "I want time to stop so I don’t have to go back. So I don’t have to figure out how to fit this version of myself, this Sarah who feels alive and real, back into that life. Back into being a wife who manages the house, a mother who solves everyone’s problems, and someone who never wants anything inconvenient."

She paused, feeling heat rise in her face. "That's selfish, isn't it?"

"It's honest."

"It's still selfish. I have responsibilities. A family. A marriage. People are depending on me."

"You're allowed to want things that don't fit neatly into those boxes, Sarah." His voice was gentle. "Wanting and doing are different things. You're allowed. Even if you can never have it."

They stood on the plateau, the valley below them, the wind blowing Sarah’s hair and making her eyes water. Or maybe it wasn’t just the wind.

"You've changed," Jack said softly. "Since that first day on the beach when you told me to mind my own business. When you sat there with your blank notebook, looking terrified, lost, and determined all at once. You're more... yourself now. More alive. Do you feel it?"

"Yes." Sarah could barely breathe, could barely force the word out. "I feel it."

"Good." He smiled, but sadly. "Don't lose that. Whatever happens when you go home - and you will go home, we both know that - don't lose this. Don't let them make you small again. Don't shrink back into who you were."

"I'm afraid I will." She whispered the words. "I'm afraid I'll go back. David will look at me the way he always does, like I'm fragile, to control, my dreams sweet but disposable, someone he says he loves but never really sees. Then I'll just shrink. I'll slip back into that role, because it's safer, easier, and fighting to be more takes a strength I don’t have."

"Then don't let him look at you that way." Jack's voice was fierce now. "Don't shrink. Don't slip back. Stand your ground. Be this Sarah, the one standing here right now. The one brave enough to admit what she wants, even when it's impossible. The one who came to France alone. The one who's writing a book. Be her. Hold onto her with everything you have."

"What if what I want is impossible?" Sarah's voice broke. "What if the life I've built and the person I'm becoming can't coexist? What if I have to choose?"

Jack hesitated, and something shifted in his expression. Vulnerable. Raw.

"What do you really want, Sarah?" His voice was barely above a whisper now. "Right now. Right here. What do you actually want?"

She looked up at him. At his kind eyes and patient face. The way he looked at her, like she was the most precious thing in the world, like he could see straight through all her defences to the truth underneath. The way his hands clenched at his sides, as if holding himself back from reaching for her.

She knew she should lie. Should say something safe and appropriate. Should protect them both from this moment, from this truth, from whatever came next.

But she was so tired of lying, of being safe, of protecting everyone else while slowly disappearing herself.

"Right now?" she said. Her voice was shaking. "I want you to kiss me."

The words hung in the air between them. Undeniable. Impossible to take back.

His face changed, showing pain, longing, close to grief. "Sarah..."

"I know." The words tumbled out. "I shouldn't want that. It's wrong. I'm married, and I love David. This is just me, confused and lonely. You're here. You see me. I haven't been seen in so long. I'm mistaking gratitude for something else and…"

"Stop." He reached up and cupped her face gently with both hands, cutting off her spiral. His palms were warm against her cheeks, his thumbs resting just below her cheekbones. "Stop. Don't do that. Don't diminish what this is. Don't minimise what you're feeling. It's not confusion, Sarah. It's not loneliness. It's not gratitude. It's real. I feel it too."

Her heart was hammering so hard she thought it might break through her ribs. She could feel his pulse in his palms against her face, could tell his heart was racing too.

"Then why don't you kiss me?" The words came out as barely more than a breath.

Jack's expression broke, and for a moment she saw everything, the wanting, the restraint, the pain of having to choose. His thumbs traced gentle circles on her cheeks, and his hands trembled.

"Because you'll regret it," he said finally. His voice was rough, strained. "Maybe not today. Maybe not tomorrow. But someday, when you're back home with your family, living your normal life, you'll remember this moment. And you'll feel guilty. You'll wonder if you ruined everything for one kiss on a hillside in France. You'll wonder if this is what broke your marriage. And that guilt will eat at you. It'll poison everything."

"And what about you?" Sarah's voice was shaking. "Will you regret not doing it? Will you wish you had?"

His expression cracked. Broke open.

"For the rest of time," he said, and his voice was raw. "I'll wish it for the rest of time. Every day. Every moment. I'll think about this - about you, about this hill, about the way you're looking at me right now - and wonder if I should have been brave enough. Selfish enough. Should have done what I wanted instead of what was right."

"Then do it." Sarah moved closer, eliminating the small space between them. Her hands came up to rest on his chest. She could feel his heart beating fast against her palms, could feel the warmth of his body through the worn fabric of his jumper. "Kiss me. Let me have this. Let us have this. Just this once."

"Sarah." It came out pleading. "Please."

For a moment, one long, aching moment, she thought he would. His hands held her face, his eyes searched hers, and she could see the struggle inside him. Want against wisdom. Desire against duty. What he felt against what he knew was right.

Then slowly, so slowly it was almost unbearable, he leaned down.

Sarah rose up on her toes to meet him, her hands sliding up to his shoulders, pulling herself closer.

Their faces drew closer. Closer. The space between them shrinking from inches to millimetres. Until they were so close she could feel the warmth of his breath on her lips. So close she could see the flecks of gold in his dark eyes. So close she could count his eyelashes. So close that when she breathed in, he breathed out, and their breath moved as one, mingled together, became inseparable.

Her eyes started to close.

"We need to stop," he whispered, his lips almost brushing hers as he spoke. She could feel the words more than hear them.

"Why?" It came out as barely a breath.

"Because this wouldn't be enough." His voice was rough with longing, with restraint that was costing him everything. "One kiss wouldn't be enough for me. And we can't have more. You know we can't. You're married. You're going home in seven days. This can't happen. Even though I want it more than I've wanted anything in... God. In so long."

They remained frozen like that. Caught in that impossible space. Close enough to kiss but not kissing. Breathing together. Hearts racing together. Neither one moving away. Neither one able to.

"I want to," Sarah whispered. "I want to so badly I can barely think. Barely breathe."

"I know." His hands trembled against her face. "God, I know. I can feel it. But I care about you too much to let you do something you'll hate yourself for later. Even if it means I spend the rest of my life wishing I'd been weaker. Wishing I'd been selfish enough to take what we both need."

A tear slipped down Sarah's cheek. She felt it track hot and wet over her skin. He caught it with his thumb and wiped it away gently.

"I don't want to be noble," she said, her voice breaking. "I don't want to do the right thing. I'm so tired of always doing the right thing, of always being good, of always putting everyone else first. I just..."

"I know." His voice was soft, infinitely gentle. "I want it too. More than you know. More than I should."

He pressed his forehead to hers, still not kissing her, still keeping that tiny distance, caught between what was and what could never be. She smelled the slight dampness of his skin and smelled his clean, simple soap.

"But you're going home soon," he continued quietly. "Back to your husband. Your daughters. Your real life. And when you do, you need to be able to look at yourself in the mirror. You need to be able to look at them. At David. At the girls. And you won't be able to do that if you cross this line. You won't be able to live with yourself."

"How can you be so sure?" Sarah's voice was barely audible.

"Because I know you." His hands cradled her face like she was precious. Something fragile. "Better than you think I do. You're not the kind of person who could do this and walk away unscathed. It would eat at you. Every time you looked at David, every time you tucked your daughters in, every time you sat at the dinner table - you'd think about this moment. About this choice. And it would poison everything. I won't do that to you. I won't be the reason you can't look your daughters in the eye."

She knew he was right. Hated it. Resented it. Wanted to argue against it with every fibre of her being.

But she knew he was right.

Very slowly, reluctantly, she lowered herself back down from her toes. Let her weight settle back on her heels. The distance between them grew from nothing to something, even though it was only an inch or two. It felt like miles.

Very slowly, reluctant, he lifted his forehead from hers. His hands stayed on her face a moment longer, his thumbs stroking her cheeks, his eyes meeting hers, everything unspoken passing between them in silence. Then he let go and stepped back.

The space between them was huge.

Sarah wrapped her arms around herself, suddenly cold despite the warm morning sun. The breeze that had felt gentle before was now cutting.

"I'm sorry," she said. The words were inadequate, but they were all she had.

"Don't be." His voice was firm. "Don't ever apologise for feeling what you feel. For wanting what you want. There's no shame in it. No guilt in desire itself. Only in actions. And we didn't... we didn't do anything."

But in a way, they had. They'd done everything except kiss, everything except cross that last physical line. But they'd crossed many other lines, emotional ones that couldn't be undone.

They started walking back down the path in silence. Not the comfortable silence of before. A heavier silence. Weighted with everything unsaid, with everything they'd nearly done, with everything they wanted but couldn't have.

Sarah's lips tingled from the breath they'd shared. From the almost-kiss that was somehow more intimate than many actual kisses she'd had. Her face burned where his hands had been, like he'd left marks on her skin. Her heart still raced, her body still hummed with need and a desperate aching that had nowhere to go.

Almost didn't count, she thought. Almost just meant not quite, not enough, wanting what you couldn't have.

And yet it was if they had. Like they'd crossed some threshold even without the kiss. Like there was a before and an after, and they were in the after now.

When they reached the village square - the familiar cobble-stones, the café where they'd shared so many coffees, the church spire pointing at the sky - it should have felt comforting, like coming home. Instead, it felt like something was ending.

Jack stopped walking. Stood there for a moment with his hands in his pockets, shoulders tense, not looking at her.

"I need some time," he said quietly.

Sarah felt her stomach drop. "What?"

"A day. Just one day." He still wasn't looking at her. "To clear my head. To think. What almost happened up there... I need to process it. We both do."

Panic rose in her throat. "You're not leaving, are you? You're not..."

"No. I'm not leaving. I'm not disappearing." He looked at her then, and his eyes were full of something she couldn't name. "I just need... I need to not see you tomorrow. Just tomorrow. Can you understand that?"

She understood. Of course, she understood. Being near each other right now was standing too close to a fire. Dangerous. Overwhelming. Impossible to sustain. The air between them was too charged. The want was too strong. If they saw each other tomorrow morning, sat at that café table, looked at each other across those two cups of black coffee...

They would break.

"How long?" Her voice was barely a whisper.

"Just tomorrow. Give us both a day to process what almost happened. What we both want but can't have." His expression softened slightly. "I'll be here the day after. Same time, same place. I promise."

"But not tomorrow."

"Not tomorrow."

Sarah nodded, not trusting her voice. One day. Just one day without him. She could manage that. She'd managed forty-three years without him.

Except she wasn't sure she could.

Because in six days, he'd become essential. Necessary. The framework around which her days were built. Morning coffee. Walks. Conversations that made her see herself differently, made her see the world differently. The way he looked at her. The way he saw her.

How had she let herself become so dependent on someone she'd known for less than a week? Someone who would inevitably disappear from her life in seven days when she got on that train back to Bristol?

"Sarah." Jack's voice was soft. "This isn't goodbye. It's just... space. Distance. We both need it."

"I know."

"Do you?"

"Yes." She took a breath, trying to steady herself, trying to be the brave person he kept saying she was. "You're right. We need space. Time to think. I'll see you the day after tomorrow."

"The day after tomorrow," he confirmed.

He reached out as if to touch her face again, his hand lifting toward her cheek, but then he stopped himself. His hand dropped back to his side, the restraint in that aborted gesture somehow more intimate than the touch would have been. Knowing he wanted to touch her but wouldn't let himself made Sarah's chest ache.

"Write," he said. "Write about what you're feeling. Don't hold back. Don't censor yourself. Just put it all on the page. Everything. Even the things you think you shouldn't think or feel or want."

"I will."

"Promise me."

"I promise."

They stood there a moment longer, neither wanting to leave first, though both knew they had to. The square bustled around them—people heading to the bakery, the market, living their usual Saturday lives, unaware that Sarah's world was shifting.

Finally, Jack took a step back. Then another.

"The day after tomorrow," he said again.

"The day after tomorrow."

Then he turned and walked away across the square. Hands in his pockets. That familiar, worn blue jumper. His dark hair caught the sunlight. Not looking back.

Sarah stood there watching him go. Memorising the way he moved. The set of his shoulders. The way he walked was as if he belonged in the world, comfortable and easy. She watched until he disappeared around a corner. Then she stood there a moment longer, trying to process what had just happened. What had almost happened. What could never happen.

Tomorrow, she wouldn't see him. Wouldn't have their morning coffee. Wouldn't hear his voice or see his smile or feel that pull between them that had become as natural as breathing.

Tomorrow, she'd be alone.

The thought terrified her. Which terrified her even more.

When did she become so dependent on him? When did his presence start to give her days meaning? She came here to find herself, to be independent, to learn to exist without always serving others. Instead, she'd just shifted her dependence from her family to a man she hardly knew.

Or had she?

She didn't know. She couldn't think clearly. Her mind was still caught on the almost-kiss, the tiny space between them, the warmth of his breath, and his trembling hands on her face.

* * *

SARAH TURNED and walked slowly back to her hotel. Her mind spun. Her heart ached. Her lips still tingled from a kiss that never happened.

She climbed the stairs to her room, each step feeling heavier than the last. Unlocked the door. Dropped her bag on the chair.

The room looked the same as always. White walls. Blue quilt on the bed. Muslin curtains moving in the breeze from the window. Her notebook on the desk, closed, holding all the words she'd written so far.

But everything was different. She was different.

She sat on the edge of the bed and put her head in her hands.

Tomorrow. She had to get through tomorrow without him. One whole day. It seemed impossible. Unendurable.

One day. Just one day. She could do this. She had to do this.

She took a deep breath. Lifted her head. Looked out the window at the slice of sea visible in the distance, glittering in the afternoon light.

Then she stood up, walked to the desk, opened her notebook, and picked up her pen.

He had told her to write. To not hold back. To put it all on the page.

So she would.

She would write about wanting and holding back. About the tiny space between almost and never. About hands that trembled on her face. About sharing breath in that small space where anything seemed possible, but nothing was allowed. About loving someone she couldn't have.

Not the comfortable, steady love she had with David. This was different. It burned. Broke her open. Made her feel everything at once.

She was falling in love with him. Had already fallen.

The thought should have terrified her. It should have filled her with guilt and shame.

Instead, it just felt true. Unavoidable. Like gravity.

And tomorrow, she wouldn't see him.

She began to write. The words came quickly, raw and honest, pouring onto the page like a confession, a prayer, or a way to let it all out.

She wrote about his hands on her face. About the almost-kiss. About breathing together. About wanting things so badly you could taste it, but knowing you couldn't have them. About restraint being its own kind of agony. About how not doing something was more intimate than doing.

She wrote for hours. The light shifted from morning to afternoon to evening. Her hand cramped. Her wrist ached. Her eyes burned. But she kept going.

When she finally stopped, darkness had fallen outside. The village lights were coming on, one by one. She'd written thirteen pages. Thirteen pages about almost kissing a man who wasn't her husband. About falling in love when she had no right to. About wanting what she couldn't have.

Sarah closed the notebook and sat back in her chair.

Her page count: one hundred and eleven pages total. She'd crossed the hundred-page threshold without even noticing.

Tomorrow. She had to get through tomorrow. One day without him.

It felt impossible.

But she would manage it. She would write. She would think. She would figure out what she was doing, what she wanted, whether any of it mattered.

And the day after tomorrow, she would see him again.

The thought was both comfort and terror.

CHAPTER 8 - ALONE

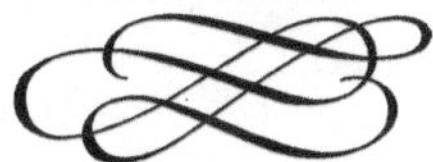

Sarah woke and for a moment forgot.

Forgot that she wouldn't see him today. Forgot the almost-kiss on the hillside, his hands trembling against her face, the inches between their lips. Forgot the way he'd said, "I need a day."

For one blissful, unconscious moment, she lay in bed thinking about walking to the café, about ordering two black coffees, about the way he smiled when he saw her approach.

Then she remembered.

And then the weight of it settled over her like a heavy blanket pressing down on her chest, making each breath a challenge.

No morning coffee. No walks through the village. She missed those conversations that made her see herself differently. He wasn't there, looking at her with those eyes that saw everything. There was no warmth beside her, only silence. Almost-touches faded into memory.

All that remained was her… alone. For the entire day.

She lay in bed longer than usual, staring at the ceiling. Outside, the village began waking up without her participation. Church bells marking the hour. Voices calling out greetings in French. Shutters being opened. The rumble of a delivery van. The familiar sounds of life continuing, unchanged, oblivious to the fact that her world had tilted.

Life continued for everyone else. While everything was different for her.

Finally, she forced herself to get up. Showered. The water was wrong against her skin - too hot or too cold, she couldn't get it right. Dressed in jeans and a t-shirt, not caring how she looked because no one would see her today. No one who mattered.

She looked at herself in the mirror over the desk. She looked the same. Hair damp. Face bare. Eyes tired from restless sleep. Outwardly unchanged.

But she was different underneath. Like a layer had been peeled away, exposing raw nerve. Like she'd been stripped down to the essential, vulnerable and new. The old Sarah - the one who'd arrived a week ago - would have barely recognised this person looking back from the mirror.

She couldn't go to the café. Couldn't bear to sit at their table without him. Couldn't order two coffees when there'd only be one person drinking them. Couldn't face the waitress's knowing look. Couldn't endure the empty chair across from her.

Instead, she walked to the boulangerie and bought a croissant and coffee to go. The girl behind the counter smiled and said

"Bonjour, madame", and Sarah managed to reply in French, but the interaction was hollow. Mechanical. Going through the motions of being a person in the world.

She carried her breakfast back to the hotel, climbed the stairs to her room, and sat at the desk by the window. The view looked the same - the village rooftops, the slice of sea in the distance, the morning light turning everything soft and golden.

But without Jack, it felt empty. Meaningless. Just scenery. Just a postcard view of a place where nothing important was happening.

The reality of his absence pressed down on her. Every routine, every habit rang hollow. The morning coffee ritual that had become sacred. The walk through the village. The conversation. The way he looked at her. All of it gone, leaving a Jack-shaped hole nothing else could fill.

How had she let this happen?

How had one man become so essential in six days? How had she become so dependent on his presence that a single day without him felt unendurable? What was wrong with her?

She opened her notebook, picked up her pen, and tried to write. But the words wouldn't come. Her mind was too crowded, too chaotic, thoughts spinning and colliding like bumper cars.

She loved David. She did. Twenty years of marriage. Two children. A home they'd bought together, painted together, filled with memories. Countless dinners. Holidays. Fights and reconciliations. The mundane intimacy of shared life. He was a good man. A good husband. A good father. Patient with the girls. Responsible. Steady. Reliable.

But.

But she was also in love with Jack.

And those were two very different things. Loving David meant reassurance and history; being in love with Jack meant immediacy and ache. Past tense versus present tense. Comfortable history versus urgent present. Settled affection versus desperate wanting.

The realisation crashed over her like a wave, knocking the breath from her lungs, leaving her gasping.

She was 'in love' with him.

Not just attracted to him. Not just grateful for his attention. Not confused or lonely or going through some midlife crisis. Actually, genuinely, terrifyingly in love. With a man she'd known for six days. With a man who wasn't her husband. With someone who would disappear from her life in six more days when she got on that train back to Bristol.

Sarah set down her pen and put her head in her hands.

This was wrong. This was so wrong. Guilt rose up, choking her, making her throat tight and her eyes burn.

She'd made vows. "For better or worse, in sickness and in health, till death do us part." She'd stood before their families and friends, before David's parents and her mother, before God if you believed in that sort of thing, promising to be faithful. Promising to love, honour, and cherish. Till death.

And here she was, in love with another man. Breaking her vows. Breaking her promises. In thought if not in deed. Becoming the kind of person she'd never imagined being.

The kind of person who had affairs. Who fell in love with strangers. Who betrayed their marriage.

Except she hadn't done anything, not really. No kiss. No crossing that line. They'd kept their restraint, even when every fibre of her being screamed to close the final gap, to feel his mouth on hers, to step from wanting to having.

But somehow not kissing was even more intimate. More significant. Like they'd chosen depth over physical satisfaction. Like the restraint meant more than the giving in would have.

And she was in love with him. That was the truth. Simple, terrible, and impossible to take back.

She needed to call home. Needed to hear David's voice. Needed to ground herself in reality, remember who she was and what she had. Remember her real life, not this bubble she'd been living in for a week.

She looked at her phone. Nine o'clock here. Eight in Bristol. Saturday morning. David would be up, probably making coffee, reading the news on his iPad. The girls would likely still be asleep - teenagers slept late on weekends, especially Betty after a match.

Sarah picked up her phone before she could talk herself out of it. Dialled David's number. Held her breath while it rang.

He answered on the third ring. "Sarah! Hello. How's France?"

His voice was so familiar. So known. So... distant. Like hearing someone speak from the far end of a tunnel.

"It's good. Fine." Her voice came out steady, which surprised her. "How are things there?"

"Oh, you know. Managing. Olivia's been a bit moody - boy trouble at school, I think, but she won't talk to me about it. You know how she is. Shuts down when things bother her." He sounded mildly exasperated. "Betty's fine. Excited about her match this afternoon. Big one against Clifton. She's been practising her corners all week."

A pang hit Sarah. Betty's match. She should be there. Should be standing on the sidelines with the other mothers, cheering, offering orange slices at halftime.

"Tell her I'm thinking of her," Sarah said. "That I hope she does well. That I'm proud of her."

"I will. She'll appreciate that." A pause. "She misses you, I think. Though she won't say it. You know Betty. All independence and bravado on the outside."

"I miss her too. Both of them."

And she did. Really did. But the missing was distant, almost muted compared to the sharp ache she felt for him. She knew she should feel more, like the volume on her maternal love had been turned down, and she couldn't quite reach the dial to turn it back up.

There was a pause on the line. Not quite comfortable. Not quite awkward. Just... there.

"How's the writing going?" David asked, finally.

"Really well, actually. Over a hundred pages now. One hundred and eleven, exactly."

"A hundred! Good lord." He sounded genuinely surprised. Impressed, even. "That's... that's a lot, Sarah. Well done."

But underneath the words, she could hear the doubt. The surprise that she'd actually done it. The assumption that this was a holiday project, a passing fancy, something she'd gotten out of her system and would now return to normal life, having ticked the box marked "write a book."

"David," she said, interrupting whatever he was about to say next. "When I come home, things are going to be different."

"Different how?" His tone shifted. Cautious now.

"I'm going to keep writing. Every morning. This isn't a holiday project or a phase I'm going through. It's..." She struggled to find the words. "It's what I do now. What I am. I'm a writer."

Another pause. Longer this time.

"Alright," he said finally. "If that's what you want."

If that's what you want. Like it was a choice. A preference. Like she was asking to join a book club or take up yoga.

"It is what I want," Sarah said, her voice sharper than she'd intended. "And I need you to support that. Really support it. Not just say 'that's nice, dear' and then expect me to go back to handling everything - all the logistics, all the emotional labour, all the invisible work - while you carry on as normal."

"I do support you, Sarah." He sounded defensive now. "I just... I suppose I don't entirely understand what's changed. You've always been so happy with our life. With being at home with the girls. And now suddenly..."

He paused. She could almost hear him choosing his words carefully.

"You know, I ran into Martin Fletcher the other day," David continued. "At the tennis club. He mentioned that the bank is looking for experienced people again. I know it's been years, but with your background in project management... I mean, if this writing thing doesn't work out, it could be a good option. Something stable. Good money. The bank would be lucky to have you back."

A chill ran through Sarah.

The writing thing.

Like it was a hobby. A whim. Work that might not "pan out" and would need a backup plan.

"I'm not going back to the bank, David."

"But why not? It was good money, and you were excellent at—"

"Because I don't want to be a banker." Her voice was flat. Final. "I want to be a writer."

"Right. Yes. Of course." A beat of silence. "I just meant as a fallback. You know. Something practical."

She could hear the doubt in his voice. The assumption that this was a phase. That she'd come to her senses. That she'd return to Bristol and slip back into her old role like putting on a familiar coat.

"I wasn't happy, David." The words came out quietly but clearly. "I was invisible. There's a difference between those things."

Silence on the other end. Then: "That's not fair. I didn't make you invisible."

"Not deliberately," Sarah said. "But you stopped seeing me. You stopped asking what I wanted or what I thought about anything beyond logistics and schedules. I became the person who makes sure everything runs smoothly, who handles all the details, who manages everyone's lives. And you forgot I was anything else. You forgot I was a person separate from my utility to the family."

"Sarah, I don't know what you want me to say."

"I don't want you to say anything." She looked out the window at the village, at people going about their Saturday, at life continuing for everyone else. "I just want you to know that when I come home, I'll be different. I've changed. And I need you to be okay with that."

Another pause. Longer. Heavier.

"Are you..." He hesitated. "Are you alright, Sarah? You sound different. Has something happened?"

She thought about Jack. About his hands cupping her face. About the almost-kiss, the inches between them, the way they'd breathed together in that impossible space. About the way he looked at her like she was the most precious thing in the world. About that terrible, wonderful feeling of being truly seen.

"I'm fine," she lied. The words tasted bitter in her mouth. "I'm just... figuring things out. That's all."

"Well. Good." He sounded relieved. "I suppose that's the point of this trip, isn't it? To figure things out. To get some perspective."

"Yes. That's the point."

"When you're back, we'll talk properly. About the writing. About... everything. We'll work it out."

We'll work it out. Like she was a problem to be solved. An issue to be managed.

"Okay," Sarah said, because what else was there to say?

"Love you," David said. His standard sign-off. Automatic. Reflexive.

"Love you too," she replied. Also automatic. Also reflexive.

But as she said it, she realised she didn't know if it was true anymore. Or what the words even meant.

When she hung up, Sarah was deflated. Hollow. Like someone had let all the air out of her.

No relief. No comfort. No sense of connection.

She'd called her husband, and it had been like talking to a stranger. Or worse - like talking to a coworker about logistics. The plumber. The girls' schedules. Betty's match. Olivia's mood. The bank job. All surface. No substance. No real seeing. No actual connection.

And then someone like Jack came along and saw you. Really saw you. Looked at you like you were a person, not a function.

Like you mattered, not just what you did for others, but who you actually were underneath all the roles.

Sarah stood at the window, looking out at the village. People going about their Saturday. A man carrying baguettes. A woman with a shopping basket. Children on bicycles. Normal life. Real life.

Her life in Bristol would be like that. Had been like that for twenty years. Would be like that when she returned. David going to work. The girls at school. Meals to cook. Laundry to do. Calendar to manage. Everything running smoothly because she made it run smoothly.

But what about her? Who was she in that life? What space did she occupy beyond all of that?

Sarah sat back down at the desk and picked up her pen.

She wrote without thinking:

> *"I love my husband. I do. But I'm also in love with someone else. And I don't know what to do with that."*

She stared at the words. The truth. Simple, terrible, impossible to take back now that it was written on the page in black ink.

She kept writing. The words poured out like a confession, like she'd been holding back for too long and couldn't contain them anymore.

She wrote about David and Jack. About comfortable love and urgent love. About the difference between being loved and being seen. About guilt and desire and the impossible space between duty and want.

She wrote about wedding vows and whether promises made at twenty-three still held when you were forty-three and had become a completely different person. About whether you could be faithful to someone who no longer saw you. About what counted as betrayal - physical acts, or the heart silently leaving long before the body did.

She wrote about his hands on her face. About almost-kissing. About restraint being its own kind of intimacy. About falling in love when you had no right to. About wanting someone so badly your bones ached with it.

She wrote about going home. About trying to fit this new Sarah back into her old life. About whether her marriage could survive her becoming visible. About whether she even wanted it to.

She wrote for hours. Hand cramping. Wrist aching. Eyes burning. But unable to stop because if she stopped, she'd have to think, and thinking hurt too much.

The light through the window shifted. Morning to afternoon. Golden to white. The church bells marked the hours. Ten. Eleven. Noon. The village moved through its Saturday rituals while Sarah sat at her desk, bleeding onto the page.

When she finally stopped, her hand trembling with fatigue, her eyes barely able to focus, she looked at the page count.

One hundred and twenty-four pages. She'd written thirteen pages. Thirteen pages about love and marriage and impossible choices. About being two different people - the wife she was and the woman she was becoming. About the unbridgeable distance between those two selves. Some things that she was writing had already been written, just from a different angle, but she instinctively knew that all of the words counted. She would write the actual book later. This draft was her way of releasing and recording the story as it unfolded. This was forming part of what would become her history.

Sarah closed the notebook and sat back in her chair. Her whole body ached, not just her hand. Like she'd run a marathon. Like she'd been physically fighting for air.

She looked at the clock. Two in the afternoon. So many hours still left in this day. So many more hours to get through before tomorrow, when she'd see him again.

* * *

THE AFTERNOON DRAGGED.

Sarah tried to read the book she'd brought from home, but couldn't concentrate on the words. They slid off the page, meaningless, jumbled.

She tried to walk through the village, but everything reminded her of him. The café where they'd had coffee every morning. The streets they'd walked down together. The garden where he'd asked about her five strengths. The path leading to the hills where they'd almost kissed.

She couldn't escape him. He was everywhere and nowhere. Present in every corner of this village, but physically absent. A ghost haunting her day.

She returned to the hotel and tried to write more, but the words wouldn't come. She'd emptied herself out in the morning session. Had nothing left.

She lay on the bed, staring at the ceiling, watching the afternoon light shift across the white paint. Thinking about David, whom she loved but wasn't in love with. About the girls, whom she missed and didn't miss in equal measure. About Jack, whom she'd known for six days and couldn't imagine not knowing. She asked herself why these questions kept appearing in her head. The same questions time and time again.

She contemplated the new Sarah - the one who wrote books and claimed space and let herself want things - being more alive than the old Sarah had ever been. More real. More honest. More herself.

But also more complicated. More conflicted. More difficult.

The old Sarah had been simpler. Invisible but simple. Managed but manageable. The path forward had been clear: be a good wife, be a good mother, keep everything running, don't want too much, don't need too much, don't be too much.

This new Sarah was a mess. All sharp edges and raw feelings and impossible wants. A woman who fell in love with strangers. A woman who questioned her marriage. A woman who was alive but had no idea what to do with that aliveness.

But at least she was awake.

At least she could feel.

At least she knew she existed, even if that existence was painful and complicated and scary.

Sarah climbed into bed at nine o'clock, not because she was tired but because she wanted the day to be over. Wanted to sleep through the remaining hours. Wanted to wake up and have tomorrow already be here.

Tomorrow. When she'd see him again.

The thought made her chest feel tight, her stomach flip, and her whole body ache with anticipation.

She lay in the darkness, listening to the sounds of the village as it settled into the night.

She thought about David, whom she loved but wasn't in love with. About their comfortable life. About whether comfort was enough. About whether she could go back to being invisible now that she'd experienced being seen.

She thought about the girls. About Olivia and her moods about a boy. About Betty and her football match. About whether they needed her as much as she'd always assumed they did. About whether her absence had actually been as catastrophic as she'd feared or whether they were managing just fine without her.

She thought about Jack. About his dark hair and kind eyes. About his worn blue jumper and paint-stained cuffs. About the way he looked at her like she was the only person in the world who mattered. About his hands trembling against her face. About the closeness of their lips. About breathing together in that impossible space where everything was possible, and nothing was allowed.

About loving someone she had no right to love. About wanting someone she couldn't have. About the fact that she'd already fallen and there was no climbing back up.

This new Sarah - the one who wrote and wanted and loved the wrong person - was awake. Was alive. Was real in a way the old Sarah had never been.

But God, it hurt. Being awake hurt. Feeling things hurt. Wanting hurt.

Invisibility had been easier. Safer. Less painful.

But she couldn't go back. Wouldn't go back. Even if she wanted to - and she didn't, not really - she couldn't unknow what she now knew. Couldn't unfeel what she'd felt. Couldn't unsee herself now that he'd had shown her who she really was underneath all the roles and responsibilities.

Sarah closed her eyes, hoping her mind would stop going around in circles.

Eventually, after what felt like hours of restless half-sleep, she drifted off.

And when she dreamed, she dreamed of him. Of almost-kisses and hands that trembled when they touched her face. Of breathing together in that impossible space where everything was possible and nothing was allowed. Of loving someone she had no right to love. Of being seen. Of being known. Of being alive.

Of wanting more than she was allowed to have.

CHAPTER 9 - THE REUNION

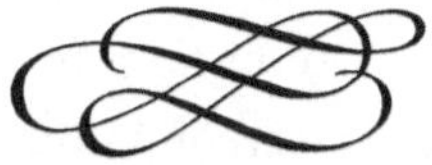

Sarah woke on the eighth morning with her heart already racing.

Today. She'd see him today.

The relief was so strong it was almost physical. It was like finally letting out a breath she'd been holding for a whole day. Yesterday had dragged on, the longest day of her life. But now it was over. She'd made it.

Today, she'd see him.

She got out of bed quickly. She didn't want to waste time lying there thinking. She didn't want to second-guess, analyse, or worry. She wanted to reach him as quickly as possible.

She dressed carefully. No more of yesterday's old t-shirt. Today she chose the blue jumper she'd bought in Bristol before the trip. It made her eyes stand out. She put on a little mascara, just enough, and a bit of lip balm.

She told herself she wasn't dressing for him. She always puts in this much effort. This was normal.

She was lying.

She knew she was lying to herself.

She was dressing for him. For the moment when he'd first see her. For the way his face would light up. For the way he'd look at her like she was the only person in the world who mattered.

She grabbed her bag and notebook, reminders that she was still a writer and still holding onto her new identity, and hurried down the hotel stairs. Her heart pounded in her chest. Her stomach fluttered with anticipation. She was a teenager again, nervous, excited, and scared all at once.

In her mind, she'd already replayed the scene a dozen times. How it would go. She'd walk to the café. He'd already be there, sitting at their table, newspaper open, that worn blue jumper, paint-stained cuffs. He'd look up as she approached. That smile. That unmistakable smile that made everything else fade into background noise. And they'd sit down, order two black coffees, and everything would be right again.

She stepped out onto the street, into the morning sunlight.

And stopped.

He wasn't at the café. He was standing across the street from her hotel, leaning against a granite wall. Hands in his pockets. Wearing that frayed blue jumper. Just standing there. Waiting for her.

When he saw her, his whole face changed. Emotions moved across his features: relief came first, quick and real, as if he'd been holding his breath too. Then came joy, open and honest. Then pain, as if seeing her hurt in a good way, like a wound that was starting to heal.

Sarah stopped on the hotel steps, her breath catching in her throat.

He'd waited for her here. Outside her hotel. Not at the café where they always met, where there would be other people and coffee and the comfortable ritual they'd established. Here. Where he could see her the moment she emerged. Where they'd be alone.

He pushed away from the wall and walked across the street to her. Sarah's heart pounded so hard she thought everyone in the village could hear it. It echoed off the cobblestones, telling the world: this woman's heart is opening. Look. See. Notice this.

"Hi," he said when he reached her. His voice was lower than usual. Rough around the edges.

"Hi." Her voice came out breathless. She couldn't help it. Couldn't make herself sound normal when everything in her body was screaming with relief at seeing him again. "You're not at the café."

"No."

"Why not?"

Vulnerability flickered across his face. Want. Raw need. All the things he usually kept so carefully controlled.

"I couldn't wait any longer," he said simply. "I tried. I went to the café, sat down, and picked up the paper like always. But I couldn't just sit there, watching other people, waiting for you to appear. Watching the street. Watching the clock. Wondering if you'd be early or late or exactly on time. It was..." He ran a hand through his hair, looking almost embarrassed. "It was driving me mad. So I came here."

Sarah's chest was tight. "How long have you been waiting?"

"Since seven-thirty."

She looked at her watch. Eight-fifteen. He'd been standing outside her hotel for forty-five minutes. Just waiting. Just hoping she'd appear.

"Jack..."

"I know." He let out a breath that might have been a laugh. "I know. I'm being ridiculous. We only took one day apart. Twenty-four hours. It shouldn't matter this much. It's absurd. But yesterday was..." He shook his head. "God, Sarah. Yesterday was the longest day ever. Every hour felt like ten. I just... I needed to see you. Needed to know you were okay. Needed to see your face."

She understood. She'd felt the same desperate, aching need, like air wasn't reaching her lungs without him.

"I missed you," she said quietly. The understatement of the century.

"I missed you, too." He looked at her with such intensity that it made her breath catch all over again. Made her forget they were standing on a public street in broad daylight. Made everything else disappear except his eyes and his voice and the space between them. "Every minute. Every hour. I kept thinking about the hill. About what almost happened. About how badly I wanted to kiss you and how right I was not to. But knowing it was right didn't make missing you any easier."

They stood on the street while people moved around them: locals going to the market with shopping bags, tourists with cameras, the baker opening his shutters. The village was waking up. Life kept going for everyone else.

But Sarah was sure they existed in a bubble. A space carved out just for them. Apart from everything else.

"Coffee?" He asked finally.

"Yes. Please."

They walked to the café. Close but not touching. His warmth at her side. The air between them was electric with everything that had built up during the day apart. A single day had made everything sharper. More intense. More urgent.

At the café, they sat at their usual table, the one that had become theirs without needing to say it. The waitress came over right away, bringing two black coffees and setting both in front of Sarah without even looking at him. The routine was so familiar now that Sarah barely noticed it.

She slid one cup across. Their fingers didn't touch, but the almost-touch was electric.

"Thank you," he said, wrapping his hands around the cup.

They sat in silence for a moment. Both of them searching for words. For how to begin. For what to say after a day of absence that had lasted a year in their minds.

"I called David yesterday," Sarah said finally. Getting it out there. Naming the elephant in the room.

His expression shifted. Caution, sliding into place. "How did that go?"

"Fine. Odd." She took a sip of coffee, grateful for something to do with her hands. "He mentioned the girls. Olivia's in a mood about some boy. Betty had a match. The usual topics. And I realised..." She paused, uncertain how to continue. How to explain what she'd experienced, or rather, what she hadn't.

"What?" His voice was gentle. Patient. Not pushing, just inviting.

"I realised I had nothing to say to him. Nothing that mattered." The words came out in a rush. "It was all logistics. Like talking to a coworker about schedules and tasks. Not like talking to someone I've been married to for twenty years. Not like someone who's supposed to be my partner. Someone who's supposed to know me."

"That must have been hard."

"It clarified everything." Sarah set down her cup. "I told him things would be different. That I'd changed. He said, 'If that's what you want,' as if it were a preference. A choice. Not a truth that's already taken hold, whether I want it or not."

"Do you think he'll be able to adapt?" he asked. "To see you differently?"

"I don't know." Sarah looked at him across the table. At his kind eyes, his patient face. "Maybe, if he tries. If he wants to. But I'm not sure he does. I'm not sure he even understands what I'm saying. He suggested I go back to the bank. Called the writing... what were his words? 'The writing thing.' Like it's a hobby. A phase I'll get over."

His jaw tightened. "He said that?"

"He did. And I realised..." Sarah took a breath. "Even if I go home and try to make it work, even if I do everything right, it might not be enough. He doesn't see me. He sees a function, a role: the person who manages the house, raises the children, and keeps everything running. But he doesn't see 'me'."

"And what has changed?" he asked. "What's different now?"

"Everything." The word came out fierce. "I've changed. I won't be invisible anymore. I won't make myself small. I won't apologise for taking up space, for having wants, or for being more than my utility to others. Even if it means..." She hesitated, words catching in her throat.

"Even if it means what?"

"Even if it means my marriage doesn't survive."

The words hung between them. Heavy. Final. Undeniable.

This was the first time she'd said it out loud. The first time she'd admitted that going home might mean ending things. That the life she'd built over twenty years might not be salvageable. Might not be worth salvaging.

As the realisation settled in her chest, everything tightened. Because it was one thing to think it, to write it in her notebook. Another thing entirely to say it out loud to another person. To Jack.

"Is that what you want?" he asked.

"I don't know." Sarah's voice was barely above a whisper. "I love David. He's a good man. A good father. We've built a life together. We have history, memories, and two beautiful daughters. But I'm not sure that's enough anymore. I don't know if comfortable love is enough after being truly seen. I don't know if that's selfish or honest or just..." She struggled for the word. "Awake. I'm awake now. I can't go back to sleep."

She met his eyes.

"You woke me up, Jack. And now I can't go back even if I wanted to.

I'm sorry."

"Don't be." The words came quickly. "I'm not sorry."

Before she could lose her nerve, before she could think about it too much or talk herself out of it, Sarah reached across the table and took his hand.

His fingers closed around hers immediately. Warm. Real. Solid. Proof that this wasn't a dream. Proof that he was here, that she was here, and that this was happening.

"I'm not sorry I met you," she said, the words tumbling out. "I'm not sorry for any of this. Even if it's complicated. Even if it hurts. Even if I don't know what happens next. I'm not sorry."

"Sarah..."

"I know what you're going to say." She squeezed his hand. "I leave in five days. This has an end. We can't have what we want. I know all of that. But right now, here in Normandy, I'm holding your hand. And I'm not sorry."

He looked down at their hands joined on the table. Their fingers fit together as if they were made for each other. She saw a change in his face: hesitation had turned into resolve.

"I'm not sorry either," he said finally.

They sat like that for a long moment, hands linked across the table, coffee growing cold. The world went on around them: people ordered breakfast, talked, laughed, and lived their usual Sunday mornings. But for Sarah, everything froze in this moment. This perfect, impossible moment.

Finally, the waitress came by, giving them a pointed look that suggested they either order more or free up the table for actual paying customers.

"Walk?" He suggested.

"Yes."

They left money on the table, enough for the coffee and a generous tip, and stood up. This time, when they reached the street, they didn't let go of each other's hands. They kept walking, fingers intertwined, as if it were the most natural thing in the world. As if they had every right to touch each other this way.

People passed them. Locals heading to the market with shopping baskets. Tourists with cameras slung around their necks, consulting maps. An elderly woman with a miniature dog. A family with children. No one seemed to notice or care that they were holding hands. No one gave them a second glance.

But Sarah noticed his hand in hers, the warmth of his palm, the roughness of his fingers, the way they fit together perfectly.

She was holding hands with a man who wasn't her husband. In public. In broad daylight. For anyone to see.

She waited for the guilt to arrive. For the shame. For the voice in her head telling her this was wrong, this was betrayal, this was exactly the kind of thing she'd never thought she'd do.

It didn't come.

Instead, something lighter settled over her. A startling sense of relief mixed with anticipation. Like she'd been carrying a weight and had finally set it down. Like she'd been holding her breath and could finally exhale.

"Where are we going?" she asked after a while.

"I don't know." He glanced at her, smiling. "Does it matter?"

"No."

And it didn't. It really didn't. They could walk anywhere, through the village, to the hills, to the beach, even in circles, and it wouldn't matter. As long as they were together.

They wandered through lanes Sarah knew and others she'd never explored. Down narrow passages where the houses leaned toward each other. Through the square where the Sunday market was being set up, vendors were arranging vegetables, flowers, and wheels of cheese. Past the church with its ancient stones and beautiful stained glass windows.

Moving together. Hands entwined. Fully present in each moment.

Eventually, they found themselves in a small public garden. The same bench where he'd had asked her about her five strengths and weaknesses. Where he'd systematically dismantled her negative self-perception and given her the gift of the word "brave."

They sat down, still holding hands.

"I wrote yesterday," Sarah said. Might as well tell him. Might as well be honest. "Thirteen pages. All about you."

"About me?" He sounded surprised.

"About being in love with you." She said it simply. Matter-of-factly. Like announcing the weather or stating an obvious fact. "About not being able to control it. About loving David but being in love with you. About how those are two different things. Past tense and present tense. History and urgency."

He went very still beside her. "Sarah..."

"I know." She turned to look at him. "I know I shouldn't say it out loud. I know it makes everything more complicated. But I spent yesterday alone with my thoughts, writing, thinking, and trying to understand what I'm feeling. And I realised I'm tired of not saying true things. I'm tired of pretending I don't feel what I feel. I'm tired of lying to David, to myself, to you."

She took a breath.

"I'm in love with you, Jack. I have been since... I don't even know when. Maybe since that first day on the beach when you offered me a penny for my thoughts. Maybe since you asked about my five strengths, I couldn't name them. Maybe since the porridge metaphor. It doesn't matter when it started. It just is. It's true. And I'm done pretending it isn't."

The silence stretched between them. Sarah's heart hammered.

She'd said it. Had actually said the words out loud. No taking them back now. No pretending she hadn't known it.

"You don't know me," he said finally. His voice was quiet. "Not really. We've known each other for eight days."

"I know enough." Sarah's voice was firm. "I know you see me. Really see me. Not the role I play or the function I serve. You see the person underneath. You're kind. You're wise. You're patient. You make me feel alive in a way I haven't felt in years. Maybe ever. When I'm with you, I'm the best version of myself. When I'm not, I miss you so much it physically aches."

He closed his eyes. "You're making this very hard."

"Good." A smile tugged at her lips despite everything. "Why should I be the only one suffering?"

He laughed, but it was a sad, broken sound that hurt to hear. "You’re not. Trust me, you’re not."

"Then tell me." Sarah squeezed his hand. "Tell me what you're feeling. Be honest with me, the way I'm being honest with you. Please."

He opened his eyes and looked at her. What she saw there made her breath catch. Pain and longing and love and grief all tangled together. All there in his expression, undisguised.

"I'm in love with you, too," he said quietly. Each word deliberate. Chosen. True. "I think I have been since you told me to mind my own business. Since you looked at me with those defiant eyes and that set jaw and told me you didn't need my help. I thought: there she is. The real her. Fighting to get out."

Tears pricked her eyes.

"And every day since then," he continued, low and intense, "I've watched you become more yourself. More visible. More alive. More brave. And I've fallen more in love with you with every conversation. Every walk. Every moment we've spent together. Every word you've written. Every time you've chosen yourself over what you think you should be."

He lifted their joined hands and pressed a kiss to her knuckles. Soft. Gentle. Reverent.

"But it doesn't change anything," he said, lowering their hands but not letting go. "It doesn't change the fact that you're going home in five days. You have a life there. A husband. Children. A home. This..." He gestured between them with his free hand. "This can't be more than what it is."

"And what is it?" Sarah's voice came out as barely a whisper.

"A perfect moment." His eyes held hers. "A gift. Memories for when you're back in Bristol. Being the new Sarah. Being visible. Being alive. Taking up space and writing your book and refusing to disappear." He paused. "But it can't be forever. It can only be now."

"Why not?" Even as she said it, she knew it was a foolish question. Knew the answer.

"Because you're married. Because you have children who need you. You can't build a life on two weeks in France." His voice was patient but firm. "Life doesn't work that way. You can't leave twenty years of marriage for someone you've known for eight days. The life you have in Bristol is complicated and messy. This..." He gestured at the garden, the village, the perfect morning. "This is a moment outside of time. A gift. But moments end, Sarah. They have to."

She knew he was right. Hated that he was right. Wanted to argue anyway.

But he was right.

"So what do we do?" she asked. "For these five days I have left?"

"We're honest." His hand tightened around hers. "We don't pretend. We don't hide. We let ourselves feel what we feel. But..." He paused, choosing his words carefully. "We don't cross lines you'll regret crossing. We don't make this harder than it already has to be when you leave."

"It's already going to be impossible when I leave."

"I know."

They sat in silence for a long time. Hands still linked. Both of them trying to accept the impossible situation they'd found themselves in. In love with each other. Admitting it. Acknowledging it. But unable to have it. Unable to keep it.

Finally, Sarah said, "I want to spend every minute I have left with you. I don't want to waste time pretending, holding back, or being careful. I just want to be with you."

"Even knowing it has to end?"

"Especially knowing it has to end." She looked at him. "Because it makes every moment more precious. More real. More worth holding onto."

He smiled, sad but genuine. "You're remarkable. You know that?"

"You've mentioned it once or twice."

He stood up, pulling her up with him. "Come on. Let's not waste these precious moments sitting on a bench being sad. Let's live them. Starting with breakfast. Proper breakfast. Have you been to the café that serves pain perdu?"

"What's pain perdu?"

"You're about to find out."

* * *

THEY WALKED BACK through the village, still holding hands. And certainty settled in Sarah's bones. Not peace, exactly. Not acceptance of how this would end. But a kind of clarity.

She was in love with Him. He was in love with her. They had five days left together. And then it would end.

She would go home to Bristol. To David, the girls, and her life. She would figure out what her marriage could or should be. She would keep writing. She would stay awake.

And Jack would... what? Stay here in Normandy? Go somewhere else? She realised she still didn't know where he lived, what his life looked like beyond these mornings with her.

But she wouldn't ask. Not now. Because asking would make the future real. Would make the separation concrete. It would make her think about the after, rather than the now.

For these five days, she would let herself have this. Would let herself be in love. Would let herself be seen. Would let herself be happy in this moment, even knowing the moment would end.

And when it was time to go home, she'd figure out what came next.

But not yet. Not today.

Today, she would just be with him. Hold his hand. Eat breakfast. Walk and talk and exist in this space outside of time.

And that would be enough.

It had to be.

CHAPTER 10 - THE LINE

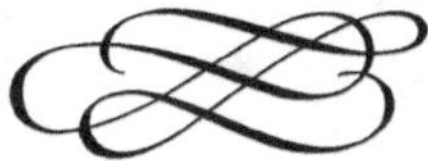

They had breakfast at a café Sarah had never seen before, tucked away on a narrow side street near the main square. It was the kind of place you'd only discover if someone brought you there, if you were lucky enough to know about it.

Pain perdu, he'd said. Lost bread. French toast, but better.

And it really was better. Thick slices of brioche, soaked in cream and eggs with a touch of vanilla or cinnamon, fried in butter until golden, then dusted with powdered sugar. Rich, indulgent, perfect.

Sarah ate slowly whilst he toyed with his food, the way Olivia does when she's on a diet again, talking about things that seemed unimportant and yet meant everything. Books they'd loved as children. Films that had stayed with them. Memories that shaped who they were.

He told her how he learned to paint as a child. His mother gave him his first set of watercolours for his eighth birthday, and he would spend hours at the kitchen table trying to paint the changing light on the wall.

"I couldn't get it right," he said, smiling at the memory. "I'd mix colours for hours trying to match it exactly. And by the time I got close, the light had moved. Changed. So I'd have to start over."

"Did you ever get it right?"

"No. Never." He took a sip of coffee. "But I learned what matters more. That light isn't static. Trying to capture a moment exactly is impossible. The best you can do is remember how it was when you saw it."

Sarah told him she had wanted to be a writer since she was eight years old. About the stories she'd written in secret note-books, hidden under her bed, where no one would find them and tell her they were silly or impractical. About characters who lived in her head, demanding to have their stories told.

"What happened to them?" he asked. "The notebooks?"

"I put them away when I got married." The admission hurt. "There wasn't time for dreams when there were nappies to change and bills to pay. When there was life to live. Told myself it was childish. That grown-ups didn't spend time on things like that."

"But you're doing it now."

"I'm doing it now."

"How does it feel?"

Sarah thought about it. Really thought. "Terrifying," she said finally. "Exhilarating. Right." She paused. "Like I'm finally who I'm meant to be. Like I've been walking around in someone else's clothes for twenty years, and I've finally found my own."

After breakfast, they wandered without a plan, moving through the village and out into the countryside. The day was beautiful, warm but not hot, with a breeze and a sky so blue it hardly seemed possible.

They held hands as they walked. Sarah was surprised by how natural it was, how right. It was as if her hand had always been waiting for this, made not just for doing things, but for connecting with someone else.

"Where are we going?" she asked after a while.

"I thought we could go to the beach," he said. "The one where we met. If you'd like."

"I'd like that."

They walked through the dunes, their feet sinking into the soft sand. The beach lay ahead, almost empty except for a few distant figures. The tide was out, leaving flat, firm sand that was smooth and untouched.

They took off their shoes and walked along the water's edge. Feet in wet sand, waves lapping their ankles. Cold. Refreshing.

"Tell me something," Jack said after a while. "Something you've never told anyone else."

Sarah thought about it. There were so many things she'd never said out loud. So many truths she'd kept locked inside.

"I'm afraid of going home," she said finally.

"Why?"

Because I'm scared I'll lose this new self. At home, with David's familiar looks, the girls' expectations, and the old routines, I'm afraid I'll shrink again. I'm afraid I'll become invisible because it's easier and because it's what everyone expects. It takes energy to stay visible and alive, and I might not have enough.

"You won't," he said with certainty.

"How do you know?"

"Because you can't unsee yourself once you've been truly seen. You can't unknow what you know about who you are." He squeezed her hand. "You might struggle. Sometimes, you'll slip back into old patterns. But you won't disappear again. Not completely. Because you'll remember this: being here, being yourself, being alive. That memory will anchor you."

"I hope you're right."

"I am right." He grinned. "I'm always right."

She laughed despite herself.

They walked in silence for a bit, just the sound of waves and gulls and their own breathing. Then he said, "My turn. What I've never told anyone."

"Alright."

He was quiet for a moment, choosing his words. When he finally spoke, his voice was low.

"I think... I think I've been waiting for you. For years. Not knowing what I was waiting for. Not knowing you existed.

Just... waiting. Feeling like a piece was missing. Like there was a space in my life that needed to be filled." He stopped walking and turned to face her. "And then you showed up on this beach with your notebook and your anger and your fear and your determination to push me away. And I thought: there she is. Finally."

Sarah's breath caught. "What do you mean?"

"I mean, you're not random, Sarah. This isn't chance." His eyes held hers. "You were supposed to be here. I was supposed to find you. Or you were supposed to find me. However, it works. I don't believe in coincidences. I believe some people are meant to meet. Meant to collide. Meant to change each other. And we were meant to meet."

"For what purpose?"

"To wake each other up." He said it simply, as if it were obvious. "To remind each other what it feels like to be seen. To be alive. To exist." He cupped her face with both hands, the gesture now familiar and cherished. "You're going to leave in five days. You're going to go home and figure out your life. And I'm going to stay here. But this - what we have right now, what we are to each other - it matters. It will always matter. Even when we're not together. Even when years have passed. This will always have mattered."

Tears slipped down Sarah's cheeks. "I don't want to leave you."

"I know." His thumbs wiped away her tears. "But you have to. You have a life. Children who need you. Things to figure out. And you can't do that from here. You can't make those decisions while you're in this bubble with me."

"I could stay," she said, even though she knew it was impossible. "I could stay here. I could…"

"No." His voice was firm but infinitely gentle. "You're not running away from your life, Sarah. You're running toward yourself. And yourself includes being a mother to Olivia and Betty. Includes figuring out what your marriage can or should be. You can't abandon all of that for two weeks in France. You can't build a new life on an escape."

"Even for you?"

"Especially for me." He kissed her forehead. "Because I care about you too much to let you make that choice. To let you become someone who runs away instead of someone who runs toward."

He lowered his hands and looked out at the sea. The endless expanse of blue-green water, waves rolling in with perfect rhythm.

"Now come on," he said, his tone shifting, becoming lighter. "Let's swim."

"Swim?" Sarah looked at him. "I don't have a costume."

"Neither do I."

They looked at each other. The moment hung between them, full of meaning and possibility, and the question of what boundaries they were willing to cross.

His name escaped her lips.

"We don't have to," he said quickly. "If it's too much. If it crosses a line you're not ready to cross. But..." He gestured at the empty beach, the endless sea, the perfect day. "When are we ever going to have this again? This moment. This place. Just us. No one watching. No one judging. Just... this."

He was right. And Sarah was tired. So tired of holding back. Of being careful. Of measuring every action against some invisible standard of appropriateness. As her hesitation faded, restraint shifted to longing.

They'd already crossed so many lines. Had admitted they were in love. Had held hands in public. Had kissed each other's hands and foreheads and existed in that charged space where restraint was its own kind of intimacy.

If everything was already irreparably tangled, why hold anything back now?

"Alright," she said. Her voice was steadier than her nerves. "Let's swim."

And just like that, Sarah made a choice the old Sarah would never have made.

Jack pulled off his jumper. Sarah stared. She'd imagined him under his clothes—of course, she had, who wouldn't? But seeing him in reality was different. He wasn't perfect, not like a magazine model. He was solid and beautiful in the way bodies are. Lean but not thin, strong but not bulky, with scars from a life lived. Real.

Sarah set down her bag and reached for the hem of her jumper. Her hands trembled slightly.

The old Sarah would have made excuses. She would have said it was too cold, too public, or too improper. She would have worried about being seen, judged, or making mistakes. She would have thought about what people would think, what

David would think, and what God would think, if there was a God.

The old Sarah would have kept her clothes on and watched from the shore while someone braver lived the moment she was too afraid to claim.

But the old Sarah had spent twenty years making herself small and invisible. She chose propriety over desire, safety over joy, and everyone else's comfort over her own sense of being alive. She kept shrinking, apologising, and fading away.

Sarah pulled her jumper over her head.

She'd nursed two babies with these breasts. They weren't the same as they'd been at twenty-three when David had first seen them, first touched them, first told her she was beautiful. Gravity had done its work. Her stomach had stretch marks - silver lines that mapped where Olivia and Betty had grown inside her, evidence of the miracle and the damage of creation. Her thighs touched. Her arms were soft. She was forty-three years old, and she looked it.

David hadn't seen her fully naked in daylight in years. She'd made sure of it. Always undressing in the bathroom. Always in darkness. Always under covers. Always hiding.

She unhooked her bra and let it fall to the sand.

The morning sun was warm on her skin. The sea breeze raised goosebumps on her arms, her chest, and her stomach. She could hear the waves, the gulls crying overhead, her own heart hammering like a drum. This was mad. This was reckless. This was completely unlike her.

And it felt extraordinary.

She stepped out of her jeans and underwear and stood there, naked on a beach in France with a man who wasn't her husband. Exposed. Vulnerable. Visible.

When she looked up, he was looking at her. Not studying her clinically. Not cataloguing her flaws. Just looking at her with such open appreciation, such genuine desire, such uncomplicated joy at seeing her, that all her self-consciousness evaporated like morning mist.

"You're beautiful," he said simply.

"You're biased."

"I'm honest."

"No." Sarah shook her head. "You're seeing me. And that's different. That's everything."

They stood there, naked in the morning sun, just looking at each other. Taking each other in. Seeing each other completely - all the imperfections, all the evidence of lives lived, all the reality of being human. And finding each other beautiful anyway. Because of it, not despite it.

Sarah felt powerful. Vulnerable. Alive. Seen. She was herself.

“It’s cold, are you sure you’re up for this?”

Sarah looked him up and down. “Not that cold, evidently”. They both laughed. Then, at the same moment, without speaking, they both reached out their hands. Their fingers intertwined. And they ran.

Ran across the sand toward the water, laughing like children, like teenagers, like people who'd just discovered joy. The water was shockingly cold when they hit it, but they didn't stop.

They plunged in together, still holding hands, and when they surfaced, gasping and laughing and alive, Sarah was more herself than she'd ever been.

The cold water on her bare skin was a shock, but a good one. It woke her up. Every nerve ending was alive, every cell aware. This was her body. Imperfect, and beautiful. It could feel cold, warmth, desire, and joy.

They swam out a little way, treading water, still laughing. The sun sparkled on the surface. The beach looked distant and perfect from here. France. A foreign country. A life outside her life.

"Cold?" Jack asked.

"Freezing," Sarah admitted. "And I don't care."

They swam back to shore, slower now, and when the water was shallow enough to stand, they did. Walking out of the sea together. Water streaming off their bodies. Sun warm on wet skin.

And when he reached for her, Sarah didn't hesitate. Didn't think. Didn't measure or calculate or worry.

She just said yes.

Yes to his hands on her face. Yes to his mouth on hers, finally, after all the restraint and waiting and choosing not to. Yes to his body against hers, skin to skin, no barriers left. Yes to being wanted this desperately. Yes to wanting him back.

They sank down onto the sand together, the beach empty, the world distant, nothing existing except this moment and this man and this choice she was making.

And when they made love - there on the sand with the sun warming their backs and the sound of waves in their ears - it was nothing like duty or maintenance or going through the motions. It was coming home. Like finding what she hadn't even known she'd lost. Like being seen, known, and wanted for who she actually was, not for what she could provide.

He touched her as if she were a mystery worth solving. Like every inch of her skin had a story to tell. Like he had all the time in the world and wanted to spend it learning the map of her body. Like her pleasure mattered. Like she mattered.

When it was over, they lay tangled together, exhausted and breathless. Sand clung to their damp skin, wetness from the sea and from each other. Sarah could feel his heart beating against her chest, feel the rise and fall of his breath gradually slowing.

She should feel guilty. Should be thinking about David, about what she'd just done, about the vows she'd broken, about the line she'd so completely and utterly crossed.

But she was simply whole. Complete. Filled with a sense of belonging she'd never known before. Like she'd spent her entire life being half a person, and had finally become full.

"Sarah," he said softly, his lips against her temple.

"Don't," she whispered. Fear flooded through her. "Don't say we shouldn't have. Don't say this was a mistake. Please."

"I wasn't going to." He pulled back slightly to look at her, brushing sand from her face with gentle fingers. "I was going to say that I will remember this - you, right here, right now, exactly like this - for the rest of time."

There it was again. That phrase. The rest of time.

"Why do you say it like that?" Sarah asked. "The rest of time. Not forever, or always, but time itself."

Something flickered across his face, maybe sadness or grief. She couldn't quite read it.

"Because some things are bigger than forever," he said quietly. "Some moments exist outside of normal time. Outside of the regular flow of life. And this is one of those moments. This matters in a way that transcends the normal measurement of hours and days."

She wanted to ask what he meant. Wanted to understand. But he was kissing her again, softer this time, and she let the question dissolve.

* * *

LATER, though she didn't know how much later because time had stopped mattering, they began to get dressed. They moved slowly, reluctantly. Sand stuck to everything—their skin, their hair, their clothes. It was evidence of what they'd done, the line they'd crossed, and the choice they'd made.

"We're a mess," Sarah said, trying to brush sand off her jeans and failing.

"We are," he agreed, smiling. "And I don't care even a little bit."

As they walked back up the beach, hand in hand, Sarah tried to process what had happened. What she'd done. What it meant.

She'd cheated on her husband. Had committed adultery. Had broken her wedding vows. All the words her mother would use, all the judgment she'd internalised about what good wives did and didn't do.

But she couldn't make herself regret it. Couldn't summon the guilt that should be there. All she was, was alive. Awake. Real.

They passed through the village's outskirts, walking in comfortable silence. And then they heard it - children's voices. High, excited, and full of joy.

They turned a corner and found themselves near a school. An old stone building with new scaffolding along one side, clearly being renovated. The courtyard gates were open, and children were streaming out, their school day finished. Seven, eight, nine years old. Backpacks bouncing. Faces bright with the freedom of being done for the day.

"Maman! Maman!"

"Papa!"

"Can we go to the park?"

"I got a gold star today!"

Pure joy. Pure innocence. Running and laughing and chattering about their day, eager to get home, to play, to live their uncomplicated child-lives where the biggest worry was whether they'd get to go to the park before dinner.

They stopped walking and stood there watching. One little girl with dark braids was spinning in circles, making herself dizzy, laughing. A boy was showing his mother what he'd made - a drawing, probably, held up proudly for inspection and praise. Two children were racing each other to see who could reach their waiting parent first.

Sarah looked at him. He was watching the children with such intensity, his face showing joy, sadness, longing, and grief.

He caught her looking and smiled, but the smile didn't quite reach his eyes.

"Do you ever think about what it's like?" Sarah asked softly. "To be that age? To have everything be that simple?"

"All the time," he said quietly. "To have your biggest worry be whether you get to go to the park after school. To believe the world is good and safe, and that all the adults around you will protect you. Not yet knowing how fragile everything is. How quickly it can all change."

"It must be nice. Being that innocent."

"It is." He squeezed her hand. "Until it isn't. But that's what childhood should be. That joy. That freedom. That belief that tomorrow will be just as good as today. That the people you love will always be there."

His voice was heavy and weighted, with what made Sarah want to ask questions. But the moment passed, and he smiled, genuine this time, and turned to her.

"Come on. Let's get you back so you can write."

They walked the rest of the way in comfortable silence, still holding hands. When they reached the village square, he stopped and turned to face her.

"Tomorrow," he said. "What do you want to do tomorrow?"

"I don't know." Sarah smiled. "Everything. Nothing. Just be with you."

"Then that's what we'll do."

He kissed her forehead, just a brief touch, but it sent warmth through her whole body.

"Write," he said. "Write about today. About what you're feeling. Don't hold back. Don't censor yourself. Just write the truth."

"I won't."

"Same time tomorrow?"

"Same time tomorrow."

He walked away, and Sarah didn't stand there watching this time. She turned and practically ran back to her hotel, her heart racing, her mind already full of words that needed to get onto paper before they disappeared.

* * *

SHE BURST through the hotel door, took the stairs two at a time, fumbled with her key - her hands still shaking - and finally got into her room. She dropped her bag, went straight to the desk, grabbed her pen, and opened her notebook.

And wrote.

She wrote about making love on a beach. About crossing lines you couldn't uncross. About choosing desire over duty and finding no guilt on the other side, just a terrible, wonderful sense of being fully alive.

She wrote about being imperfect. About making choices that

didn't fit neatly into boxes of right and wrong. About how perfection was a prison and messiness was freedom.

She wrote about her body. About reclaiming it. About the difference between being needed and being wanted. Between someone touching you because they want to and wanting to be touched.

She wrote about David. About the sex that was scheduled. Tuesdays and Saturdays, usually. After the girls were asleep. Before they were too tired. A maintenance task, like changing the oil in the car. Necessary. Mostly pleasant. Occasionally annoying when you'd rather just go to sleep. The same moves in the same order. Reliable. Efficient. Done.

And then she wrote about Jack. About being touched, as if she were a mystery worth solving. Like her pleasure mattered. Like she mattered.

She wrote about loving two men at once - David with the comfortable love of shared history, Jack with the consuming love of being truly seen. And how both were real. Both mattered. Both were valid even though they contradicted each other.

She wrote about watching children run from school. About their laughter. About the way he'd looked at them with such complicated emotion. About innocence and fragility, and believing tomorrow would be just as good as today.

She wrote about not knowing what came next. About having four days left. About terror and exhilaration existing side by side.

The words poured out faster than she could catch them. Her hand cramped, but she refused to stop. The light through the window shifted from afternoon to evening, and still she wrote.

When she finally stopped, her wrist throbbing, her eyes burning, she looked at the page count.

One hundred and forty-two pages. She'd written eighteen pages. Eighteen pages about one day. About crossing the line. About choosing to be alive.

Sarah closed the notebook and sat back in her chair.

She'd cheated on her husband. Had broken her marriage vows. Had done the thing she'd always said she'd never do. Had become the person she'd judged others for being.

And she couldn't make herself regret it.

She went to the window and looked out at the village. Lights coming on in windows. People making dinner, living their normal lives. Tomorrow would be Monday. The ninth day. Four more days. Then the train home.

To David, the girls, her life. To the choices she'd have to make about what came next.

But not tonight.

Tonight, she would just sit with what had happened. With who she'd become. Given that she was alive, awake, and real.

CHAPTER 11 - THE HILL

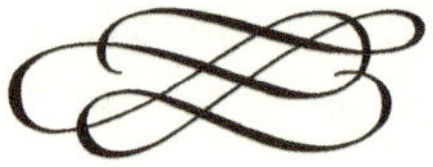

Sarah woke feeling... good.

It wasn't just okay or fine. It was genuinely, surprisingly good. She lay in bed, savouring the feeling and letting it wash over her like sunlight through the window.

When was the last time she'd woken up feeling this way? This at ease in her own skin? This comfortable with herself? This alive?

She couldn't remember. Maybe never.

Last night she'd written eighteen pages. They poured out so fast she could barely keep up. Her hand cramped, but she refused to stop. Words about desire, bodies, and being alive. About making love on a beach without shame. About crossing lines and finding freedom. About choosing yourself even when it was complicated.

She stretched under the sheets, feeling the cool linen against her bare skin, and realised her body was humming. Awake. Aware. Wanting.

Her hand moved down her body slowly. At first, she was tentative, then grew more confident. The first time in the shower, she had been nervous, guilty, and worried about the maid. Now, no hesitation. Only curiosity, anticipation, and the gentle rush of pleasure. The simple, surprising joy of a body that truly felt.

She thought about him. About yesterday on the beach. About his hands on her skin and his mouth on hers and the way he'd looked at her like she was everything. Like seeing her gave him pleasure. Like her body was beautiful, worthy, and desired.

The pleasure built slowly, warmly, spreading through her like honey. And when it crested, she gasped softly into the morning quiet, her body arching, every nerve alive.

Afterwards, she lay there catching her breath, a smile spreading across her face. And then she started to laugh. Quietly at first, then louder, her shoulders shaking with it.

My God, Sarah, she thought. You're turning into some sort of vixen.

Six months ago, or even six weeks ago, she had just gone through the motions. She touched her husband dutifully, efficiently, and quietly, and it was over quickly. She had forgotten her body could feel pleasure. She thought desire faded with age, motherhood, and marriage - something you were supposed to outgrow.

And now here she was, in France, pleasuring herself in the morning light and laughing about it instead of feeling guilty. Thinking about a man who wasn't her husband and feeling no shame. Just joy. Just aliveness.

Who was this person, she wondered—this version of herself, unafraid, open to experience, living so differently than before?

She liked her.

Then she glanced at the clock, and her eyes went wide.

Nine o'clock.

She was late. Really late. Usually, she got to the café by eight-fifteen at the latest. He would already be there. Waiting. Probably wondering where she was. Worried something had happened.

She threw off the covers and rushed through her morning routine. She took a quick, efficient shower with no lingering. She put on the first clothes she grabbed. Her hair was pulled back while still wet. There was no time for mascara. She grabbed her bag and notebook and ran down the stairs, through the lobby, and out onto the street.

The village was already fully alive with the sounds of a new day. People going about their business. Shutters open. The boulangerie door propped wide, the smell of bread filling the air. Normal Tuesday morning life.

Sarah hurried through the streets toward the square, her heart pounding from more than just the rushing. She was nearly an hour late. What if he'd left? What if he'd waited and given up? What if he thought she'd changed her mind about seeing him?

* * *

WHEN SHE REACHED THE CAFÉ, breathless from hurrying, he wasn't there.

She stopped at the edge of the square, confused. He was always there. Every single morning. Already sitting at their table, newspaper in hand, that worn blue jumper, waiting for her with that smile that made everything else fade away.

But today, the table was empty.

Sarah felt her stomach drop. Was he upset she'd kept him waiting? Was he hurt, or did he believe she'd changed her mind? Her mind raced through scenarios: maybe he'd waited, then left in disappointment, or perhaps he thought she didn't care enough to arrive at all.

She walked to their table and sat down anyway. Tried to catch her breath. Her mind spun with possibilities.

The waitress appeared almost immediately. "Café, madame?"

"Oui, s'il vous plaît. Un café noir."

Just one. Because he wasn't here.

The coffee arrived. Sarah wrapped her hands around the cup but didn't drink; she just stared at the rising steam, trying to figure out what to do. Where would he be? Should she go look for him? Where would she even start?

"Pardon, madame."

Sarah looked up to see an old man beside the table. He must have been in his eighties, maybe nineties. His snow-white hair and deeply lined face spoke of a long life lived. His eyes were kind, gentle. He wore a worn cardigan despite the warmth and leaned on a walking stick, his hand gnarled with age.

"Oui?" Sarah said, her French rusty and uncertain.

He gestured at the empty chair across from her. "Je peux?"

"Oh. Yes, of course." Sarah gestured for him to sit, grateful that someone might be able to help. "Please."

The old man lowered himself carefully into the chair, settling his walking stick against the table with a soft thunk. For a moment, he just sat there, looking at her with those kind eyes, a small smile on his weathered face.

"Are you looking for Jack?" he asked in heavily accented English.

Sarah felt her breath catch. "You know him?"

The old man's smile grew. "Everybody knows who Jack is." He paused, and something flickered across his face. Something she couldn't quite read. "But not everybody sees him."

"I'm sorry, what?"

"Jack. He was here this morning. At this table. Waiting for you, I think." The old man nodded toward the empty chair. "But then he left."

Relief flooded through Sarah so intensely that she was dizzy. Her breath caught, and her hands trembled. He had been here. He had waited for her. She hadn't imagined him, lost him, or driven him away by being late.

"Where did he go?" she asked.

"Up to the hill. The one overlooking the sea." The old man pointed vaguely toward the edge of the village with his walking stick. "He goes there sometimes. To think, I believe. To be alone. You could find him there, if you like."

"Thank you." Sarah stood quickly, already reaching for her bag. She left coins on the table for the coffee she hadn't touched, probably too much, but she didn't care. "Thank you so much."

"De rien, madame." The old man smiled up at her, that same unreadable expression in his eyes.

Sarah started to walk away, then paused and turned back. Something about what he'd said was nagging at her. "What did you mean? That everybody knows who Jack is, but not everybody sees him?"

The old man's smile grew sad. Almost pitying, though not in an unkind way. "Some people walk through the world, and everyone notices them. Everyone sees them. They cannot help but be seen." He paused, choosing his words carefully. "Jack is not like that. He is here, but..." He gestured vaguely with his hand. "Not everyone has the eyes to see him. You do, though. You see him very clearly, I think. Very clearly indeed."

It was a strange thing to say. An odd turn of phrase. But Sarah didn't have time to puzzle over it. She just nodded her thanks and headed toward the path that led up the hill.

As she walked through the village and out toward the countryside, Sarah found herself turning the old man's words over in her mind.

Everybody knows who Jack is. But not everybody sees him.

What did that mean? She mulled over the phrasing. Why 'knows who Jack is' instead of just 'knows him'? Was the old man implying he had a reputation, a significance that set him apart? Did people talk about him in the village, or was there something she was missing? The uncertainty nagged at her as she walked.

Maybe he was more well-known than he'd let on. Maybe his paintings sold for serious money. Maybe he was recognised in art circles, celebrated in galleries. Maybe people in the village knew he was someone important, even if they didn't personally know him. That would explain why the vendors at the market never spoke to him directly. Why did the waitress always look at Sarah instead? Not because they couldn't see him, but because they were giving him space. Respecting his privacy. The way you might with a celebrity or someone who clearly prefers to be left alone.

It made sense. Artists could be reclusive, protective of solitude. He'd said as much. If he was successful, as he must be to spend his time painting and live in Normandy without financial worry, then people would know of him without knowing him. They might recognise his presence but not approach.

That was all the old man had meant. Jack was a known artist. Recognised but private. Famous enough that people were aware of him, reclusive enough that they'd learned not to bother him.

Sarah was relieved to have an explanation. The comment had been strange, but there was a perfectly logical reason for it.

The path grew steeper. Sarah focused on her breathing. She placed her feet carefully on the uneven ground. The village fell away behind her, getting smaller. The sounds faded. Ahead, she could see the top of the hill. Grass waved in the breeze.

And there he was, sitting on the grass looking out at the endless sea.

Even from a distance, even with his back to her, she knew him. The set of his shoulders. The way he held himself. That worn blue jumper. Paint stains on the cuffs, she could imagine, even if she couldn't see them from here.

Her heart lifted, sending lightness surging through her tired limbs.

"Jack!" she called out, breathless from the climb and from relief and from seeing him.

He turned at the sound of his name, and when he saw her, his whole face transformed. Relief. Joy. Something that looked almost like pain, but the good kind.

He stood as she reached him, and without thinking, without hesitating, Sarah walked straight into his arms. He caught her, held her tight, his face buried in her hair.

"I thought you weren't coming," he said, his voice muffled. "I waited and waited, and when you didn't show up, I thought... I don't know what I thought. That you'd changed your mind. That yesterday had been too much. That you'd woken up and realised what we'd done and decided you couldn't see me anymore."

"I'm sorry," Sarah pulled back to look at him. "I woke up late. Really late. I completely lost track of time, and then I rushed to the café, but you weren't there, and I didn't know where you'd gone and…"

"It's okay." He cupped her face with both hands, that gesture she'd come to love. "You're here now. That's what matters."

They stood there, holding each other, and Sarah felt the tension drain from both of them. The fear. The worry. The relief of finding each other again.

"How did you sleep?" he asked, his lips against her hair.

"Really well, actually." Sarah smiled against his chest. "I wrote eighteen pages last night. The words just poured out. And then I slept like the dead." She pulled back to look at him. "You?"

"Not as well." His expression was troubled. "I kept thinking about yesterday. About you. About..." He gestured at the sea, the endless horizon, and the world below them. "About the fact that we only have three more days. Two after today. And then..."

Sarah's throat closed. "Can we not think about that yet? Please?"

"I'm trying not to." His hands moved to her shoulders, his grip gentle but firm. "But it's hard to ignore when every morning I wake up and think: three more days. Two more days. One more day." He paused, his eyes searching hers. "I'm trying to memorise you. Every expression. Every word. Every laugh. Every moment. Because when you leave, that's all I'll have left. Memories. I want them to be complete."

“Jack”…

"I know. I'm being morbid. I'm sorry." He dropped his hands and managed a smile. "Tell me about your morning. You said you woke up late?"

Sarah's cheeks heated. "Yes. I was... distracted."

"Distracted how?"

"Just..." She couldn't quite meet his eyes. "Thinking about yesterday. About you. About... things."

A slow smile spread across his face. "Things?"

"Yes. Things."

"What kind of things?"

"Jack."

"I'm just asking." But he was grinning now, and Sarah felt her embarrassment shift into something else. Amusement. A lightness that made her want to laugh.

"Fine." She lifted her chin, meeting his eyes. "I was touching myself, if you must know. Thinking about you. About the beach. About how you looked at me and touched me and made me feel. And I completely lost track of time. Happy now?"

"Extremely." He pulled her close again, his voice dropping low and intimate. "And were you? Happy, I mean?"

"Yes."

"Good." His breath was warm against her ear. "You should be. You should feel pleasure. You should touch yourself thinking about me. You should wake up late and rush through the village with" he paused, reaching up to pull a grain of sand from behind her ear. He showed it to her on his fingertip. "Evidence of what we did is still on your skin."

Sarah laughed despite herself. "I showered!"

"Not thoroughly enough, apparently." He blew the sand grain away, watching it disappear into the breeze. "Though I'm glad. I like knowing yesterday is still with you. That I'm still with you."

They sat down on the grass together, looking out at the view. The sea stretched endlessly before them, blue-green and sparkling in the morning sun. The sky was that impossible shade of blue. The whole world spread out like a gift.

"I spoke to an old man at the café," Sarah said after a moment. "He told me where to find you."

"Did he?" His expression shifted. Became more guarded.

"He said something strange." Sarah watched him carefully. "He said everybody knows who Jack is, but not everybody sees you."

Jack went very still beside her. "What else did he say?"

"Nothing. Just that you'd been at the café waiting and then left for the hill." She turned to face him. "What did he mean by that? About not everybody seeing you?"

"I don't know." But his voice was too casual. Too dismissive. "Old men say strange things sometimes."

"But you know what he meant."

"No, I..."

"Jack." She took his hand, lacing their fingers together. "I've noticed it too. The way people look through you sometimes. The way vendors at the market talk to me but not to you. The way the waitress never addresses you directly, always sets both coffees in front of me. At first, I thought I was imagining it, but I'm not, am I?"

He was quiet for a long moment. When he finally spoke, his voice was careful. "No. You're not imagining it."

"So what is it? Why don't people see you?"

"Because I don't want them to." He squeezed her hand. "I'm a private person. I keep to myself. I don't engage with people, don't make eye contact, don't invite interaction. So they've learned not to see me. To look past me. It's easier that way."

"Easier for whom?"

"For everyone."

"That doesn't make sense."

"It doesn't have to make sense." He turned to look at her, and she saw fear in his eyes.

"It just is. But you see me, Sarah. You've always seen me. From that first day on the beach when you told me to mind my own business. You saw me clearly. That's what matters."

Sarah wanted to push further. Wanted to ask more questions. Wanted to understand why a man would make himself invisible, why he'd train an entire village to look past him. But something in his expression stopped her. He looked almost fragile. Like if she pushed too hard, he might break. Or disappear.

"Alright," she said softly. "I won't push. But Jack... if there's anything you need to tell me. Anything I should know. You can trust me."

"I know I can." He lifted her hand to his lips and kissed it. "And if there was something to tell, I would. But there isn't. I'm just a private man, an artist who happened to meet you at exactly the right moment. That's all."

It wasn't all. Sarah knew it wasn't. Could feel it in the way he held himself, in the careful way he'd answered, in what he wasn't saying.

But she let it go. For now.

They sat in silence for a while, just looking out at the sea, hands linked, breathing together. Two people on a hillside in France with three days left before everything changed.

Finally, he said, "Tell me what you're going to do when you go home."

"I don't want to think about going home."

"I know. But we should." His voice was gentle but firm. "Because in three days, you'll be there. You'll be back in Bristol with David and the girls and your life. And I want to make sure you're ready. That you know what you're going to do. That you don't lose yourself the moment you step off that train."

Sarah sighed. "I don't know if I'll ever be ready."

"You will be. You already are." He shifted to face her fully. "So. You get home. David picks you up from the train station. What happens?"

"I suppose..." Sarah tried to picture it. "We drive home. The girls will probably be out or in their rooms. David will ask about France in that polite way he has, like I've been to a spa or retreat. I'll say it was good. We'll settle back into routines. Life will continue."

"And then?"

"And then the next morning, I'll wake up and write. Like I've been doing here. Because I'm a writer now. That's who I am."

"Good. Where will you write?"

Sarah thought about it. "The kitchen table, probably. That's where I usually…"

"No." His voice was firm, almost sharp. "Not the kitchen table where everyone can interrupt you. Where David can walk through and ask what you're doing. Where the girls can come down for breakfast and need things. Where you're in the middle of everything instead of having your own space." He looked at her intently. "Where will you really write?"

Sarah thought about her house. About the spare room upstairs, the one they'd used for storage for years. "We have a spare room," she said slowly. "It's full of boxes and old furniture that we never use. But I could clear it out. Make it into an office."

"Perfect. That's exactly what you'll do." He nodded. "In the first week home, you clear out that room. You claim it. You make it yours. A door you can close. A desk by the window. A space that's just for your writing. A room of your own."

"David might not like that."

"David will have to accept it." Jack's voice was fierce. "You're not asking permission, Sarah. You're informing him. 'I'm turning the spare room into an office. I'll be writing every morning from seven to noon. The girls can handle their own breakfast. You can handle getting yourself to work. I'm not available during those hours.' Clear. Direct. No negotiation."

"That sounds harsh."

"It sounds clear. There's a difference." He squeezed her hand. "You've spent twenty years being unclear about what you need. Being accommodating. Making yourself flexible, available, and small. That stops now. You claim your space. You claim your time. You write every single day. No exceptions."

"And if David doesn't support it?"

"Then you do it anyway." His eyes held hers. "His support would be nice. But you don't need it. You're doing this for you, not for him. This isn't about his approval. It's about your life. Your identity. Your work."

Sarah felt tears prick her eyes. "What if I can't? What if I get home and fall right back into old patterns? What if I'm not strong enough?"

"You won't. And you are." He cupped her face gently. "Because you've changed, Sarah. Fundamentally. You can't unsee yourself once you've been truly seen. You can't unknow what you know about who you are." He paused, his voice softening. "You're a writer. That's not a hobby. That's not something you do in your free time when everyone else is taken care of. That's who you are. And you protect who you are. Fiercely. Even when it's uncomfortable. Even when people push back. Even when it would be easier to give in."

"You make it sound easy."

"It's not easy. It's necessary. There's a difference." He smiled. "But you're strong enough. You've proven that already. You came here alone. You wrote a book. You let yourself want things. You chose yourself. That takes strength most people never find."

"I had help. I had you."

"I was just the mirror." He kissed her forehead. "You did the work. And you'll keep doing the work when you go home. You'll finish your book. You'll figure out your marriage. You'll be a mother, a writer, and whatever else you want to be. And you'll do it without disappearing."

"What if my marriage doesn't survive this?" The question came out as barely a whisper. "What if David can't accept this new version of me? What if he wants the old Sarah back?"

He was quiet for a moment, considering. "Then it doesn't survive. And that will be hard, sad, and complicated. But Sarah..." He waited until she met his eyes. "A marriage that only works when one person makes themselves small isn't a marriage worth saving. You deserve to be seen. To be valued. To have a partner who celebrates who you are, not who you've been pretending to be."

"I do love him, you know." The words came out fierce. "David. Despite everything. Despite being here with you. Despite what we've done. I still love him."

"I know you do." His voice was infinitely gentle. "And that's okay. Love doesn't make everything simple. Sometimes loving someone means recognising that you've grown in different directions. That which worked for twenty years doesn't work anymore. That you need different things now." He paused. "But that's for you to figure out. Not me. Not David. You. You get to decide what kind of life you want.

What kind of marriage. What you're willing to accept and what you're not."

He was quiet for a moment, then added, "And Sarah... maybe David has changed too. While you've been away."

Sarah looked at him, surprised. "What do you mean?"

"You've had two weeks to think. To reflect. To figure out who you are without him. Maybe he's had the same time. Maybe he's been sitting at home, washing his own dishes, making his own meals, handling bedtime routines, managing everything you usually manage. Maybe he's realised how much he misses you. How much he took you for granted. Maybe he's had time to think about your marriage, about what went wrong, about what he wants."

Sarah hadn't considered that. "You think so?"

"I don't know. But it's possible." His voice was thoughtful. "You're not the only one who can grow and change. Maybe when you get home, when he sees you - really sees you - he'll fall back in love with who you actually are. Not the accommodating wife who manages everything. Not the invisible woman who makes everything work. But you. The writer. The woman with dreams and desires and needs of her own. Maybe that will wake him up."

"Or maybe it won't."

"Maybe it won't," he agreed. "But Sarah... It's not all his fault. You said it yourself: you made yourself invisible. You trained him for over twenty years to see you as someone who didn't need anything. That's not all on him. You both contributed to what your marriage became."

"I know."

"So maybe now is the time to rebuild. To have honest conversations. To tell him what you need and ask him what he needs. To see if you can create a new partnership together. One where you're both seen and valued and celebrated." He squeezed her hand. "He might surprise you. He might be ready to meet you halfway. And if he is, if he's willing to do the work, then maybe your marriage can survive this. Maybe it can even be stronger."

"And if he's not? If he wants the old Sarah back?"

"Then you'll know. And you'll make your decision from there." He smiled sadly. "But don't assume he hasn't changed. Don't assume the worst. Give him a chance to show up. To see you. To choose you the way you're choosing yourself."

He paused, then added quietly, "He might be a fool if he doesn't. But maybe he won't be a fool. Maybe he'll realise what he almost lost and fight to keep it."

Sarah felt something loosen in her chest. On her shoulders. She'd been so focused on her own transformation, her own needs, her own changes, that she hadn't considered David might be having his own revelations. That these two weeks without her might have shifted something in him, too.

"You're very generous," she said softly. "About David. Considering..."

"Considering I'm in love with you?" he smiled, but it was tinged with sadness. "Yes. But I also care about you enough to want you to have a good life. Whatever that looks like. Even if it means staying married to him. Even if it means being happy with someone who isn't me."

"That's..." Sarah's voice broke. "That's really kind."

"It's honest. I love you, Sarah. Which means I want what's best for you. Even when what's best for you isn't me." He pulled her close. "Even when it breaks my heart to say it."

They sat there holding each other for a long time. Sarah felt her emotions settle into clarity. There was still fear and definitely uncertainty. But also determination and purpose. She felt she could do this. She could go home, claim space, and keep writing. She could have honest conversations with David. She could see if their marriage could survive, or even thrive, with both of them being honest about what they needed.

And if it couldn't... well. She'd face that when she had to.

But she wouldn't assume the worst. She'd give David a chance. Give them both a chance to build anew.

"Come on," he said eventually, pulling back. "Let's go back."

They stood and started back down the hill, hand in hand, taking their time. No urgency now. Just walking together through the afternoon.

And as they walked, Sarah realised: three more days.

Just three more days with him.

And then she'd have to let go.

The thought made her chest ache. But she pushed it away. Not yet. She didn't have to think about leaving yet.

For now, she had this. This moment. This man. This feeling.

CHAPTER 12 - LITTLE HOBBY

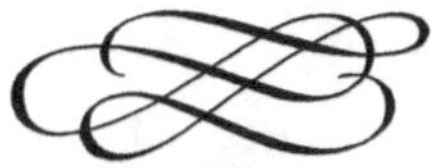

Sarah woke feeling unsettled. Off-balance. Wrong.

She'd dreamed about David. Not the familiar David she'd lived with for twenty years, the man who read the paper at breakfast, forgot his socks, and fell asleep watching television. But the David she'd married: young, hopeful, who'd looked at her like she was everything.

In the dream, she stood on the beach with Jack, holding his hand. David called her name from far away, over and over. She couldn't decide whether to go to him or stay. Dream-David sounded hurt, confused, lost.

She'd woken with that sound still echoing in her head. Her name in David's voice. A plea she couldn't answer.

She lay in bed, caught between sleep's warmth and a sharp, rising unease. The fading images tightened her chest, a mix of longing and dread.

Two more days. Just two more days with Jack, and then she'd have to go home and face David and figure out what her marriage could or should be. Two more days of being seen. Two more days of being alive. Two more days before she had to choose between the life she'd built and the woman she'd become.

She looked at the clock. Seven-thirty. Early still. At home in Bristol, it would be eight-thirty. Morning routine time. David is getting ready for work. The girls are getting ready for school. Life continues without her.

On impulse, or maybe it was guilt, or the dream still lingering, Sarah reached for her phone on the bedside table and called home.

It rang three times. Four. She almost hung up. Then David answered.

"Sarah! Hello." He sounded surprised. Pleased. "Is everything alright?"

"Yes, everything's fine." Her voice came out steadier than she felt. "I just... I wanted to call. Hear your voice."

"Oh." A pause. She could hear him moving around, probably in the kitchen, probably getting his work things together. "Well. That's nice. How's France?"

"Good. Really good. How are things there?"

"Fine, fine. Busy, you know how it is." In the background, she heard the kettle boiling, or maybe it was the radio. "The girls have already left for school. Olivia had an early drama rehearsal. Betty had football practice before class."

"Right. Of course." Sarah had forgotten the time difference, and that routines happened an hour earlier there. Life continued, schedules kept, and children got to school on time. All without her. "How are they doing?"

"Fine. Olivia's been a bit moody, but that's normal at her age. Betty's excited about her match this weekend. Another big one." Another pause. "When do you get back again?"

"Day after tomorrow. Sunday."

"Right, right. I'll pick you up from the station. What time does the train arrive?"

"Around six, I think. I'll text you the details."

"Good. Good." She heard keys jingling. He was probably picking up his briefcase, getting ready to leave for work. "So. How's the writing going? Still working on your little hobby?"

The words hit her like cold water to the face. Like a slap. Like being jerked out of one reality and shoved back into another.

Little hobby.

"It's not a hobby, David."

"What?" He sounded genuinely confused.

"My writing. It's not a hobby." Sarah sat up in bed, anger hot and sharp in her chest. "It's what I do. What I am. I've written nearly two hundred pages. That's a book, David. An actual book."

"Well, yes, of course." He was backpedalling now. "I didn't mean..."

"You did mean it. You always do." The anger rose, unstoppable. "You think this is just to keep me busy, a cute project. Like knitting, or a book club. Just to fill my days while the girls are at school."

"Sarah, that's not fair. I'm being supportive..."

"You're being patronising. There's a big difference." She was fully awake, fully present, fully angry. "I told you before I left. I told you last week. This isn't a holiday project. I won't do this for a few months and stop. This is who I am now. When I come home, I'm going to keep writing. Every day. I need you to take that seriously."

Silence on the other end of the line. Long enough that Sarah thought the call might have dropped. Then: "I do take it seriously."

"Do you? Because calling it my 'little hobby' doesn't sound like taking it seriously."

"I'm sorry." He actually did sound sorry. Confused and hurt and sorry. "I didn't... I didn't realise that would upset you. I think I just don't know how to react because this is new, and I'm not used to you doing things like this. I'm not sure what it means yet, but I want to understand. I'm trying to adjust."

"Well, adjust faster." Sarah's voice was hard. "Because I'm not going back to being the old Sarah. The one who had no dreams or ambitions or needs beyond making sure everyone else was okay. That version of me is gone, David. She doesn't exist anymore."

"Sarah..."

"I mean it." She cut him off. "When I come home, things will be different. I'm claiming space, time. I'm writing every morning. You and the girls will have to handle breakfast and getting ready. I won't be available."

More silence. Then, quietly: "Have I done something wrong? Have I... have I upset you somehow? Beyond the hobby comment, I mean?"

The genuine hurt in his voice twisted Sarah's chest. The anger faltered. Guilt rose to replace it.

"No." Her voice softened. "Yes. I don't know." She rubbed her eyes, exhausted. "It's not that you did anything wrong, David. It's about me finally doing what’s right. For myself. I need you to really support that, not just say the words and expect everything to go back to normal."

"I want to support you. I do. I just..." He took a breath. "I don't entirely understand what's changed. Why is this suddenly so important? You've always seemed happy with our life. Being home with the girls. With... everything."

"I've changed. That's what's changed." Sarah looked out the window at the morning light over the French village. The life she'd lived here for two weeks felt more vivid than the last twenty years. "I've remembered who I am, underneath all the wife-and-mother stuff. And I'm not willing to forget again."

"Alright." Another pause. Then: "Alright. When you come home, we'll talk. Properly. About what you need. About what's changed. About... everything."

"Good."

Another pause. Longer this time. Then: "Sarah?"

"Yes?"

"I love you." His voice was quiet. Almost hesitant. "I know I don't say it enough. I know I take you for granted. But I do love you. And I miss you."

The words hit her like a blow. Knocked the breath from her chest.

I love you. I miss you.

Simple words. True words. From her husband. The man she'd promised to love and honour and cherish. The man she'd stood beside for twenty years. The father of her children.

The man she'd betrayed. The man she was currently betraying.

"I..." Her voice caught. Stuck in her throat. "I have to go. I'll call you before I leave. To confirm the train time."

"Alright. I..."

She hung up before he could finish. Before he could say anything else, that would make it harder. Before she had to say I love you back and feel like the biggest liar.

She sat on the bed, phone in hand, guilt crashing in like a wave. Like drowning. Like being pulled under by a current too strong to fight.

I love you. I miss you.

David loved her. David missed her. And while he was at home missing her, working, taking care of their children, managing everything she usually managed, she'd been here in France making love to another man on a beach.

God. What had she done? What was she doing?

Sarah showered and dressed mechanically, her mind spinning. The anger from the phone call, from the sneering "little hobby," still burned in her chest, hot and raw. He'd dismissed her. Minimised her. Everything she'd worked for was belittled and shrunken to a joke.

But.

But he also loved her. Missed her. Said so in that uncertain voice, like he was afraid she might not know. Might not feel the same.

And she'd hung up on him. She couldn't say I love you back. The words would have been true and false at once. She loved him and had also fallen for someone else. Both were true; she didn't know how to hold them.

I love my husband, she thought. I betrayed him. I made love with someone else. I don't regret it.

All of it true. All exist simultaneously. Impossible to reconcile.

* * *

SHE WENT TO THE CAFÉ, her stomach knotted with dread and uncertainty. Each step was heavy. Each breath, difficult. She didn't know if she could look him in the eye.

But he was already there, at their table, and when he looked up and saw her expression, his face immediately shifted to concern.

"What's wrong?" he said as she sat down.

"Nothing. Everything. I don't know."

The waitress appeared with two coffees. Sarah automatically pushed one across, the ritual so familiar now that it happened without thought.

"Talk to me," he said gently.

"I called David this morning."

"Ah."

"He called my writing a 'little hobby.' Made me furious. We argued. I told him things would be different when I got home." She wrapped her hands around her coffee cup. "Right at the end, he said he loved me. That he missed me."

He said nothing. Just waited.

"And that made me feel guilty," Sarah finished quietly. "Because I'm here with you."

"Yes."

"What am I doing?" She looked up at him, tears in her eyes. "I have a husband who loves me. Children. A life. And I'm here having an affair and falling, no, fallen in love with someone I've known for less than two weeks. What kind of person does that?"

"A human one."

"That's not an answer."

"It's the only answer." He reached across the table and took her hand. "You're not a villain, Sarah. You're not a bad person. You're someone who was drowning and found air. Someone who was invisible and found someone who could see her. That doesn't make what we're doing simple, easy, or without consequences. But it doesn't make you bad."

"I betrayed him."

"Yes."

"I made love with you, and I didn't feel guilty until just now."

"Yes."

"And now I feel terrible."

"I know." He squeezed her hand. "Do you want to stop? Do you want to spend these last two days apart so you can go home with a clearer conscience?"

Sarah thought about it. Really thought about it. Imagined spending today and tomorrow alone. Going back to her hotel room. Writing. Walking by herself. Not seeing him. Not being with him.

"No," she said finally. "I don't want to stop. I don't want to spend these days apart. I want to be with you. Even knowing it's wrong. Even feeling guilty. I still want it."

"Then that's your answer."

"What answer?"

"That you're capable of holding two truths at once." His voice was patient. Understanding. "You love David. You also love me. You feel guilty. You also don't regret what we've done. Both things can be true. You can go home and try to fix your marriage while also treasuring what we had here. They don't cancel each other out."

"How do you always know the right thing to say?"

"Because I've had a lot of time to think about complicated feelings." His expression shifted. Something sad. "About loving someone and losing them. About regret and choice and the messy reality of being human." He lifted her hand to his lips and kissed it. "You're allowed to feel guilty, Sarah. You should feel guilty. What we're doing has costs. Real costs. But that doesn't mean it wasn't also necessary. Doesn't mean you should regret it entirely."

"I keep thinking about going home. About looking David in the eye. About whether I'll be able to."

"You will be. Because you'll tell him the truth."

Sarah's stomach dropped. "What?"

"Not about me. Not about this specifically." His voice was careful. Measured. "But about what happened to you here. That you changed. That you found yourself. That you fell in love with writing, with being visible, with being your own person. That's the truth that matters. The rest..." He shrugged. "The rest is detail."

"You think I shouldn't tell him about you."

"I think telling him would be for your benefit, not his." He held her gaze. "It would make you feel better - cleaner, more honest. Less guilty. But it would hurt him. Badly. And for what? So you can feel less guilty? So you can transfer your discomfort onto him?" He shook his head. "Some things you carry yourself. Some guilt is yours to bear. That's part of the cost of the choice you made."

Sarah sat with that. Let it sink in. "So I just... what? Pretend this never happened?"

"No. You let it inform who you become. You let it remind you that you're capable of wanting things. Of choosing things. Of being more than you've been allowed to be. But you don't weaponise it. You don't use it to hurt David just so you can feel cleaner."

"That seems... cowardly."

"It's kind. There's a difference." He paused, then leaned forward slightly. "What would telling him accomplish? Really? Would it make your marriage better? Would it help him trust you? Would it serve any purpose other than transferring your guilt onto him so you don't have to carry it alone?"

"No. I suppose not."

"Then don't. Carry it yourself." His voice was gentle but firm. "That's the price of what we've done. You carry the guilt. The complexity. The knowledge that you're capable of betrayal. And you use that knowledge to be better. To be honest in the ways that actually matter. To never disappear again. To never let him not see you again." Tears slipped down Sarah's cheeks. "I hate that you're right."

"I know." He smiled sadly. "But I am right. And you know it."

They sat in silence for a while, Sarah crying quietly, Jack holding her hand across the table. Other people came and went. The waitress refilled their coffees. Life continued around them while Sarah's world shifted and settled into a new configuration.

Finally, she said, "I'm sorry. This is our second-to-last full day together, and I'm crying about my husband."

"Don't apologise." His voice was warm. "This is real. This matters. Your marriage matters, even if it's complicated. Especially because it's complicated."

"I don't deserve you."

"You deserve everything good, Sarah. Including guilt when appropriate. Including hard choices. Including figuring out how to live with complexity." He stood and offered her his hand. "Come on. Let's walk. Let's spend today together. Really together. And tomorrow. And then you'll go home and do the hard work of building your life. But today? Today we just be."

Sarah took his hand and let him pull her to her feet.

* * *

THEY WALKED through the village hand in hand, not talking much, just being together. The morning was beautiful: warm sun, gentle breeze, the kind of perfect day that made you want to hold onto every moment. It made you notice how time passes, how days end, how everything is temporary.

Two more days.

Two more days of being with him. Of being seen. Of being this version of herself. And then she'd go home. And carry the guilt. And try to be honest in the ways that mattered. And see if her marriage could survive.

Two more days.

He led her down to the beach, the one that felt like theirs, where they'd first met, where she'd told him to mind his own business, where everything had started. They took off their shoes and walked along the water's edge, feet sinking slightly into the wet sand, waves lapping at their ankles.

"Tell me something," Sarah said after a while. "Something I don't know about you."

"What do you want to know?"

"Anything. Everything." She looked at him. "I have two days left, and I still feel like you're a mystery to me. Like, there are whole parts of you I haven't seen. Haven't understood."

He was quiet for a moment, thinking. Then he said, "When I was young, really young, maybe seven or eight, I used to think I could fly."

Sarah smiled despite the heaviness in her chest. "Like Peter Pan?"

"Not exactly. I didn't think I could fly like a bird. But I thought if I concentrated hard enough, if I believed hard enough, I could make myself lighter and lift off the ground." He paused, looking out at the sea. "I'd stand on my bed and jump, flapping my arms, believing with everything in me that this time I'd stay up. This time I wouldn't fall."

"Did it ever work?"

"No." He laughed, a soft, sad sound. "But I kept trying. For months. Until one day, my mother found me jumping off the furniture and told me I was going to break my neck. That I needed to stop believing in impossible things." He paused. "I've often wondered if that was good advice or terrible advice."

"What do you think?"

"I think some impossible things are worth believing in. Even if you never achieve them. Even if they break your neck trying." He looked at her, his eyes intense. "Like this. Us. Impossible from the start. But worth believing in anyway."

"We're not impossible."

"Aren't we?" His smile was sad. "You're married. You have a life. I'm..." He trailed off. "We only ever had two weeks, Sarah. That's not nothing, but it's not forever either."

"It feels like forever."

"I know." He squeezed her hand. "But it's not. And that's okay. Some of the most important things in life are temporary. That doesn't make them less meaningful. Sometimes the temporary things are the most meaningful of all."

They walked in silence for a while. Sarah tried to memorise everything. The feel of the sand under her feet. The sound of the waves. The warmth of his hand in hers. The way the light caught his hair. The way he moved. The way he existed in the world.

"Do you believe in fate?" she asked suddenly.

"What do you mean?"

"Do you think we were meant to meet? That there's some bigger reason I came here at this exact time and found you on this exact beach? That this was all... I don't know. Destined?"

Jack smiled. "I think believing in fate is another way of believing in impossible things. But yes. I believe we were meant to meet. I believe you needed to find yourself, and I needed to help you do that. I believe this matters, even if it has to end. Especially because it has to end."

"What did you need?" The question came out quietly.

"What?"

"You said I needed to find myself, and you needed to help me. But what did you need? What did you get out of this? Out of us?"

He stopped walking and turned to face her fully. "I got to love you. I got to be seen by you. I got to feel alive again in a way I haven't been in..." He paused. "In a very long time. You gave me that. You reminded me what it feels like to matter to someone."

"You matter to me more than you know."

"I know." His eyes held hers. "And that's enough. That's more than enough. That's everything."

They stood there on the beach, looking at each other, and Sarah realised that her heart was breaking even though nothing had ended yet. Just the anticipation of loss. The knowledge that in two days, she'd have to let go.

* * *

THEY SPENT the rest of the day on the beach. Found a sheltered spot in the dunes where the wind couldn't reach them and just lay there together on the sand, talking about everything and nothing.

He told her stories about growing up. About his mother and the kitchen with the light on the walls. He talked about learning to see the world through an artist's eyes, how once you learned to really see, you could never unsee. The world became both more beautiful and more heartbreaking.

Sarah told him about the girls when they were small. About Olivia's first day of school, when she'd cried and clung to Sarah's leg and refused to let go. About Betty scoring her first football goal and doing a victory dance that made everyone laugh. About the good parts of motherhood, the parts she'd forgotten in all the exhaustion and invisibility and constant giving.

"You're a good mother," he said.

"I don't know about that."

"You are." His voice was certain. "You love them. You see them. You want them to be happy, whole, and themselves. That's what matters."

"I also resent them sometimes." The admission came out quietly. "For needing so much. For taking so much. For the way they've consumed my entire identity."

"That's normal. You're allowed to love your children and also need space from them. Those aren't contradictory feelings. They're just... human."

They lay in comfortable silence, watching the clouds move across the sky. Jack pointed up.

"That one looks like a dragon."

Sarah squinted at the white shapes. "I don't see it."

"There. The head. The wings. The tail curving."

"That's just a blob."

"You're not looking at it right." He turned to her, smiling. "You have to let your eyes unfocus. Stop trying to see what it really is and instead see what it could be."

Sarah tried. Softened her gaze. Stopped trying to force the cloud into a recognisable shape. And suddenly, there it was. A dragon in the clouds.

"I see it!" She laughed. "I actually see it!"

"Good. Now what else do you see?"

They spent the next hour finding shapes in clouds. A castle. A ship. A face. A tree. Each one requiring that same trick - stopping trying to see what was really there and instead seeing what could be there if you just looked differently.

"That's what you did for me," Sarah said quietly.

"What?"

"You helped me stop seeing what I really was - invisible wife, tired mother, woman with no dreams - and instead see what I could be. You helped me unfocus. See the possibility instead of just the reality I'd resigned myself to."

"You always had the possibility in you. I just pointed it out."

"Still. Thank you."

When the sun started to sink lower in the sky, turning everything golden, they walked back along the beach toward the village. Their last walk along this beach as... whatever they were. Lovers. Friends. More complicated than either. There was no woird for it.

At the edge of the dunes, where the path led back to the village, Sarah stopped.

"Jack.”

"Yes.”

"Tomorrow." Her voice caught. "Our last day together. I'm scared. Scared of saying goodbye. Scared of going home. Scared of losing this. Losing you."

He pulled her close, wrapping his arms around her. "I know."

"I don't want tomorrow to be sad. I don't want us to spend the whole day crying and being maudlin about endings. I don't want that to be how we say goodbye."

He was quiet for a moment. When he spoke, his voice was careful. Measured. "Tomorrow will be what it needs to be. Not sad, exactly. But... important. Meaningful. We'll be together. We'll be honest with each other. And yes, there will probably be some sadness because endings are sad. But there will also be..." He paused, choosing his words. "There will also be clarity. Understanding. Things you need to know."

Sarah pulled back to look at him. "That sounds ominous."

"Not ominous. Just... significant." He cupped her face gently. "Trust me. Tomorrow matters. More than you know. And I promise you, by the end of it, you'll understand everything."

"Understand what?"

"Everything that's happened between us. Why it had to happen this way. Why it has to end this way." He kissed her forehead. "I know that's cryptic. But trust me. Please."

"I trust you."

"Good." He smiled, but there was deep sadness in it. "Tomorrow we'll spend the day together. All day. And we'll talk. Really talk. And then... then you'll know what you need to know. And you'll understand. And it will make sense. I promise."

They walked back to the village hand in hand. At the square, they stopped.

"Tomorrow," Jack said. "Same time, same place?"

"Same time, same place."

He kissed her - properly, deeply, a kiss that made her toes curl, and her heart race, and her whole body ache with wanting.

"One more day," he whispered against her lips.

"One more day."

Then he walked away, and Sarah stood there watching him go, her lips still tingling, her heart already aching for tomorrow.

One more day.

Just one more day.

And then... what? She'd understand everything. What did that mean? What was there to understand beyond the simple fact that this was ending, she was going home, he was staying here, and they'd never see each other again?

She pushed the thought away. Tomorrow would come soon enough.

Tomorrow she'd understand.

Whatever that meant.

CHAPTER 13 - THE TRUTH

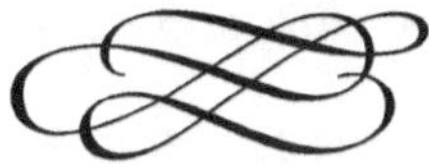

Sarah woke on the eleventh morning, her last morning, and found she couldn't breathe.

Panic gripped her lungs. Grief jabbed at her consciousness like needles. She bolted upright in bed, gasping, swallowing hard against the dread threatening to drown her.

One more day.

Just one more day with him. And then, tomorrow, she'd get on a train and go home, never to see him again. Never hold his hand. Never hear his voice. Never be seen by him again.

The thought was suffocating.

She got up, showered, and dressed. When she looked in the mirror, she saw someone completely different from the woman who had arrived nearly two weeks earlier. Now, her cheeks had colour and her eyes were bright. She looked alive. Awake. Real.

But her heart still ached with every beat. Underneath all her new energy, there was a deep pain. Being alive, she thought, meant feeling everything, even loss.

* * *

SHE MADE her way to the café, and he was already there.

When he saw her, his whole face transformed. Joy, sorrow, and love collided in an expression so raw it made her chest ache.

"Hi," he said.

"Hi."

She sat across from him. They looked at each other. So much to say, so little time. Every word was final.

The waitress brought two coffees without being asked. Sarah pushed one across. The ritual was so familiar it happened without thought.

"How did you sleep?" he asked.

"Terribly." Her voice was hoarse. "I kept waking up thinking: tomorrow I leave. Tomorrow this ends. Tomorrow I never see you again."

"I know." His expression was pained. "I didn't sleep much either."

They sat in silence, both grasping for words to define what this day meant, both haunted by the looming end. Their last shared moments pressed in with sorrow and urgency.

Finally, Sarah said, "Can I ask you something?"

"Of course."

She took a breath. "If things don't work out with David. If I go home and try and it just... doesn't work. If we can't fix it, can't build anew." She paused, gathering courage. "Could I come back here? To you?"

His expression crumpled. "Sarah..."

"I know it's not fair to ask. I know you said this is just these two weeks. But I need to know." Her voice quivered, hope and fear tangled together. "If I'm free, if my marriage ends, could we... could we have more than this?"

"No." The word was gentle but absolute.

"Why not?"

"Because these two weeks are all we have, Sarah. That's the rule, the boundary. I wish I could promise more, but I can't. I would give anything for more time with you, but it's just not possible."

"How does what work? You're not making sense."

"I know it doesn't make sense now. But later today, I'll explain everything, and it will all be clear. Until then, please trust me, you cannot come back. This is our only chance. When you leave tomorrow, you must let me go completely. No looking back, no what-ifs. Please, Sarah, this is how it must be."

Tears slipped down Sarah's cheeks. "I don't think I can."

"You can. You're strong enough. You'll go home, and you'll fight for your marriage, or you'll end it. You'll write your books. You'll be visible. You'll live your life fully, loudly, and beautifully. And I'll be..." He paused. "I'll be here. Always here. But you can't come back."

"You said I'd understand everything today. That things would become clear."

"They will."

"Then tell me now." Sarah's voice was almost pleading. "Tell me what's going on. Tell me why we can't have more than two weeks. Tell me why you're saying these cryptic things that sound like goodbye before goodbye."

"Not yet. Later. When we're at the right place. When you're ready to hear it." He squeezed her hands. "Trust me. Please. Just trust me for a few more hours."

Sarah wanted to push, to demand answers. The confusion and fear were almost too much. But his eyes, so vulnerable and almost frightened, stopped her.

"Alright," she said finally. "I'll wait. But Jack... you're scaring me."

"I know. I'm sorry." His smile was infinitely sad. "But I promise, by the end of today, you'll understand everything. And then..." He paused. "And then you'll be able to let me go."

"I don't want to let you go."

"I know. But you'll have to. And you'll be okay. Better than okay. You'll be amazing."

They finished their coffee in weighted silence. Then Jack stood and offered his hand.

"Come on. Let's make the most of today. Let's have one perfect last day together."

Sarah took his hand and stood.

One last day.

* * *

THEY WALKED through the village hand in hand, taking their time, noticing things they'd often passed by. Every moment felt precious. Every breath might be their last together.

They went to the market, wandering between the stalls. The same vendors Sarah had seen every few days, selling their tomatoes, cheese, bread, and flowers.

"Bonjour, madame," the tomato vendor said, smiling at Sarah.

"Bonjour." Sarah smiled back, her French more confident now.

The vendor said something in rapid French that Sarah caught only pieces of: belle journée - beautiful day.

"Oui, très belle," Sarah agreed, though her eyes were shining with unshed tears.

The vendor must have seen something in her expression because she packed up some tomatoes - the ripest, most beautiful ones - and handed them to Sarah with a warm smile.

Sarah tried to pay, but the woman waved her off. "Pour vous. Un cadeau." A gift.

"Merci," Sarah said, tears pricking her eyes now. "Merci beaucoup."

They walked on, Sarah carrying the tomatoes, feeling the weight of a stranger's kindness. From a woman who'd never once acknowledged his existence but who'd seen Sarah every time she'd come to the market. Who'd watched her transform over two weeks from an invisible woman to someone visible.

They passed the school. It was mid-morning, so the children were inside, but Sarah could hear them through the open windows - voices reciting something in unison, a teacher's patient correction, bursts of laughter.

He stopped and looked at the building for a long moment. His face showed joy, longing, grief, and an emotion Sarah couldn't name.

"You always look at the school like that," Sarah said quietly. "Like it means something to you."

"It does."

"Why?"

"You'll understand. Soon. I promise."

They walked on, and as they crossed the square, Sarah saw the old man sitting on his usual bench. The one who'd told her where to find him. Who'd said that strange thing about everybody knowing who Jack was but not everybody seeing him?

They both waved to him.

The old man waved back, his lined face breaking into a smile. "Bonne journée!" he called.

"Bonne journée," Sarah called back, wondering if she'd ever see him again. Wondering if any of this would feel real once she left.

And then they were past him, walking toward the edge of the village, toward the coastal path that led away from everything familiar.

"Where are we going?" Sarah asked.

"Somewhere important." He squeezed her hand. "Somewhere you need to see. It's not far. Just a walk along the coast."

The path was beautiful, with cliffs on one side and the sea on the other. The sun was warm and the breeze gentle. Everything about the day seemed to go against the tension in Sarah's heart.

But Sarah's shoulders were tense with anxiety. She could sense something building between them. Something electric and fragile. Every glance he gave her felt desperate, like he was trying to memorise her. Like he was trying to hold this moment forever because he knew it would end.

They walked for maybe twenty minutes, not talking much. Just being together. Just existing in the same space while they still could.

And then he stopped walking. Turned to face her. Took both her hands in his.

"Sarah," he said, his voice serious. Solemn. "I need you to remember this. Whatever happens. However long you live. Always remember: I was deeply, deeply in love with you."

"Jack..."

"Let me finish. Please." He squeezed her hands. "Love isn't always about being together. Love is about letting go when needed. About wanting what's best for the other person even when it breaks your heart. That's what this is. Me loving you enough to let you go home. To let you live your life. To let you be free."

"You're scaring me."

"I know. I'm sorry." He pulled her close and held her for a long moment, his face buried in her hair, his arms tight around her. "But I needed to say it. I needed you to know."

He pulled back and cupped her face with both hands.

"Come on. There's something I need to show you."

* * *

THE PATH OPENED up to a small clearing, and there, overlooking the sea, stood a memorial.

It was simple and dignified: a large stone monument with bronze plaques, and red and white roses climbing the trellis behind.

As they got closer, Sarah could read the inscription at the top:

À LA MÉMOIRE DE CEUX QUI SONT TOMBÉS

6 JUIN 1944

In memory of those who fell

June 6, 1944

"A war memorial," Sarah said softly. "For D-Day."

"Yes. For the men who died here. Who gave everything for freedom."

Sarah walked up to the memorial slowly and with respect, reading the names carved into the bronze plaques. There were so many names, so much loss. Some of the young men were barely twenty, others in their thirties. British, American, Canadian, French. All gone.

She read slowly, respectfully, her fingers tracing over the carved letters. Each name representing a life cut short. A family destroyed. Someone's son, brother, husband, father. The weight of it was overwhelming.

Her fingers moved down the list of British soldiers:

JAMES HARRISON, AGE 23

THOMAS FLETCHER, AGE 29

JACK HARTLEY, AGE 32

WILLIAM COOPER, AGE 21

Her finger stopped. Lingered on one name.

JACK HARTLEY, AGE 32

Jack.

The same name as...

Her heart started to pound. Slowly at first, then faster. Her mind refused to make the connection her body had already made.

Not turning around yet, her finger still on the carved letters. Her voice sounded strange. Distant. "There's somebody here with the same name as you. Jack Hartley. That's... that's an odd coincidence, isn't it?"

Silence.

Complete, absolute silence.

"Jack?"

She turned around.

He was gone.

The clearing was empty. Just her and the memorial and the roses swaying gently in the breeze.

"Jack?" she called, louder now. Panic rising in her throat. "Jack!"

Nothing. No one. Just the sound of the sea and the wind and her own ragged breathing.

Sarah spun in a circle, looking for him. He'd been right there. Right there a second ago, holding her, touching her face, telling her he loved her.

Where could he have gone?

The path was open and completely visible in both directions. She would have seen him if he walked away. She would have heard his footsteps on the gravel.

"Jack!" Her voice was rising now, panic fully taking hold. "This isn't funny! Where are you?"

Only silence answered.

She ran to the edge of the clearing, looked down the coastal path in both directions. Empty. No one. Nothing. Just grass and rocks and the endless sea.

He was gone.

Completely, impossibly vanished.

Sarah stood there, breathing hard, her mind spinning. This didn't make sense. People didn't just vanish. They didn't just disappear into thin air like smoke.

Unless...

Unless they weren't really there to begin with.

She turned back to the memorial, walked slowly toward it like moving through water, and found that name again. Read it more carefully this time.

JACK HARTLEY

WAR ARTIST, WAAC

BORN: 12 MARCH 1912

DIED: 6 JUNE 1944

AGE 32

Born in 1912.

Died in 1944.

Eighty-one years ago.

Sarah's legs gave out. She sank to the ground in front of the memorial, shock and disbelief crashing through her like waves. A cold numbness spread through her entire body as she stared at the name. Pain so sharp it was physical.

No.

No, that was impossible.

Jack was real. She'd touched him. Held his hand. Kissed him. Made love with him on a beach. He was solid, warm, and alive. You couldn't touch a ghost. You couldn't make love to someone who'd been dead for eighty-one years.

Could you?

She pressed her hands to her face, trying to think, trying to make sense of anything. Had she imagined it all? Had she had some kind of breakdown? Come to France and lost her mind and invented a man who understood her, who saw her, who made her feel alive?

But that didn't make sense either because other people had seen him. The old man. The old man in the square who'd told her where to find him. He'd known Jack. He'd waved to him just this morning.

So he had to be real. Other people had seen him.

Except... had they?

The memories came flooding back, each one a piece of evidence she'd ignored:

The waitress had never looked at him. Never addressed him. Always gave both coffees to Sarah.

The vendors at the market had never spoken to him. Never acknowledged him. Only ever looked at Sarah.

The old man had said, "Everybody knows who Jack is." But not everybody sees him.

Oh God.

He wore the same jumper every day, the same worn blue one with paint stains. She had thought it was just his artistic style. But what if it was the only thing he owned? The only thing he had died in?

His vague answers about his past. The way he'd never really told her where he lived or what his life was like before.

The way he talked about time. "I'll remember this for the rest of time." Not forever. Not always. Time itself.

His lost love, Elizabeth, whom he couldn't go back to "because of circumstances."

The way he'd said "I've been waiting for you. For years."

The coldness in places when she was with him. The way the air was sometimes different.

He never actually ate. She'd seen him order food, move it around on his plate, but had she ever actually seen him eat?

He knew things about the village, about history, like he'd been here forever.

The way he watched the school with such longing. A man who'd died at thirty-two, who'd never gotten to have the family he wanted.

"Love is about letting go."

"This is borrowed time."

"You can't come back to me."

"Tomorrow we say goodbye, and you don't look for me."

All of it. Every strange thing. Every moment that hadn't quite made sense. Every clue she'd noticed and explained away because you couldn't fall in love with a ghost.

Except she had.

She'd fallen in love with a man who'd been dead for eighty-one years.

Sarah sat there on the ground in front of the memorial, shaking, crying, her mind refusing to accept what her heart already knew.

It had been real. He had been real to her. But he'd also been dead.

How was that possible? How could any of this be possible?

She didn't know how long she sat there. Minutes. Hours. The sun moved across the sky. The shadows lengthened. Her tears eventually stopped, leaving her empty and hollow and numb.

Finally, when she had no tears left, she stood up on shaky legs.

She touched the carved letters of his name one more time. Pressed her palm against the cool bronze.

Jack Hartley. War Artist. Thirty-two years old. Someone who'd died on D-Day. Someone who'd impossibly, miraculously, come back for two weeks.

For her.

To save her.

"Thank you," she whispered to the memorial. To him. To wherever he was. "Thank you for seeing me."

Then she turned and walked back down the coastal path toward the village, each step heavy, each breath difficult. Her mind kept circling back to the same impossible questions:

Was it real?

Was any of it true?

Had she actually spent two weeks with a ghost?

Or had she imagined the whole thing? Created an entire person out of her desperate need to be seen?

But she had the writing. Over two hundred pages. That was real. The changes in herself were real. She'd called David. She'd talked to people in the village. She'd bought things from vendors and stayed in a hotel. All of that had happened.

But Jack?

She didn't know. She didn't know anything anymore.

When she reached the village, the square was quiet, evening settling in. The café was closing up for the night. A few people were heading home, shops shuttering, the daily rhythm winding down.

The old man wasn't on his bench.

Sarah walked back to her hotel in a daze. Climbed the stairs. Unlocked her door. Went inside.

The room looked the same as always. Her notebook on the desk. Her clothes in the wardrobe. Everything normal. Everything real.

She sat at the desk and opened her notebook. Two hundred and sixteen pages of her story. About a woman finding herself.

About a man who helped her see who she really was. About falling in love.

About the impossible.

Her hands were shaking as she picked up her pen.

And she wrote.

How do you write about loving someone who doesn't exist?

How do you make readers believe in what you can barely believe yourself?

The protagonist had fallen in love with a ghost. Say it out loud, and it sounds absurd. Ridiculous. The stuff of cheap romance novels, not serious fiction about middle-aged women finding themselves.

But it had happened.

He had been real. The truest thing she'd ever felt.

His hands on her skin – real. His voice in her ear – real. The way he looked at her like she mattered, like she was visible, like she was everything – real.

All of it real. And all of it impossible.

He'd been dead for eighty-one years. Died at thirty-two. Never got to have the life he wanted. The family he wanted. The future he'd imagined.

And then, impossibly, he'd been given two weeks.

Two weeks to exist again. To love again. To feel alive again.

He'd used those two weeks on her.

Why? Why her? A middle-aged English housewife who'd forgotten she existed? What was so special about her that he would choose to spend his precious, borrowed time helping her remember who she was?

"Because you needed me," he'd said. "And I needed you."

She wrote until her hand cramped. Until her eyes burned. Until there was nothing left to say except:

Thank you.
Thank you for seeing me.
Thank you for saving me.
Thank you for letting me go.

Sarah closed the notebook. Two hundred and thirty pages. A complete book.

Tomorrow she'd go home. Tomorrow, she'd get on a train and go back to David and the girls and figure out her life.

Tomorrow, she'd start being the visible Sarah in the world.

Tomorrow.

But tonight, she sat at her desk in a hotel room in Normandy and let herself feel everything. The confusion. The loss. The love. The questions that had no answers.

Real or not real.

Dead or alive.

Gone either way.

She looked out the window at the dark village. One more night. One more night in France.

And then she'd go home.

Home to a life that felt less vivid than two weeks with a ghost.

But she'd go. Because he'd asked her to. Because he'd loved her enough to let her go.

Because that's what love was.

* * *

SARAH WOKE EARLY the next morning - her last morning in France - and packed her bag with care. Made the bed even though housekeeping would do it. Tidied the room. Left everything neat for the next guest.

Someone who would never know that a woman had been remade here. That he had been loved here. That the impossible had happened in this quiet room overlooking a French village.

She looked around one last time. The desk where she'd written two hundred and thirty pages. The window that looked out over the village. The bed where she'd dreamed of him and woken wanting him and learned what her body could feel.

Two weeks. Just two weeks in this room.

And she was leaving as someone completely different.

What surprised her, what caught her off guard as she picked up her bag and notebook, was that she didn't feel devastated. She had expected to be broken this morning, unable to function, destroyed by loss.

But instead, she felt something else. Vast and warm and whole.

Love.

Just love. Pure and uncomplicated and enormous.

She understood now what he'd said about Elizabeth. "I hope she found someone who made her happy. I hope she had a good life." That was love. Real love. Wanting the best for someone even when you couldn't be part of it.

He had loved Elizabeth enough to hope she'd moved on.

And he'd loved Sarah enough to send her home.

Love isn't always about being together. Sometimes love is about letting go.

She picked up her bags and left the room.

SHE HAD one last coffee at the café. Sat at their table - what had been their table. The waitress brought one cup without being asked and set it in front of Sarah with a kind smile.

"Dernier jour?" Last day?

"Oui," Sarah said. "Dernier jour."

"Bon voyage, madame."

"Merci."

The coffee was hot, black, and perfect. Sarah wrapped her hands around the cup, looking out at the square. The same view she'd had every morning for nearly two weeks. Same cobblestones, same buildings, same morning light.

But no Jack. Never Jack again.

"Pardon, madame."

She looked up to find the old man standing beside her table, leaning on his walking stick.

"Oui?"

He gestured at the empty chair. "Je peux?"

"Of course. Please." Sarah gestured for him to sit.

The old man lowered himself carefully into the chair, his chair, and set his walking stick against the table. He looked at her with kind, knowing eyes.

They sat in silence for a moment. Sarah gathering her courage.

Then she took a breath and said, quietly but directly, "He was a ghost, wasn't he?"

The old man tilted his head slightly. "A ghost? No. No, not a ghost."

"Then what was he? Because I saw his name on the memorial. Jack Hartley. Died June 6, 1944. Eighty-one years ago."

"That is true."

"So he's dead."

"Yes. He is dead. But he is not a ghost." The old man smiled gently. "He is very real. Very real to some of us."

"I don't understand." Sarah's voice broke. "How can he be real if he's been dead for eighty years? How could I see him, but other people couldn't? You said everyone knows who he is, but not everyone sees him. What does that mean?"

The old man was quiet for a moment, choosing his words carefully.

"You saw him because you needed to. Because you were... how do you say... lost? And he helps people who are lost. Has helped them for a very long time."

"But why here? Why this village? The memorial said he died on the beach. On D-Day."

"Ah. No." The old man shook his head. "The memorial is for all who died at that time, in this region. But he did not die on the beach. He died here. In this village. Three days after the landing."

Sarah felt her breath catch. "Here?"

"Yes. The Germans were retreating. They were shelling the village as they left. And the school..." He gestured toward the school building visible across the square. "The school was hit. It caught fire. And there were children inside. Hiding in the cellar. Terrified."

Sarah's hands were shaking. "What happened?"

“He was attached to an infantry unit that had just arrived. Not as a soldier, you understand, but as a war artist. To document what he saw." The old man's voice grew thick with emotion. "They heard the children screaming. And Jack... he went inside. Into the burning building. He brought out one child. Then another. Then another."

The old man's eyes were wet now.

"He kept going back. Again and again. Until all the children were safe. Eight children. All saved."

"And then?"

"And then he went back one more time. To make sure. To be certain, there was no one left inside." The old man wiped his eyes. "But the building... it collapsed. The smoke, the fire... He did not come out again."

"Oh God." Sarah felt tears streaming down her face.

"He was thirty-two years old. An artist. A good man. And he gave his life to save children he had never met. Children who were not his to save. Just... children who needed saving."

"That's why he watches the school," Sarah whispered. "That's why he looks at it with so much emotion."

"Yes. It is his place. Where he gave everything. Where he stayed."

They sat in silence for a while. Sarah crying quietly. The old man waiting patiently.

Finally, Sarah said, "How do you know all this?"

The old man smiled, tears now running freely down his weathered cheeks.

"Because I was one of those children. I was six years old. Hiding in that cellar with my sister and six other children. Terrified. Certain we would die." His voice broke. "And then this man appeared through the smoke. This man with kind eyes. And he picked me up and carried me out. Told me I was safe. Told me to be brave."

He wiped his eyes.

"I am eighty-seven years old now. I have lived my whole life because of Jack Hartley. I married. I had children. Grandchildren. Great-grandchildren. All of it... all of it because he saved me."

"That's why you can see him."

"Yes. Those of us he saved, we can see him. Or we could, when we were younger. As we get older, it becomes harder. But I still see him sometimes. I still recognise him. Still remember."

"And me?" Sarah's voice was barely a whisper. "Why could I see him?"

The old man reached across and patted her hand gently.

"Because you needed saving, too. Not from fire. Not from Germans. But from disappearing. From being invisible. He saw that in you. And so you saw him." He smiled. "He is very good at finding people who need help. Always has been. Even now."

Sarah couldn't speak. Her whole body trembled with understanding and gratitude and grief.

"He loved you, you know," the old man said gently. "I saw you together. The way he looked at you. He loved you very much."

"I loved him too."

"I know. And that is a gift. For both of you. He got to love again. To feel alive again. And you..." He squeezed her hand. "You got to be seen. To be saved. To remember who you are. That is love, madame. Real love."

"I don't want to leave him."

"I know. But you must. You have a life to live. A long life, if you are fortunate. And he... he will be here. Always here. Watching over this village. Helping people who need help. That is his purpose. His gift. But you cannot stay. You know this."

Sarah nodded, tears blurring her vision. "He told me that. He said I had to let him go."

"Then you must. For him. And for yourself."

They sat in silence a moment longer. Then the old man stood, carefully, using his walking stick for support.

"Bon voyage, madame," he said. "And thank you. For seeing him. For loving him. For giving him those two weeks. It is more than most ghosts ever get."

"I thought you said he wasn't a ghost."

The old man smiled. "He is not. But he is not alive either. He exists in between. A beautiful impossibility." He tipped his cap. "Safe travels."

"Wait," Sarah said. "What's your name?"

"Jean-Paul," he said. "Jean-Paul Marchand."

Sarah watched as Jean-Paul walked away across the square. Slowly. Carefully. An eighty-seven-year-old man who'd been saved by him when he was six.

One of eight children who owed their entire lives to a thirty-two-year-old artist who'd run into a burning building again and again until every child was safe.

One of eight reasons why he had stayed. Why he watched the school. Why he helped lost people.

Why had he been waiting for her?

Sarah looked down at her coffee, cold now, untouched.

She stood, left money on the table, picked up her bags, and walked away from the café for the last time.

Time to go home.

CHAPTER 14 - HOME

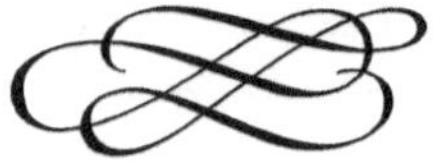

She stood in the hallway with her suitcase by the door, listening to familiar sounds: the hum of the refrigerator, the tick of the living room clock. She heard the floorboards creak upstairs. David was putting fresh sheets on their bed. Their bed. The word was strange now, like clothing that no longer fit.

"Mum's home!" Betty's voice carried down the stairs, followed by the thunder of footsteps.

Sarah barely had time to brace herself before her daughters appeared, Olivia leading the way with Betty close behind. They wrapped around her like they used to when they were small, and Sarah closed her eyes, breathing in the scent of Betty's strawberry shampoo, feeling the familiar weight of Olivia's head against her shoulder.

"We missed you," Betty said, her voice muffled against Sarah's coat.

"I missed you too. So much."

When they finally pulled back, Sarah saw David standing at the top of the stairs, watching. He gave her that gentle, familiar smile and came down to take her suitcase.

"I'll put this away," he said. "Girls, give your mum space. She's had a long journey."

The girls retreated to the kitchen, already talking over each other about what had happened while she was gone, and Sarah followed David upstairs.

He set her suitcase on the bed and turned to her, his hands in his pockets. "How was the trip back?"

"Long," Sarah said. She sat on the edge of the bed, suddenly exhausted. "David, we need to talk."

He nodded slowly, as if he'd been expecting this. "I know."

“I changed in France," Sarah began, choosing her words carefully. "I found something I didn't even know I'd lost. A sense of myself. Of who I am beyond being a wife and a mother."

"I noticed," David said. His tone was neutral, but his eyes were guarded.

"I need that to continue," Sarah said. "I need to keep writing. I need time and space to be myself, not just the person everyone else needs me to be."

David was quiet for a long moment. Then he said, "I understand that you feel that way."

"But?"

He looked at her, struggling with words, and in his eyes she saw something that made her heart sink. "But I liked you the old way, Sarah. The way you were before."

The words hung between them like smoke.

"The old way," Sarah repeated softly.

"You were happier," David said. "You didn't question things. You were content with our life, with the family. You were... easier."

"Easier."

"I didn't mean it like that…"

"Yes, you did." Sarah stood, her legs suddenly unsteady. "You meant exactly that. I was easier when I was invisible. When I didn't have needs of my own."

"That's not fair," David said, but there was no conviction in his voice.

Sarah looked at her husband, this kind, decent man who had shared her life for twenty years. For the first time, she saw clearly that he didn't want her to grow. He wanted her to shrink back into the shape she'd been before, the shape that fit comfortably into his life without disrupting anything.

"Maybe we should talk to someone," she said quietly. "A therapist. Both of us."

David's face softened with relief. "Yes. I think that would be good."

* * *

THE THERAPY STARTED IN SEPTEMBER.

Sarah went alone first, then David went alone, and then they went together. Dr Morrison's office was in a converted Victorian house with high ceilings and large windows that let in generous light. Sarah found herself watching the dust motes drift through the sunbeams as she and David sat in matching armchairs, trying to explain to a stranger what they couldn't explain to each other.

"What do you need from this marriage?" Dr Morrison asked Sarah during their third joint session.

"To be seen," Sarah said. "To be a full person, not just a role."

"And you, David?"

"I need stability," David said. "I need to know that the life we've built together still matters."

"It does matter," Sarah said quickly. "But I can't go back to who I was."

"I'm not asking you to…"

"Yes, you are. Every time you say you preferred me before, that's exactly what you're asking."

Dr Morrison made a note. "David, can you understand why Sarah experiences your preference for 'before' as a rejection of who she is now?"

David was quiet. Then he said, "I suppose I can. But I don't know how to want anything different from what I want."

In her individual sessions, Sarah talked about France. About writing in the garden. About Jack, though she didn't mention that he was a ghost. She talked about feeling alive for the first time in years, about discovering that she was capable of more than she'd believed.

"Do you love your husband?" Dr Morrison asked one afternoon in October.

Sarah thought about it, really thought about it. "Yes," she said finally. "But like a brother. Like family. Not the way I know in my heart that I can love someone."

Dr Morrison nodded. "And does he know this?"

"I think he's always known," Sarah said. "I think we both have."

* * *

THE MONTHS that followed developed a rhythm.

Firstly, with much sweat and not a few swear words, Sarah cleared out the spare room. Taking old furniture to the tip, putting up framed photographs, cleaning and making it her space. Lastly putting a few sprigs of lavender in a vase on the desk. She purposely hadn't asked for help because this was her space from start to finish.

Sarah wrote in the mornings until lunchtime, the house quiet around her as she poured herself onto the page. The book was no longer about him or her, not really. It was about a woman who learned to see herself, who discovered that invisibility was a choice she could refuse.

She and David moved through the house like dancers who knew the steps but had forgotten the music. They were kind to each other. Careful. They attended Olivia's sixth-form events together, cheered at Betty's football matches, and had dinner as a family every Sunday. To anyone watching, they might have looked fine.

But at night, Sarah lay in their bed. David kept to his side, she kept to hers. She stared at the ceiling, wondering how long they could keep up this careful pretence.

In November, Olivia announced she wanted to visit King's College London.

"It's supposed to have an amazing medical program," she said over dinner, her face bright with excitement. "And the city is so vibrant. Can we go look at it?"

Sarah glanced at David, saw the same mixture of pride and panic she had. Their eldest daughter is preparing to leave. She had always known that Olivia was the more academic of the two girls. Betty was more creative, like her—still bright but with a different attitude to life.

"Of course we can," David said. "We'll make a weekend of it."

They drove up on a Friday in late November, the four of them squeezed into the car like they used to on family holidays. Olivia chattered about course options. Betty read aloud from the university prospectus. Sarah watched the countryside roll past the window, thinking about beginnings and endings, and all the ways they were sometimes the same thing.

London was everything Olivia had hoped for. The sights, the sounds, the whole place had an energy that Bristol lacked. They toured the college, sat in on a sample lecture, and walked along the riverbank as the winter sun set early and cold.

"I can see myself here," Olivia said, and Sarah heard in her daughter's voice the same note of discovery she'd had in France. The sound of someone finding where they belonged.

On the way home, both girls asleep in the back, David said, "She's going to leave us."

"She's going to leave home," Sarah corrected gently. "That's what children do."

"I know. But it makes everything feel so... temporary."

Sarah looked at him in the dim light of the car. "Everything is temporary, David. That's what I learned. We can hold on so tight we crush what we love. Or we can let it grow, change, become what it's meant to be."

"Even if what it becomes a life without 'us'?"

"Even then."

* * *

THE DINNER HAPPENED on a Tuesday in early December.

Sarah had made lasagna, Betty's favourite, and they were all sitting around the table, the conversation flowing easily. Olivia was talking about her chemistry teacher when Betty interrupted.

"I'm going to start life drawing in January," she announced.

Olivia grinned. "You're going to draw nude people?"

Sarah nearly choked on her water.

"Don't be so stupid," Betty said, rolling her eyes. "It's drawing fruit and things on a table."

Sarah set down her glass carefully, able to breath again. "Actually, love, that's called still life. Life drawing is when you draw from a live model, which sometimes includes nude figure studies. But at your age, it would probably be clothed models or anatomical studies."

"Oh." Betty's face went red. "Right. Still life then. That's what I meant."

They all laughed, the kind of genuine, unforced laughter that had been rare in recent months. The sound filled the kitchen, warm and easy. For a moment, Sarah had a pang of loss for what they were about to lose.

As the laughter died down, Betty turned to Sarah, her expression suddenly serious. "Mum, are you and Dad getting divorced?"

The question hung in the air. Sarah felt David stiffen opposite her.

"We're... working through some things," Sarah said carefully. "We've been seeing a therapist to help us figure out what's best."

"That's not really an answer," Olivia said quietly.

Sarah looked at David, saw him nod slightly. Permission. Or perhaps resignation.

"You're right," Sarah said. "The honest answer is that we probably are heading toward separation. We're trying to be thoughtful about it, to make sure we're doing what's right for everyone, but yes. That's likely where we're heading."

She braced herself for tears, for anger, for the inevitable teenage drama. Instead, Betty just nodded and said, "Yeah, we kind of figured."

"You did?" David sounded genuinely surprised.

"You sleep in separate beds now," Olivia pointed out. "And you're always so... polite to each other. Like you're roommates, not married."

"Are you okay with this?" Sarah asked, searching their faces.

Betty shrugged. "I mean, it's not great. But it's also not, like, the end of the world. Emma's parents got divorced last year, and she's fine. Better, actually, because they stopped fighting all the time."

"We haven't been fighting," David said.

"Exactly," Olivia said. "That's kind of the problem, isn't it? You're just... existing. It's sad to watch."

Tears pricked Sarah's eyes. When had her daughters become so perceptive? So mature?

"We love you both very much," she said. "That won't change, whatever happens."

"We know," Betty said. "Can I have more lasagna?"

And just like that, the conversation moved on. Sarah caught David's eye across the table and saw the same mixture of relief and sadness she felt. Their daughters were going to be okay. Perhaps better than okay.

Perhaps they were all going to be okay.

* * *

SARAH MET Margaret Thornton for coffee on a Wednesday afternoon in mid-December. They sat in a café near the cathedral, the Christmas decorations twinkling in the windows, the smell of cinnamon and coffee filling the air.

"So," Margaret said, stirring sugar into her cappuccino. "How was France?"

Sarah laughed. "That's rather a loaded question."

"I know. That's why I'm asking." Margaret leaned back in her chair, studying Sarah with those sharp, knowing eyes. "You look different. In a good way. Like you've finally woken up."

"I have," Sarah said. "In more ways than I can explain."

"Try."

So Sarah told her. Not about Jack, she couldn't tell anyone about him, not really. But she told her about the writing, about the beach, about discovering that she'd been disappearing for years. About coming home and realising she couldn't go back to being invisible, even if it meant her marriage ending.

Margaret listened without interrupting, her expression thoughtful.

"You know," she said when Sarah finished, "I wondered if this might happen. That's why I encouraged you to go. I could see you fading. Like a photograph left in the sun too long."

"You saw that?"

"I'm a librarian, Sarah. I'm trained to notice the stories people aren't telling." She took a sip of her coffee. "So what now?"

"Now I finish the book," Sarah said. "And I figure out what my life looks like on the other side of my marriage."

"How's David handling it?"

"He's... processing. We're in therapy. He wants me to go back to being who I was before, but I can't. I won't."

"Good," Margaret said firmly. "You shouldn't. That woman was half-asleep. This woman," she gestured at Sarah, "is fully alive. Don't you dare apologise for that."

Sarah felt tears welling up. "Thank you. For sending me to France. For seeing me when I couldn't see myself."

"Thank you for having the courage to go," Margaret replied. "Most people don't, you know. They see the opportunity to change, and they run the other way. You ran toward it. That takes bravery."

They talked for another hour about books, about children, about the complicated reality of wanting more from life than what you have. When Sarah finally left, walking through the Christmas-lit streets toward home, she was lighter than she had been in months.

Margaret had seen her. Jack had seen her. And now, finally, she was learning to see herself.

* * *

THE EMAIL ARRIVED on a Friday in late January.

Sarah was in her study - the spare bedroom that she had cleared a few months ago, working on revisions to chapter twelve, when her phone buzzed.

From: Rebecca Chen, Literary Agent

Subject: YOUR BOOK. THEY LOVED IT!!!

SARAH CLICKED ON IT, her heart suddenly racing.

Sarah,

I just got off the phone with the publishers. They're making an offer. A GOOD offer. A VERY VERY GOOD OFFER. They absolutely love The Man on the Beach. The editor said it's the most emotionally resonant thing she's read in years. She cried three times. AND I'M CRYING NOW LOL

I'll send you the full details this evening, but I wanted you to know immediately. YOU DID IT. What you've written is truly special, and people will read it, love it, and see themselves in it.

Call me when you can. And maybe open a bottle of wine.

Rebecca

Sarah read the text twice. Three times. Then she set down her phone and stared at her laptop screen, at the words she'd been revising, at the story she'd poured her heart into.

They wanted it.

Someone wanted to publish her book.

Her book about a ghost who taught a woman how to stop disappearing.

She stood up, walked to the window, and looked out at the garden. It was winter now, everything dormant and grey, but spring would come. Things would grow again. They always did.

Her phone buzzed. A text from David downstairs:

> Girls want pancakes. Should I tell them to start the batter or wait for you?

Sarah looked at the message. Six months ago, she would have dropped everything and rushed downstairs. Would have made the pancakes herself, served them with a smile, cleaned up afterwards while everyone else dispersed to their own activities.

Now she typed:

> You and the girls can start preparing the pancake batter without me. I'll be down in twenty minutes.

She saved her document, closed her laptop, and sat back in her chair.

Visible. Awake. Alive.

The way he had always seen her.

The way she'd finally learned to see herself.

* * *

THE LETTER ARRIVED the next morning.

Sarah found it in the stack of mail David had left on the kitchen counter, a cream envelope with French stamps, her name written in careful, old-fashioned handwriting.

The return address was the hotel in Normandy.

Her hands shook as she opened it.

Dear Madame Mitchell,

I am writing to inform you that Monsieur Jean-Paul Marchand passed away peacefully in his sleep on January 15th. He was 87 years old.

Before his death, he left instructions that I should write to you. He also left you a letter, which I have enclosed.

Monsieur Marchand spoke of you often in his final weeks. He said you were someone who understood. Someone who had been saved, as he was saved. I did not understand what he meant, but he insisted I send you this letter.

With deepest sympathies,

Marie Rousseau

Proprietor, Hotel Belle Vue

Sarah's vision blurred. Jean-Paul. The old man who had sat with her in the café that last morning. Who had told her about Jack, about the children, about being saved.

With trembling fingers, she opened the second envelope.

The handwriting was shaky but clear:

Dear Sarah,

If you are reading this, then I am gone. I am not sad about this. I have lived a long and full life, much longer than I had any right to expect. Every day past June 9, 1944, has been a gift.

I saw Jack again, the day after you left. I was walking past the school and there he was, standing by the gates where I always see him. He was smiling. Not sad at all.

I said to him, "I thought you would be sad. The English woman is gone."

He said, "My work here is done now. You are the last of the children from the school, Jean-Paul. And you have lived a full and long life. I stayed to watch over you all, to help when I could. But you don't need me anymore. None of you do."

I said, "Where will you go?"

He said, "I have learned what matters. I am capable of both being in love and being loved again. For eighty-one years, I thought that part of me died with Elizabeth. But Sarah showed me it didn't. And now I know, it's time for me to pass to the other side."

I said, "Will you see Elizabeth again?"

He smiled and said, "I hope so. I have a lot to tell her."

That was the last time I saw him. I have gone to the school every day since, but he is not there. I think he is truly gone now. I think he has finally moved on. Finally at peace, a peace that he truly deserves.

I hope, by the time you receive this letter, that I will have met him again. On the other side. So I can thank him one more time for saving my life. And so I can tell him that the woman he saved in his final act, you Sarah, she is going to be just fine.

Thank you for seeing him. For loving him. For giving him that gift.

May you live a long and full life, as I have done. Every day is a gift.

With warmest regards,

Jean-Paul Marchand

SARAH READ the letter three times. Then she folded it carefully, held it against her chest, and let herself cry.

Jack was gone. Really gone. Not standing watch over a village anymore. Not waiting by a. Not helping lost people find themselves.

He had moved on. Because of her. Because she had shown him he could still love and be loved.

And somewhere, somehow, she hoped he had found Elizabeth again. Hoped they were together, the way they should have been eighty-one years ago.

She stood, walked to the window, and looked out at the winter garden. The sun was coming up, pale and cold, casting long shadows across the dormant earth.

"Thank you," she whispered to the empty room. "Thank you for seeing me. Thank you for saving me. Thank you for showing me how to live."

The room was silent. Still. But something shifted inside her, a final letting go, a final acceptance.

Jack was at peace.

And so, finally, was she.

She wiped her eyes, folded the letter, and made a cup of tea. This is when my life really starts again. Her real, messy, complicated, beautiful life was waiting; she instinctively knew the story was not over. There was more to write. She took a new notebook from her bag and took it upstairs.

THE END

ABOUT THE AUTHOR

Ollie Llewellyn writes stories about transformation, resilience, and the quiet courage it takes to reclaim yourself.

After a long career dedicated to others, Ollie now spends days walking windswept beaches with a loyal dog companion, where the rhythm of waves and the vastness of the horizon provide the perfect backdrop for dreaming up stories. These coastal wanderings have become a meditation on the human spirit—its capacity for reinvention, its hunger for connection, and its remarkable ability to find hope even in the most unexpected places.

Drawn to tales of ordinary people discovering extraordinary truths about themselves, Ollie's writing explores the spaces between who we think we are and who we're capable of becoming. Whether it's a woman finding her voice in a foreign country, or the ghosts of the past teaching us how to live in the present, every story is an invitation to look more closely at the beautiful complexity of being human.

When not writing, Ollie can be found in nature - watching the light change over coastal cliffs, listening to birdsong in quiet forests, or simply sitting in the garden with a cup of tea and a notebook, always ready to capture the next fleeting moment of inspiration.

Seen is Ollie's debut novel, a story born from those long beach walks and a deep belief that it's never too late to become visible in your own life.

www.ingramcontent.com/pod-product-compliance
Lightning Source LLC
LaVergne TN
LVHW091026080826
845145LV00002B/376

* 9 7 8 1 9 1 9 5 4 1 1 0 5 *